Handwritten: 378 306

PIRATES IN CALUSA COVE

EVERGLADES OVERWATCH

BOOK TWO

ELLE JAMES

JEN TALTY

TWISTED PAGE INC

ISBN EBOOK: 978-1-62695-649-0

ISBN PRINT: 978-1-62695-661-2

AUTHORS' NOTE

USA Today Bestselling authors Elle James and Jen Talty
join forces in an electrifying collaboration born from an
author retreat in paradise. Inspired by the lush land-
scapes of the Florida Everglades, their latest venture
blends heart-pounding suspense, sizzling romance, and
gripping action. With their signature storytelling prow-
ess, Talty and James weave a thrilling tale that will keep
readers on the edge of their seats, proving that when
two powerhouse authors unite, the result is pure magic.

EVERGLADES OVERWATCH
Secrets in Calusa Cove
Pirates in Calusa Cove
Murder in Calusa Cove
Betrayal in Calusa Cove

PIRATES IN CALUSA COVE

EVERGLADES OVERWATCH BOOK #2

New York Times & *USA Today*
Bestselling Author

ELLE JAMES

USA Today
Bestselling Author

JEN TALTY

PROLOGUE

A YEAR AGO...

TRINITY STEVENSON STEPPED from behind the protective windshield. Her ponytail smacked her face. The wind howled, and the seas kicked up angrily as if Poseidon himself was about to emerge from the depths of the ocean floor, waving his trident.

This storm had collided with another system, changed direction, and came at her so fast she'd barely had a chance to get her bearings. What had started as a few hours alone to collect her thoughts, to decide if she would believe him—again—had turned into a death grip on her survival instincts.

She squinted, searching and scanning the wild waters for the green and red bow lights. Or the white of the stern light. There had been another boat out there. She'd seen it. And they were charging into the storm, being tossed around by the raging waves like a rag doll. She suspected the small fishing boat to be eighteen to twenty feet long. Way too small to be out here in these conditions. Heck, her forty-footer, while built for the ocean and to handle a good storm, struggled with waves this tall. But Trinity couldn't, in good faith, just leave them out here to be swallowed by the sea gods.

Who was she kidding? She was about to be upside down if she didn't point this vessel toward shore and head in soon. She blew out a puff of air, stared into the darkness, and waited for another flash from the heavens. All she needed was a few seconds of visibility. Something to give her a better gauge of where those red and green lights were bobbing up and down in the open waters.

Thankfully, those lights appeared through the wind, waves, and rain. It rolled down with a massive crest before turning up toward the sky. Once again, she squinted, focusing solely on the small vessel, which was struggling to stay afloat and quickly losing the battle.

She reached for the radio, glancing at the channel setting, which was already set to sixteen. "Pan-Pan, Pan-Pan, Pan-Pan. This is *Princess Afloat*."

Pushing down on the throttles, she cut through the top of a massive wave. Quickly, she eased up on the power of the engines, allowing the boat's bow to rise, before giving it more gas to cut through another wave. Salt water splashed across the windshield. It sloshed over the top of the cuddy and landed right on her head. She wiped her face with her forearm and repeated the maneuver, ensuring her boat didn't go sideways.

"This is the US Coast Guard. What's your situation, *Princess Afloat*?"

She rattled off where she believed she was because she couldn't take her eyes off the waves before her to check the exact coordinates. She knew these waters like she knew the back of her hand. She knew, within a quarter of a mile, how far offshore she was and in what direction. "There's a boat in trouble about a mile and a half from my location... Oh my God. No." The vessel in question pitched sideways with the wave and rolled. A bolt of lightning lit up the sky. A clap of thunder that sounded more like gunfire rattled her teeth.

A second clap echoed in the night.

Followed by a...flash? Or a spark.

She swallowed her pulse.

"Ma'am. Are you okay?"

"Um, yes. I think so," she managed. "There's a second boat. No lights, and the other one... It capsized, and it's... Oh God, it's sinking."

"Ma'am. We're four miles from your location. Flash your spotlight."

She did as instructed.

"We can see you," the man said. "Look to your port. You'll see us."

Bang!

"Oh my God." She crouched behind the steering wheel but not too low. "The other boat fired a weapon," she said as calmly as she could.

The vessel circled—danced—around where the white glow of a stern light disappeared into the dark ocean.

Pirates? This close to shore? While it was always possible to come across a pirate wanting to steal a boat's navigational system and anything else of value in the open waters, she had never heard of one doing so this close to civilization..

Bang! Bang!

They must have seen the signal between her and the Coast Guard.

"Ma'am, are you okay?"

"Oh, my God. That was gunfire," she said into the mic. She sucked in a deep breath, staring at the white water being churned up by the boat heading right for her.

"Ma'am, can you maneuver and head toward the island barriers?" the gentleman on the other end asked. Another voice—a familiar one—muttered a few expletives in the background.

"Yes. I can do that."

"Trinity, get your ass back to the docks, now," Dawson, the new chief of police, said with real bite laced to his words.

"What about the boat that sank? I know what I saw."

"You need to be more worried about the one headed in your direction that we need to deal with," Dawson said. "Now, head home."

She glanced over her shoulder. She couldn't see anything but waves, rain, and lightning. She couldn't hear anything but the howl of the wind. No boat chasing her. The only other vessel was the Coast Guard, less than a mile away now, and racing toward the open ocean. She let out a huge breath. "Heading in." She hooked the mic to the handle and stared at the roller cresting at the top. It wasn't just any crest, either. It was the kind of wave that movies were made about. "Well, crap." She hit the throttle, spun the wheel, and braced for impact.

Princess Afloat pitched starboard as a twelve-foot swell crashed into the hull awkwardly. Gripping the steering wheel with one hand, she pushed the throttle down harder because speed was her friend right now. Rollers, she could handle. Waves that turned into surf machines, well, she couldn't risk going sideways. Her boat was too small for that, and she'd surely capsize.

Riding the wave wasn't smart, either. She needed to get in front of it. But the swells were coming closer and faster. She would have to make sure she stayed between the waves as much as she could. Or get on top of one and ride it downward before it crested. Not a fun drive.

A clap of thunder rattled the boat right before the evening sky lit up with five flashes of lightning. Usually, she loved a good lightning storm. That was when she was sitting on her front porch, watching the storm roll in from the comforts of home.

The wipers sloshed salty water across the windshield, but it did nothing to help with visibility. Flicking the spotlight on, she found the spot between the grouping of islands that led into Chokoloskee Bay from the north. She'd be protected from the massive waves once she was between the islands and the shoreline.

It was navigating through them, alone, in these conditions, that was the challenge.

She'd been a water baby her entire life. However, to most people of Calusa Cove, she was a spoiled rich girl with servants. It wasn't a falsehood. She'd been born with a silver spoon in her mouth. She'd grown up eight miles from the center of town—in a mansion. The only one in the zip code.

Her mother had never worked a day in her life, and that included housecleaning and cooking. They had a staff for that. They had a staff for everything.

Audra McCain had once joked that she wouldn't be surprised if Trinity had someone to wipe her ass. Trinity chuckled at the memory. Why did Audra, of all people, pop into her head at a time like this? She had no idea. She hadn't heard of or seen Audra in sixteen years. She wondered what had happened to the local *Stigini*. Poor girl had also gotten the short end of the stick when it came to this town. Lucky her for getting out and staying out.

Trinity had her reasons for coming back two years ago. No one in this town knew. They suspected, and some had the story half right.

A man had broken her heart. Crushed it. Tore it from her chest and utterly destroyed it. But that wasn't the worst of it. He'd taken her dignity. Her self-worth. And he stripped her of her confidence.

But that was one of the best-kept secrets of Calusa Cove.

However, she had a better understanding of her mother now. However, she hadn't wanted to bond with her mom because of it. There was too much pain over her own childhood. She hadn't even told her mother she'd been pregnant. She'd told her father, and she didn't blame him for what happened next. He'd done what any normal father would in that situation.

Hours after she'd miscarried, her mother had done the rarest thing. She'd called. She'd asked to visit and to comfort her in her time of need.

Her mom had come to Calusa Cove for an entire week. It had been the worst week of Trinity's life. Not just because she'd ended a relationship with an abusive man, but because she'd lost something she hadn't known she'd wanted.

A child.

Her mother had been a miserable woman, and everyone who had ever met her knew it. Her mom had packed her bags and left the second Trinity graduated from high school. The ink on her diploma hadn't even had the chance to dry before her mom had been on that plane.

Her mother had hated everything about Calusa Cove, and up until a few years ago, so had Trinity. Now, Calusa Cove offered her a sanctuary from her past pains and an opportunity to be the person she'd always wanted to be.

Another clap of thunder rattled her brain. The boat vibrated, starting at her toes and landing between her temples.

More lightning lit up the night skies. She was thankful for the few seconds of brightness guiding her home.

But the waves tossed her cruiser around like a freaking dingy.

Silas had warned her—more like sneered at her—that a storm was brewing. She'd checked all the weather apps and had known the sea was ripe for a storm today. However, the open water gave her peace and tranquility, and after the lunacy of her mother's call that morning, she sure as heck needed it.

Silas had pissed her off as well. Well, he and Dewey, the mangrove trimmer. Especially Dewey. He was always sitting down at the docks when he wasn't working, staring at her, waiting for her to crash her shiny, expensive boat. He'd waggle his long, crooked finger at her, reminding her that she didn't fit in and that she'd smash her boat one day.

There wasn't a scratch on her baby because she was a darn good boat driver.

But people didn't see her as Monty Stevenson's daughter, the rising star who had left on a full-ride scholarship, started a medical-tech company, and then sold it for millions after he'd gotten burned out and realized he missed small-town life.

Nope. They saw her as Porsche Stevenson's kid—the one who had brought sushi to school for lunch and, at one time, had been just like her mother.

As the islands came into view, the waves crashed into them with unrelenting force. She swallowed her pounding pulse. This had to be the worst she'd ever driven in, and frankly, she didn't ever want to do it again.

Easing up on the throttle, she made her way between two stretches of land. It was known as the Ten Thousand Islands. A chain of islands and mangrove islets that stretched from Cape Romano to Lostmans River. This area could be treacherous on a sunny day because of oyster bars and shallow waters. A captain needed to understand the tides and the area.

No matter what anyone said about her, she knew both, but that didn't make this any less dangerous.

She made it through the first set of islands and eased back even more on the throttles, letting out a long sigh of relief. The waves had reduced to four to five feet, and she could see the inlet leading her to Mitchell's Marina.

Thank God.

No. Thank Poseidon.

But oh, she could hear the crap she was going to catch from Baily, the owner of the marina and now one of her best friends. That friendship was one of the best things about returning to Calusa Cove. She'd never really had girlfriends before. She'd thought she did, but they had all turned out to be rich, prissy snots.

Kind of like she used to be.

She narrowed her gaze as she pulled down the narrow channel toward the dock she rented. A couple of dozen people were lined up along it. Some wore appropriate rain gear, others made do with what was nearby, like garbage bags. Most people in Calusa Cove were dirt-poor, and the town's population, at last count, was four hundred and twenty-eight.

Silas waved his fist in her direction as he raced across the edge of the shore toward the docks with the new sexy Fish and Wildlife guy right on his heels.

Wonderful.

This was the last thing she needed. A lecture by one of Fletcher Dane's friends and Silas, the resident grumpy old man, who occasionally had a heart of gold if you took the time to get to know him.

She spun the boat, pulling in backward, as she always did. Mainly to show off. To prove she was a master at the helm. It was childish—she knew it—but she wanted respect.

Few gave it to her.

Raindrops the size of mosquitoes pelted her eyes. As quickly as she could, she tossed the stern line to Silas.

Keaton Cole managed to snag the bowline before she could reach the front of her vessel.

"I warned you," Silas said, taking her hand. "Why didn't you come in sooner?"

"Because someone needed help," she managed to say above the roar of the wind whipping and swirling through the marina. The palm trees bent over. "I tried to help, but I couldn't get to them. Pirates did and, unfortunately, they sank." She steadied her bare feet on the dock, holding her wedges in her other hand. "I radioed the Coast Guard. And before both of you lay into me, I already got barked at by Dawson and ordered back to the docks."

"I'm not sure what to think of that man." Silas shook his head. "You're crazy, you know that? You had us all worried. I was sitting here enjoying a beer and watching those two systems collide, but there was no Trinity. I stood out there for over an hour while I watched that storm turn into a nightmare, and no Trinity. Waves like that will take even a boat your size."

"I'm well aware of what the sea can do." She blinked. "Are all the boats from this marina back? Do we have any idea who could've sunk out there?"

"You were the only one we've been waiting on," Silas said.

She shifted her gaze toward Keaton, who had served

in the Navy with Dawson Ridge, the new chief. "Why was Dawson with the Coast Guard?"

Keaton arched a brow. "He asked if he could because that's what he does when one of his townspeople doesn't come in and there were reports of pirates in the area."

"Oh." Wonderful. Here came another flipping lecture.

Keaton jerked his head toward the main building. "Let's get you inside and warmed up. You looked like a drowned rat."

"Gee, thanks. Just what a girl wants to hear." She figured she had mascara running down her cheeks. Some habits died hard, and she was still a vain woman, even if she wasn't trying to impress a man. At least not this man.

She had a man. It was a new relationship. They'd only been dating for two months, and she'd thought Fenton would be different.

Well, at first, he had been. And he didn't bark at her like Keaton did.

While Fenton worked at one of her father's many car dealerships, he didn't see her for her bank account. Fenton made good money. Perhaps not the kind she'd been born and raised with, but enough to shower her with some very nice gifts.

Though not too many. He was a man who believed everyone should live within their means, which sometimes caused a few interesting discussions. She made good money as a data scientist, a career that allowed her to work from home and live anywhere. But again, old habits died hard, and she wasn't about to give up the things she enjoyed.

Shoes, handbags, and designer clothes.

She no longer paid full price because that was just stupid. She didn't have to have top-of-the-line everything. Nor did she have to have…everything. But yeah, she liked her BMW.

To say she lived within her means was a bit of a stretch. Daddy had bought her boat, so there was that. She understood this made it harder for her to get the one thing she wanted more than anything—respect from the people of Calusa Cove. She did want them to see her in a different light.

Fenton didn't seem to care about her princess status or her father's money. But earlier today, she'd picked up his cell and found a weird text on it. It was from someone named Al. Just Al. At first, she hadn't thought anything of it, but when it had dinged in her hand and a second text came over that was sexual in nature, her heart had stopped.

Fenton had gotten defensive at first. But he'd softened, saying it was just some guy he knew, being a dick.

She'd struggled to believe it, though she'd wanted to, and it was why she'd gone for a late-night boat ride when she hadn't planned on it.

Keaton pressed his hand on the small of her back.

Her body responded, and that annoyed her on more than one level. "I have a boyfriend." She wasn't sure if that was for her benefit or Keaton's.

"I'm well aware. His name is Fenton. He drives a flashy Range Rover." Keaton did not remove his hand.

"Only he doesn't deserve you, and he doesn't come around much."

"He works a lot." She glanced over her shoulder. Silas turned and headed toward the parking lot. The gathering of people had dissipated, but not without muttering a few nasty little whispers. This town always had to have something to gossip about.

Lately, it was her.

The hum of car engines filled the air as vehicles pulled out into the street.

"While it was mighty nice of you to try to help whoever was out there, you should've just radioed and come in." Keaton nudged her closer to the main building. "I heard they fired a few shots at you."

The front door opened, and Baily stood in the entrance, holding a tall mug of something.

"Not sure it was at me," she mumbled. "And I didn't even see the pirate boat at first. Once I did, I had no intention of staying out there. Once I got hold of the Coast Guard, and they were on the way, I turned around and came home."

"It's the part where you stayed until you saw the Coast Guard, even though you were in danger, that concerns me." He stepped aside, letting her enter the marina first.

"Oh my God. You do not listen. I didn't know I was in danger at first. Once I did, I turned around. I'm not stupid." She took the mug of steaming coffee that Baily offered and smiled. "Thanks. I really need this."

"I put a shot of something else in, too," Baily said

with a sweet smile, which quickly turned into a frown as she suspiciously eyed Keaton.

Trinity knew the history. They'd spoken of it, though not at great lengths, and while she more than understood why Baily felt the way she did about Fletcher, his friends, and what that meant, she didn't agree.

"I wouldn't mind a cup of that," Keaton said. "Especially when chatting with this one is like talking to a brick wall." He lowered his chin. "You were in danger the second those storms collided."

"Anyone ever tell you you're a bully?" Trinity asked.

"You. Every time we find ourselves in a discussion." He pointed toward the far counter. "Coffee?" he asked Baily.

"You can help yourself." Baily glared. "Feel free to donate to the coffee fund."

"As if I'd take a free one." Keaton shook out his coat, stomped his muddy boots, and strode past.

When it came to the Baily and the guys, Trinity bit her tongue. This wasn't her battle. She had her own problems—not that she'd shared them with anyone. Not even Baily. It wasn't about the shame. Not anymore. It was about taking back control and being in charge of her own destiny.

The radio behind the counter crackled to life.

She and Baily raced to it, staring at it as if it yielded great power.

Dawson had only been chief for a few weeks, but he'd been one of Ken's best friends. It didn't matter if she wanted to blame Ken's military brothers for his death—she did have a heart, and no one wanted to see a storm take one of Calusa Cove's finest.

"Lost visual of pirate ship. No visual of wreckage at sea, halting search," a male voice boomed over the radio. "Heading back to port."

"This is heartbreaking," Trinity whispered. "I feel so bad for whoever was out there."

A strong hand came down on her shoulder.

She flinched.

"That could've been you." Keaton's hot breath tickled her neck. "Don't you ever pull a stunt like that again."

She whipped her head around. "Excuse me?"

He stared deep into her eyes. A hint of anger was etched into his dark brown irises. "Dawson went out there with the Coast Guard to look for *you*. We were all worried that something had happened to *you*." Keaton exhaled through his nose, and a second later, he inhaled sharply. She hadn't known him all that long, but she didn't have to. From the moment they'd met, they'd been like oil drizzled on top of water with a lit match dropped on top.

The instant heat—instant attraction—had been palpable, and she knew it hadn't been one-sided. No. He'd looked her over like a tongue licking a Popsicle on a hot summer day. They had stared each other down like a couple of sex-starved teenagers. Then one of them had opened their mouth, and the next thing she knew, they were fighting.

Every day it was the same. She did something he found offensive or reckless, and he was overbearing and opinionated.

It didn't matter that he was sexy as hell. He drove her crazy.

Besides, she had a boyfriend, something she constantly forgot about whenever she was in Keaton's presence.

She pursed her lips. "If I needed help, I would have radioed. I'm not stupid."

He cocked his head. "But you didn't think to radio anyone to tell them you were safe or what you were doing. Or that you were helping someone or even heading in until after you'd been in that storm for a good forty minutes to an hour." He jerked his thumb over his shoulder. "Do you think those people were standing out there to watch you back your pretty toy into the dock? No. They were worried that something bad had happened to you. We all were. I would've hated to have to call that boyfriend of yours to tell him you'd been lost at sea." He turned on his heel and marched his sexy ass right out the door.

"Jeez, that was totally unnecessary," she mumbled.

"I can't believe I'm going to side with him, but no, it wasn't." Baily sighed and leaned across the counter, taking Trinity's hand. "I tried to radio you, but you never answered."

"Crap. I switched to channel sixteen when the storm hit, and the reception was spotty anyway with all that rain and wind. Why didn't you try me on—"

"That's for emergencies. Two is what we use for marina chatter. You know that."

"You're right. You're right. I'm sorry, Baily. It won't ever happen again. I swear." The old Trinity would have gotten her panties in a twist and huffed out. But not the new and improved Trinity. No, this version valued and respected her friends and their feelings.

She could admit when she was wrong.

And this time, she could have been dead wrong.

* * *

THE FOLLOWING MORNING, Trinity raced out her front door and flew down the porch steps, flinging herself at Mallary Shaw. She pulled her friend into her arms and hugged her tightly. "I'm so sorry, Mallary." Tears poured out of her eyes. "If I had known that Jared was on the boat that sank last night, I would have..." A guttural sob filled her throat, choking off the rest of her...what? Words? There were no words to express the horrible guilt and the terrible sadness that swirled around in Trinity's heart.

"I can't believe he's gone," Mallary whispered. Her shoulders bobbed up and down. Her body grew heavy as she collapsed onto the steps.

Trinity sank with her friend, clinging to her, wishing she could take away all the pain, but not even time would do that. She cradled Mallary in her arms, stroking her hair, letting her friend purge all the emotions. No amount of caring and kind words would ever make this okay.

She stared out over the ocean. Barely a ripple showed on the water as the calm sea gently lapped against the shore. Not a single cloud in the sky intercepted the bright sunrays as they stretched long fingers, warming her skin. She blinked. So many questions might never be answered.

But Trinity knew what she'd seen... a boat lost to the sea.

She was told that Keaton, Dawson, Hayes, and Fletcher had volunteered to scuba dive in the area where the vessel may have gone down, but no one was sure of the exact location. They were trained Navy SEALs. If anyone could find the boat—and Jared—it would be those four men. She glanced at her watch. They would already be a hundred feet down by now.

But Trinity, a certified deep scuba diver herself, knew how hard that would be. She knew how deep those waters could be, how the currents and the wind from the storm could have taken Jared's body farther out to sea. It might be a futile attempt. Even the boat could have twisted, turned, and landed in a very different location. However, she was grateful they were good enough men to go out there and try.

That included Keaton.

No matter how much they clashed, she couldn't rid herself of the attraction. And she tried.

"I don't understand why my brother was out there alone. He said he was taking his new friends with him. I hate those guys. Especially that Ralph idiot. He's bad news." Mallary pushed from Trinity's embrace.

Trinity had never met Ralph or his friends. But she'd heard all about them from Mallary, and how Mallary had believed they were a bad influence on her little brother, how they'd been using Jared and his kindness. His generosity and his desire to be liked and accepted by his peers were things Trinity understood all too well.

"I know taking a gap year isn't a bad thing," Mallary said, swiping her cheeks. "Jared wanted to stay and work with our dad. He loved fishing. They talked about taking over Daddy's business all the time. He thought he should spend a year seeing how things were done in all facets of the charter business before spending four years in business school. I supported that idea. I mean, I took a gap year, and it was the best decision I ever made." Mallary spoke so fast it was amazing she managed to choke up a few sobs. "His mother hated everything about that idea. She bragged about how she finished her four-year degree in three and a half years and had just turned twenty-one. Of course, I reminded her that she ended up pregnant by a man twice her age. I know my dad loves her, though I can't fathom why. She's a brainless twit and not half the woman my mother was. I'm not bitter, but I miss my mother so much right now. Her death was so pointless, and I still don't understand it. She had so much to live for."

"I know. I know." Trinity had met Mallary years after her mother had died by suicide. She had swallowed a bunch of pills that no one had known she'd been taking for anxiety and depression. Not even Mallary's father had known. It had all been a shock, and Mallary had been so close to her mom. She had shared pictures of them going to get their hair and nails done—always with big, bright smiles.

"I wanted to like my stepmom, but she tried too hard to be my mother. It was gross." Mallary sniffled. She tilted her head and smiled. "I did, however, adore my half-brother. He was sweet and pure and didn't deserve to be lost at sea. Do you think he might still be alive?"

What a loaded question. There was always the possibility. Stranger things had happened. But she didn't want to give her friend false hope, especially since that storm had rumbled on until four in the morning, twisting and turning the ocean with waves uncharacteristic for this time of year.

Trinity looped her arm around one of the few true friends she'd managed to make—and maintain—from her years at university. She held Mallary's gaze. "I know it's crazy to hope for a miracle, but I reached out to an old charter buddy of my dad's, and he said he heard of people being found days after their boat went under. So, no, it's not crazy. If I had a brother, I'd be doing the same thing. Plus, Jared was a good captain. He would've done all the right things."

"You watched his boat capsize." Mallary sighed.

"We don't know it was his vessel," Trinity said. "There are two other missing boats from nearby coastal towns. It could've been one of them."

"But you told me you witnessed a boat go down. One that looked similar in size. You also said there was a possible pirate ship in the area." Mallary hiccupped. "You heard gunshots. The Coast Guard said all the same things, and my brother never came home. Why? Why my brother?" Mallary shot her hand up. "That was a rhetorical question. I'm not expecting an answer."

"Do you have any idea what he was doing or why his friends didn't go with him?"

"All I know is my dad said Jared asked if he could use one of the charter boats to go fishing with his friends. My dad reminded him that a storm was brewing off the coast and to be mindful of the weather. He never worried about Jared on the water." Mallary shook her head. "He trained us both to handle ourselves out there. The lessons were sometimes tough, but Jared really knew what he was doing. He loved the ocean so much—more than I ever did. I could take it or leave it. Growing up, we used to call Jared *Baby Aquaman*. If there was rough weather coming, Jared would've come in. He didn't take chances. He knew how devastating the sea could be."

"I can tell you it was bad out there, and Jared's little fishing boat could've easily capsized."

"You're not helping." Mallary glared, blowing out a puff of air. "Bethany babied that poor kid. She wanted him to be an overachieving pencil-pushing nerd. Sometimes, I swear she wanted him to take over that flower shop, as if that were a place for Jared."

"Maybe not, but flowers could have gotten him laid," Trinity said, desperately needing to lighten the mood. She pushed down her aversion to the concept of receiving such a thoughtful gift, reminding herself that, somewhere, there was a man who presented a woman with flowers for no other reason than that he cared.

Mallary dropped her head back and burst out laughing. "At least I can be happy he got to experience sex before he died."

"No. Seriously?" Trinity jerked her head. "Little Jared? With whom?"

"This marina babe. A girl by the name of Valerie. A real looker, too." Mallary heaved in a breath and let it with a big swoosh. "I miss him so much already. When I was his age and my friends would all complain about their pain-in-the-ass little siblings, I didn't understand. He was just a baby back then, and I couldn't get enough of him."

"I remember when we met in college. I first thought you were a teenage mom."

"I thought of myself that way with him," Mallary whispered. "What am I going to do? My dad is dealing with so much because Bethany has completely lost her shit. The worst part is she's blaming me—and my dad— for what happened as if we told him to go out there alone. Now, everyone believes he might've had something to do with the jewels stolen from Ralph's parents."

"I heard that." Trinity nodded. "Dawson, you met him, the new chief of police of Calusa Cove. I overheard him telling his buddies that they believe either pirates heard Jared must've had the jewels from the *Flying Victoria* or that he was meeting pirates out there to sell them."

"That's utter crap. My little brother would never do something like that." Mallary's face hardened. She stared at Trinity with daggers shooting from her unwavering gaze. "I bet it was Ralph who stole that jewelry. That kid is a no-good little twit. But it still doesn't explain why Jared went out there alone, and my ugly stepmother will never forgive either me or my dad."

"Oh my God. That's so unfair. Neither of you were even out there."

"Doesn't matter. My dad handed him the keys, and once again, I took my dad's side. She's always feeling ganged up on by us. It's my fault he deferred college for a year, and now she's going to blame his death on me for as long as she has breath in her lungs."

Trinity understood a little something about blame. Totally different situations, and she wouldn't compare —not out loud anyway. But her mother blamed her very existence for her misery. If Trinity hadn't been born, her father might never have moved back to Calusa Cove to show her something other than the station to which she was born. And her mother would have never blamed her for all the pain she suffered.

"Right now, all you can do is allow yourself to grieve," Trinity said softly. "You have to do that. You have to let the emotions in—and out. Don't fight it. Plus, your dad is going to need you. His heart is breaking just like yours. So is Bethany's, even if she doesn't empathize with anyone other than herself. Remember, I'll be here every step of the way. Whatever you need."

"Do you mean that?"

"Of course I do."

"My dad wants to have a memorial service. I think it's too soon, but I won't argue with him. He asked me to help him plan the memorial. You know how much I hate things like that."

Oh boy, did Trinity know that. When they'd been in college, a friend—not a close one, but someone who had lived in their dorm—had died in a horrible accident. They had all been drinking that night at a party, but

Amber had been a hot mess and remained behind when the rest headed back to their dorm. They'd all drawn straws to decide who would pick her up, and Mallary had gotten the short one. But when she'd gone to collect Amber, she'd disappeared. They'd all searched for her for over an hour. No one could find her. The next day, the police found her body. She'd stumbled into someone's backyard and fallen into their pool. They'd all been utterly heartbroken.

"My dad also wants me to speak at this...thing. He believes Jared would've wanted me to, but I haven't a clue as to what to say."

Trinity squeezed her friend's shoulder. "We'll figure it out together."

"I don't know what I'd do without you."

"Ditto." Trinity's phone vibrated. Quickly, she pulled it from her pocket and glanced at the text. She'd ignored Fenton since their fight yesterday, other than to let him know she'd made it in safely. She'd neglected to tell him anything about her adventure at sea. He'd learn about it soon enough.

Although it appeared from his worried text, he might have already been told.

She frowned.

"What's wrong?" Mallary asked.

"Nothing." Trinity tucked her cell back in her pocket. She'd deal with Fenton later.

"Come on. I need something to distract me from what's happening. My brain can't stop going back out there." Mallary pointed to the open ocean.

Trinity sighed. While Mallary could be high maintenance as friends went, and she wasn't always there when Trinity needed her most, she was a good person. She was kind and decent, and if she needed a distraction, Trinity could give her that. "It's Fenton. We got into a fight yesterday. It's why I went out on the boat instead of going out with him."

"Oh. I didn't know that." Mallary brushed her hair from her face. "What happened?"

"I saw a text. He says it was from some dude, but the words on the screen screamed some girl he was sexting with—not some random old buddy sending him sex jokes. I'm not stupid. It was dirty talk, and I can't do another cheating man again."

"Seriously?" Mallary jerked her head back. "Fenton? No way. That man adores you. He worships the ground you walk on. I can't believe he'd be chatting with another chick. He wouldn't do that. No way. You totally misinterpreted that text."

Trinity wanted to believe that. She really liked Fenton. He was normal, if there was such a thing. He wasn't needy. He didn't demand all her time. The only thing he did was occasionally get jealous.

Of Keaton.

Granted, she did find Keaton sexy as hell—in the looks department. But his personality was sometimes a little too rough around the edges—at least toward her.

"I don't think I misinterpreted it," Trinity admitted. "And this isn't the first red flag." However, this was the first time she was talking about it with anyone.

"What do you mean?" Mallary crinkled her nose.

"I found an earring in his car a week ago."

"What did he say about it?" Mallary's eyes went wide. She swiped at her cheeks.

"He told me he let one of the girls in the office take his car to get lunch."

"Well, there you have it." Mallary lowered her chin. "I get you're wounded. I know you have some trust issues. I would, too. But come on. Fenton is a keeper. He's super sweet. He's kind, and generous—and he's good to you. He wouldn't cheat. He's so not the type."

He was a man. He had a dick. That made him "the type" in Trinity's book. But she wasn't about to argue with Mallary. That woman thought Fenton was the perfect man for Trinity.

For a hot minute, so had Trinity, but she wasn't so sure now.

"Call him back." Mallary nudged her. "Make up with him. Life is too short."

Trinity sighed. She understood shock, and that was the only explanation for what was happening here because the only thing that mattered was Jared.

CHAPTER 1

KEATON STUFFED his marshmallow on the end of the stick and held it over the open flame, waving it back and forth, but that didn't stop it from catching fire. "Crap," he mumbled. He hated burnt white mush. He raised his stick, blew, and tried again.

This time, he had a little better luck. But not much. Damn thing still had a crusty outside.

Kind of like his mood.

"What's got your panties in a twist?" Dawson tugged at his jeans and sat down.

"Long day." Except, it had been an easy day—a sunrise tour for Everglades Overwatch airboat tour company that he owned with his three best friends, and then a lazy day working for Fish and Wildlife, and he hadn't given out one ticket. He wasn't even tired. But he was annoyed. He'd known Trinity Stevenson now for a year. One full flipping year. He didn't deny—at least to himself—that he found her attractive, even if he didn't go for chicks with painted nails, designer bags, and heels.

Okay, so what hot-blooded male didn't like a woman in three-inch heels?

But he had kept his distance from Trinity for two reasons. First, she came off as a spoiled woman who cared more about her BMW than the environment or people.

However, that assessment had been proven wrong on a stormy night when she'd put herself in danger to help someone else. Noble but reckless, and the constant recklessness was the second reason he kept her at arm's length.

He couldn't go down that road again.

"Is it that or the fact that one blond-haired female isn't here?" Dawson leaned back, folding his arms across his chest, and gave Dawson that look. The one where he thought he'd hit the nail on the head.

Well, he had, and that annoyed Keaton even more.

"I saw her before she went out on her boat today. She said she's coming after she's done with her deep dive." Keaton blew on his marshmallow before shoving it in his mouth. He set his stick aside and reached for his beer, taking a healthy swig. He sighed. "She shouldn't be out there doing that alone. It's dangerous."

"We've both done deep dives alone," Dawson said, cocking his head and arching a brow, daring Keaton to find some explanation for how what she was doing was different.

"We're SEALs, and we generally don't do that when our emotions are running hot." Keaton had contemplated asking out Trinity when he'd first met her, but she'd had a boyfriend, and he didn't insert himself into other people's relationships. However, that excuse had ended pretty quickly, ruining his excuse to stay away.

But she also ran around town like she had something to prove to everyone. It was frustrating as hell. However, he could understand that part because the good people of this town still treated her as if she were that rich, bratty teenage girl no one liked because she thought she was entitled simply because she existed. Or that she was plain better than everyone else.

But Trinity Stevenson had depth. She was super smart. She often amazed him with the way she held her side of a conversation. Or the things she knew. It baffled him why she thought she needed to be so damned impetuous impetus all the time. That wasn't how she was going to gain the respect she desired. Besides, she had it from the people who mattered.

Who cared what anyone else thought?

"That girl is about as obsessed with finding that wreckage as you are with her," Dawson added.

"I'm not obsessed. What I am is tired of watching her do things that could potentially land her in the hospital or worse." Keaton shot his friend a fiery glare. "She needs backup. She needs someone to temper what's driving her to spend all her free time looking for a sunken ship, lost treasure, and a dead man."

"That's a crappy way to put it," Dawson said. "Why can't you admit you like her?"

"Never said I didn't. I'm just not interested in asking out a woman who doesn't give a damn about her own safety. Scuba diving alone might not be reckless for some people, but this is personal for her, and the more she goes out there, the more desperate she becomes to find answers."

Dawson waggled a finger. "If you're not interested, then she's not your problem. You shouldn't be so upset over it."

"This coming from the man who can't utter the words 'I love you' to his girlfriend." That was a horrible analogy, but Keaton didn't care. He wanted off the subject. Trinity had crawled under his skin and into every waking thought. She'd even entered his endless dreams. He couldn't get rid of her, and boy, had he tried.

Dawson groaned. "It's not that I can't. It's just that we decided, now that she's moved into the big house and not crashing with me, to take things a little slower."

Keaton's lips curved into a massive smile. Laughter bubbled in his throat. He tried like hell not to let it roar, but it became impossible. "You and Audra have one speed. You'll be living in the big house by the end of next week."

"Half my stuff's already there." Dawson raised his beer. "And I can't say I've slept in the cabin in the last week. But this thing with us happened so fast. It's only been a couple of months. I'm still dealing with the fallout from the Massey case. He and his son managed to get some fancy high-priced attorney, and I hear they are talking plea deals for protection from the cartel. Agent Pope was able to put a good dent in the Mendoza's operation—a big one, especially with Trevor rolling over on them. But Paul Massey still has information Pope wants."

"Would trading that information be so bad?" Keaton asked.

"No, and it's the same thing we promised Trevor, but I want justice for Audra and the murder of her dad. I want to make sure that's not part of the deal. They got Paul and Benson on multiple drug and arms charges. But murder could keep them both in prison for life. I need to give that to her." Dawson ran a hand over his mouth. "It would suck if that didn't happen."

"I get it." Keaton nodded. "Any news on how involved Ken was back in the day? Or is that story still the same?"

"It's shifted a bit, but nothing concrete. Trevor swears Ken only knew about what he and Benson were doing, and while I do believe Trevor, I'm not sure that our good friend Ken had been completely honest with us all those years. Anna and I have been searching for Trip's notebook, but we keep coming up empty-handed. Trevor had some ideas on where his dad might have hidden it, but part of me wonders if he's leading me on a wild goose chase. His dad could have intel in that book that could hurt Trevor. Or save him. No one knows." Dawson glanced over his shoulder. "I'd rather not talk about all this with Baily so close. She gets upset when it comes to Ken."

"Understood."

"The whole case is a shit show."

"It still has this town upside down. But it has nothing to do with you telling Audra you love her, because I don't want to have to beat the crap out of you if you screw up the best thing that's ever happened to you outside of me, Hayes, and Fletcher."

Dawson chuckled, shifting his gaze. He waved to Audra, who leaned against the railing of the big house while she sipped wine and chit-chatted with Baily. "Neither one of us is the romantic type, but I want to do that right."

"Don't. You'll make an ass out of yourself, and it won't be authentic. Just look into her eyes and say it."

Dawson tilted his head and stared into the fire. "The only other time I've said those words was to Liz. Besides not meaning them, I damn near choked on them. I do love Audra. I can say that to you. I can say it to myself. I don't want to lose her, but I'm afraid if I move too fast or come in too hot, I'll scare her away."

"Take it from a man who's loved and lost. The longer you hold out, the more you'll regret not saying it." Keaton reached out and gave his buddy a little love punch on the shoulder.

Dawson lowered his chin and his eyelids at the same time. Slowly, he nodded his head but said nothing. He didn't have to. Everyone on the team had known Petra. They'd been there when Keaton had met her, and they'd stood by him when he'd buried the love of his life.

But he would always have one big regret when it came to Petra. Well, two regrets, wrapped into one messed-up childish decision that had changed him forever.

Keaton didn't often openly talk about what had

happened, but there were moments it bubbled to the surface. Normally, he pushed them down.

However, this was one of those rare times that he believed sharing his personal, private hell might help one of his best friends past an important hurdle.

"I fought with Petra the week before she died," Keaton said softly. "I was too stubborn to call her before we were deployed. It didn't matter what the fight was about, we always said we loved each other before I left, and we didn't that one time. She died without hearing those words come out of my mouth, and trust me, man, they are not just words." Keaton sighed. The emotion stuck in his throat, then dropped to his heart.

Dawson knew there was so much more to this story. It wasn't just that he'd failed to tell the woman he loved how he felt, but he'd also forgiven her for breaking his trust. He understood her reasons. He could have accepted they weren't ready. But she'd never given him the chance, and he'd let her die believing he not only didn't love her but wasn't sure if they could stand the test of time.

He would always love Petra. There could never be another woman for him, which was why this thing with Trinity made him so crazy. The blond-haired beauty had gotten under his skin like a toxin. For the last year, she was all he could think about. He'd blink his eyes open in the morning and wonder what she'd be doing that day. Would he see her when he showed up at the docks? Or run into her in town? He found himself stopping at the local coffee shop almost every morning in hopes of running into her, only to get pissed off because he'd learn she was doing something stupid again.

Petra had died because she'd thought she was invisible. She'd lived her life on the edge. Adrenaline meant almost more to her than he did. At first, that's what had drawn him to Petra. He'd loved how much she'd enjoyed the outdoors. She'd try almost anything. About the only thing she hadn't liked was fishing because the woman couldn't sit still unless she was strapped to something going a hundred miles an hour.

As they'd gotten older, a little more mature, her wild nature had become a concern. He'd wanted her to stop seeking out everything that could kill her. He'd started to worry she had a death wish that he hadn't noticed before. And maybe she had. Maybe she'd gone up in that plane and performed those tricks with reckless abandon, not caring if she'd lived or died.

Her motto had always been, *Babe, you only live once. Might as well live like you're dying.*

Trinity wasn't like that. He knew she didn't want to die—well, maybe Petra hadn't wanted to either, but she also hadn't been afraid of it.

Trinity wanted to prove she wasn't some spoiled rich bitch who needed the world to serve her, that she could do what everyone else in Calusa Cove did. That she wasn't afraid to take risks.

But this scuba diving alone thing was making him crazy. She could die under the water, and no one would know—and for what? To prove what? This wasn't her battle. It belonged to someone else.

"I know you're right about Audra. I'm just scared it's too soon, and she'll run," Dawson said.

Keaton smiled. "That chick isn't afraid of much, and I'm pretty sure she feels the same way." The sound of big-ass tires kicking up pebbles tickled his ears. He waved his finger toward Hayes's souped-up truck. "Did you know that Hayes managed to get Chloe's personal cell phone number and has been texting her for a week straight?"

"As in the FBI agent who's been in town a couple of times looking for those missing young adults?" Dawson asked.

"That's the one." Keaton chuckled. "Talk about a man with a hard-on. The last time she showed up in town, his eyes nearly popped right out of their sockets. He's not even subtle about it."

"Looks like he's got Fletcher with him." Dawson stood. "Want another beer?"

Keaton closed one eye and peered into his longneck. "Yeah." He downed the last two swallows, handed the empty to his buddy, and watched him walk away.

Dawson stopped on the front porch, took Audra by the hand, and led her inside the big house. They were about two months from the grand opening of Harvey's Bed and Breakfast. Keaton didn't understand why on God's green earth they hadn't changed the name. Granted, Harvey's Cabins had been a staple in the community for years. It was a well-known name, but Dawson owned the establishment now. Turning that house into a B&B and slapping someone else's name on it seemed strange.

"Well, dang. I didn't mean say it right now," Keaton mumbled.

"What are you babbling about?" Fletcher slapped his shoulder.

"Oh, Dawson's about to tell Audra he loves her for the first time." Keaton shook his head. This team didn't have any secrets. Well, at least the living didn't. They'd recently learned that their good friend Ken—Baily's brother, the man who had died in combat and was one of the reasons they'd come to Calusa Cove a little over a year ago, had a few secrets.

One, they knew.

The rest? Well, a picture was forming, and it wasn't pretty.

"Not the most romantic moment, but good on him." Fletcher snagged a stick and the marshmallow bag. He plopped himself down in a chair and tossed the bag to Hayes. "I see that idiot Decker Brown is back in town." He jerked his thumb over his shoulder. "I don't like that guy."

"You barely even know him," Keaton said. "None of us do. Besides, Dawson did a basic check on the man. His story is legit."

"I don't care," Fletcher huffed. "He's a land developer. His job description goes against everything we all stand for, not to mention his current project is over on Marco Island. Why does he keep coming around here—specifically, showing up at the marina to have a cup of coffee with Baily?"

"Ah. I see." Keaton leaned back and folded his arms across his chest. "You're jealous."

"Not the right word," Fletcher said. "I don't trust him. It's a long commute to deal with a project when he comes to town, which is way too often. Dawson should tell him he doesn't have any vacancies."

"Decker's a paying customer." Keaton shook his head. "Besides, Trinity told me Baily's not interested."

Fletcher arched a brow. "You managed a civil conversation with her? Wow. Impressive."

"I have my moments." Keaton chuckled.

"Hey, Baily, are you going to join us?" Fletcher called, waving to Baily.

"If I'm forced." Slowly, she came down the steps. She strolled across the path and to the fire pit, taking a seat across from Fletcher. The tension between the two had eased somewhat over the course of the last year.

Baily and Audra had gotten close again, and that seemed to make things even better, but Baily still resented the entire team. It was complicated and Keaton understood better than most. He and the rest of the team were a constant reminder that Ken hadn't returned.

Baily checked her watch. "Trinity should have been here by now."

Keaton sat up taller. "Did she come back before you left the marina?"

"No, but—"

"Jesus. She could still be out there." Keaton jumped to his feet.

"Relax." Baily held up her hand. "She called me to tell me she was going home first. Something about wanting to take a look at an image she took underwater. I just didn't think it would take this long." Baily jerked her thumb over her shoulder. "Knowing Dawson and Audra, they're probably inside having a quickie, and I don't want to be stuck alone out here with you three."

"We're not that bad," Fletcher said. "And Dawson and Audra are kind of disgusting."

"Leave Mommy and Daddy alone," Hayes said. "I, for one, think they're cute."

"That texting with Chloe must be going really well," Keaton said.

"Nah. Crashed and burned." Hayes shrugged. "She told me her caseload was too much, and while I *intrigued* her, she wasn't dating."

"Seriously? You've been chatting with her for an entire week. It took that long to hit the ground in flames?" Keaton asked.

"I tried more than once." Hayes shrugged. "I just finally gave up today. There are more fish in the sea. Only, just not in this town."

Dawson and Audra came out of the big house, all smiles, holding hands. Dawson carried a small cooler in his free hand. Thank God. Keaton could sure use that fresh beer.

It warmed Keaton's heart to see his buddy so happy. Deep down, he was a hopeless romantic. He totally believed in love.

But that ship had sailed.

Dawson set the cooler down and flipped open the lid. "You idiots can help yourself." He took a seat next to Baily, and Audra eased onto his lap, gazing into his eyes.

They'd said the words. Keaton knew it. Felt it deep

in his bones. He gave them six months before wedding bells were ringing, and he and the rest of the guys were arguing over who would be the best man.

But they all knew how it would play out. All or no one.

"What are we talking about?" Dawson asked.

"Hayes's love life, and the fact that the FBI agent turned him down."

Dawson laughed. "Sorry, man. But I was struggling to see it anyway."

"Trinity's friend Mallary is single," Baily said.

"Nope." Hayes let out a long breath. "She's nice. She's intelligent. And she's pretty. But she turned me down, too. Said she's got too much going on with what happened to her brother, and I understand that."

Dawson scratched his jaw. "I've been following that case. I even looked at the police file."

"Does Trinity know you did that?" Baily asked.

"She asked me to." Dawson nodded. "I can't tell her much, but I did tell her and Mallary that I find some of the statements suspicious."

"What do you mean?" Baily leaned forward. "Exactly."

"You've all read the newspapers. Those boys all tell the same story. They thought they were going on a little fishing trip with their buddy. They were excited. But then came the reports of the storm, and they thought better of it. They told Jared not to go, but Jared got mad, called them names, and told them he'd never ask them to go fishing again."

"Something tells me you don't believe them," Baily said.

"Half the town says Jared was a sweet kid, who was kind to everyone and wouldn't hurt a fly, much less steal anything." Dawson cocked a brow. "The other half now believe he was a thief, made worse by the fact that one of the boys says he overheard Jared whispering about the jewels while on his phone, saying that he'd do it—that he'd handle it whether he had help or not."

"There were many stories that came out right after the incident," Audra said. "Jared had never been in trouble before. The other boys didn't have glowing reputations, but they weren't painted as bad kids who would lie."

"Yeah, but since then things have snowballed. Other kids have come out to say that Jared had changed in the last few months before he died," Baily said. "Even some very reputable adults have come forward with credible stories about Jared and his strange, secretive behavior."

"Even the police chief on Marco Island told me that his own father stated that Jared had been late to work or had come back late from lunch and lied about where he was," Dawson said. "His dad said that it was because he'd been seeing this marina babe, Valerie, but that girl has said more than once she never dated Jared. That they were barely friends."

"Didn't Mallary swear she set her brother up with that young girl?" Keaton asked.

"She did, and now it's become a he-said/she-said kind of situation." Dawson ran his hand over his face.

"It's hard to figure out the truth when one of the players is dead."

"There have been some *so-called* credible things said about me and my dad in this town." Audra twisted her hair. "For years, people in Calusa Cove believed horrible things about me, and only about an eighth of them were true."

"Don't get mad at me, babe, but you didn't help yourself with some of the things you said and did." Dawson pressed his finger on Audra's lips to keep her from blurting out a typical retort consisting of a few curse words.

Keaton stared at his friends. Sometimes, he found himself simply watching their interactions with each other. It was so nice to see two people who genuinely loved, valued, and respected one another.

"After looking at everything I could about the case and doing my own little mini-investigation, the circumstantial evidence points to Jared, but that doesn't mean I'm going to believe everything I hear," Dawson said. "Without the boat or the jewels, there isn't much to go on."

"What are you going to do about it?" Baily asked.

"Not much I can do. Everyone thinks the jewelry is back at the bottom of the ocean, and Jared's the one responsible." Dawson wrapped his arms around Audra, who rested her head on his shoulder. "I've spoken to the lead detectives. They did everything by the book. Unless that boat is brought up from the bottom of the sea, or the jewels are found, Jared is, right now, the only plausible suspect."

"I feel so bad for Mallary and her family," Baily said. "Her father's business has taken a big hit because of this. Even if Jared did do it, they shouldn't suffer more. Right now, it's just rumors. I wish I could say I didn't believe how fast a town could turn on someone, but we all did the same thing to Audra."

"The worst part is all the speculation is twisting partial truths into absolute facts," Audra said. "That marina babe—Valerie—her story did change a little bit. She first indicated that she and Jared were closer—until her parents got involved. I get they want to protect her, but they're doing so at the expense of a potentially innocent dead kid. And for what? To maintain her popularity status?"

"That's harsh," Baily said.

"But not necessarily untrue." Audra cocked her head. "Mallary swears Valerie and Jared had sex. Valerie's still in high school. She's head cheerleader. Class president. Besides virgin status, she has a reputation to maintain."

"I wouldn't want to be a teenager again," Keaton said. "The pressure to be cool, to be popular—it's exhausting."

Hayes tossed a marshmallow. It bounced off Keaton's nose. "What are you blustering about? You were always popular. Class president. Captain of the football team. Voted most likely to succeed. You were even voted most popular."

"That may be true, but there are pressures in being the kid everyone thinks they want to be. Or wants to be friends with. I hated it most of my youth. I'd look at the kids in school who weren't popular and often wished I were them. I wanted to blend into the woodwork." He smacked his forehead and chuckled. "I remember once thinking if I went out for something I wasn't good at, people might see me as normal, instead of some kind of superhero. So, I started with the chess club. I had never played the dumb game, but it turned out that I'm great at it. I went out for three different things that I'd never done and—"

"Oh, shut up," Hayes said. "We get it. You're the golden boy. Good at everything you touch, even flipping gymnastics." He jerked his thumb. "You know, this guy was actually on the team his junior year of high school. Competed and everything."

"No way?" Baily laughed. "You did a floor routine? I'd like to see that."

"Absolutely not," Keaton mumbled. "And for the record, I wasn't that good, just good enough to make the team."

"And get a couple of silver medals, or whatever they call it at the high school level," Hayes said.

"And he can still do a backflip." Dawson wiggled his finger. "I'd give it a seven. His form sucks."

"You're all assholes." Keaton downed half his beer. His teenage years had been rough, but it was difficult to explain why. He'd had everything growing up. Loving parents. Great siblings. A cool older cousin named Foster, who, to this day, he still looked up to, even if he couldn't get the guy to move to Florida now that he'd left the Air Force. No, Foster had decided on the

Oregon Coast. Well, it was a nice place to visit, and Keaton had spent his first few years as a boy living there. Not that he had any ties to Oregon, because he didn't, but he had a bond with Foster.

Keaton's family wasn't rich, but they weren't poor either. He'd wanted for nothing.

And yet, he'd craved everything.

Mainly, he hadn't wanted to be seen as special.

The day he'd enlisted in the Navy, he'd discovered he was just another sailor. He might have joined the elite SEALs, but especially there, he wasn't anything to write home about, because every man was the best, and no one was treated as though they were "better than."

He'd found home.

And he'd found Petra.

For some reason, that brought his mind right back to Trinity. Damn woman wouldn't get out of his thoughts.

As if on cue, her pretty BMW SUV rolled into what would be the parking area of Harvey's B&B.

She flew out of that vehicle as if it were on fire. Her blond hair was pulled back in a high ponytail with a few strands dangling around her face. Her pale-blue eyes sparkled against the flames reaching toward the clear night sky.

And those damn freaking wedge heels, or whatever they were called... She was going to break her neck running on gravel like that, but of course, she managed to make it look graceful.

"Sorry, I'm late." She waved something over the top

of her head. "But I think I might have found something out there today."

Keaton closed his eyes and counted to ten, promising himself he wouldn't argue with her tonight— but knowing he'd break that promise the second he lifted his lids.

CHAPTER 2

TRINITY SKIDDED TO A STOP, breathless. Her gaze locked with Keaton's, and her heart dropped to her stomach, lurched back up, and lodged in her throat, pounding like a pulsating balloon.

She'd long gotten past being slightly fearful of Keaton. Not of him, but afraid of her feelings for the man. He wasn't anything like Fenton. Not even close. She knew that, but she couldn't trust herself around Keaton. The attraction was palpable.

Even if he didn't share it.

Every time she saw him, it was the same thing.

You're going to get yourself killed.

You're reckless.

Or her favorite.

Don't go alone. I'll go with you.

Right. The man was always working, and it was worse since he'd been promoted to head of the Fish and Wildlife Department of Calusa Cove. When he wasn't busy with that, he was running tours for the airboat company he owned with his buddies. A couple of times, she'd agreed to his help, but it had been on his terms, and she wasn't one to sit around and wait.

She was an experienced scuba diver. Much to her mother's dismay, she'd been doing it since she was fifteen. She knew the dangers. Prepared for them. It wasn't unheard of for someone with her level of expertise to go on a solo adventure. It was actually quite a common practice.

Keaton was just being controlling and, well, Keaton.

She'd learned over the year she'd known him that he was a bit of a rules guy and a safety nut. Perhaps not totally strange for a man who had once been what most considered a thrill-seeker. But she would have expected that behavior more from Hayes, the firefighter, or Dawson, the cop.

"What's got you all excited?" Keaton stood, reaching for the photograph in her hands.

Instinctively, she pulled it to her chest.

He arched a brow. "You don't want me to see that?"

"Oh. No, I do. Well, I'd rather they all look at it first, tell me what they think, and then you can tell me I'm crazy and lecture me about scuba diving on my own like I'm a toddler and you're my daddy."

"Let the record show I did not start this argument." Keaton snatched the picture right from her fingertips. "What am I looking at?"

"Anyone ever tell you you're a jerk?"

"Yeah, you, every time I see you."

She planted a hand on her hip and resisted the urge to stick her tongue out. God, this man often brought out the worst in her, and that made her emotions even more confusing. She shouldn't want a man so badly who made her this crazy.

He took out his cell and tapped the screen, turning on the flashlight, nearly blinding her. "I'm going to ask you again. What am I supposed to see in this murky image?"

"That. Right there." She leaned over and tapped the image. "My tank was low, and it was getting late. But that's a boat. I think it might be Jared's."

"I can't tell anything from this picture." Keaton brought the image closer. "It's a big shadow. It could be almost anything."

"Maybe that's what it looks like on paper, but I know what I saw, and Mallary finally got her deep dive certification. We're going out again tomorrow after lunch."

"At least you won't be going out there alone," Keaton mumbled.

"Can I see that?" Dawson asked.

"Sure." Trinity snatched it from Keaton and marched across the grass. "I get it's hard to see, but that's Jared's boat. I know it."

"Even if it is, what's it going to tell you?" Keaton eased back into his chair and sipped his beer. "What kind of answers do you honestly think you're going to find?" He held up his hand. "Because if the jewels from the *Flying Victoria* are down there and you bring them back up, it's not going to do anything but make Jared look guilty."

The blood in her veins boiled. "Why do you always have to do that?"

"Do what?" Keaton glared. "Be realistic? Tell you the truth about your actions? Because sometimes, I swear that, for a smart woman, you simply don't think."

"Jeez, Keaton. You're being a bit harsh, don't you think?" Audra said. "Mallary and the rest of her family have been through hell. They want to clear Jared's name, or at the very least, find the truth. I might know a little something about what that feels like."

"Trust me, I get it." Keaton set his beer on the ground, rested his forearms on his thighs, and leaned forward, holding Trinity's gaze with a scrutinizing glare. She saw a hint of something else behind those intense, dark eyes.

She always saw a twinge of kindness. A softness. Deep down, she knew the man had a heart. She saw it in the way he was with his team. He had their backs and not just with his brawn. He would die for those three men because he loved them with every ounce of his heart. He'd welcomed Audra into his fold. He'd do anything for her, and the same went for Baily. But for whatever reason, he often treated her as if she had some sort of death wish.

Or worse, that she wasn't capable.

"Why don't you let me and the guys go and poke around down there, and if there's a wreck, we'll investigate," Keaton said. "We can go the next time Dawson has a day off. I'm sure we can all manage to work out our schedules to fit that."

"While I appreciate that you want to help," she muttered, managing to let those words roll off her tongue without choking on them. "Mallary doesn't want to wait. She's worked hard to get her deep dive certification, and even if I hadn't seen anything—or that doesn't turn out to be Jared's boat—she wants to look. She needs to search for answers. To do something other than sit on her thumbs and listen to people whisper as she walks through town. Her family needs peace."

Slowly, methodically, Keaton rose. He inched closer.

The air in her lungs was trapped, caught somewhere between an inhale and an exhale.

He palmed her cheek, his touch so tender. So soft.

She blinked.

"I can understand how truly painful this has been for them." His thumb rubbed across her cheek, and it was as if time had stopped. As if the crackle of the fire had been put on pause and her friends weren't sitting around the pit, staring at her and Keaton sharing an odd moment of... she had no idea. "Dawson has spent countless hours looking into this. Every single one of us has taken our free time searching for clues, trying to figure out what could've really happened out there and why so many people were so quick to judge and turn on Jared." He dropped his hand. "It's frustrating that you can't see that and constantly have to go it alone. You're a stubborn woman, and you're going to wind up getting yourself or Mallary hurt."

"Do not start that crap with me again." She poked him in the chest. "Do you have any idea how many years I've been scuba diving? How many solo dives I've done? I understand the dangers better than most. I'm not reckless, and I resent you constantly telling me that I am."

53

Keaton cocked his head. "The fact that this is personal—and you're trying to prove yourself to God only knows who—makes you reckless."

"You don't have a clue regarding anything about me." She lowered her chin and dug her wedges into the ground. "You're a misogynistic pig who—"

"That's enough, children," Dawson said.

"You would think that," Keaton mumbled, tossing his empty beer in the recycling bin. "It's time to call it a night. I'll catch everyone later." He turned, took three steps, and glanced over his shoulder. "Be careful out there."

"I always am." She let out a big sigh and plopped herself in one of the chairs.

"Hey, man, don't go." Fletcher chased Keaton across the lawn and into the gravel driveway.

"You shouldn't have called him that," Dawson said. "It couldn't be further from the truth."

"Seriously?" Trinity's eyes narrowed. "Then why is he always being a jerk about the things I do? All starting back on the night Jared died. I mean, I could rattle off a dozen comments over the last year. Hell, he got bent out of shape about me changing a flat by myself. As if my being a woman meant I couldn't do it."

Hayes smacked his forehead. "You were on the side of a highway. Alone. During rush hour."

"I had hazard cones set up." She folded her arms.

"It was getting dark. You should've had flares, and when Keaton drove by, he saw cars zooming way too close," Dawson said. "You have AAA. You should've called them, or hell, called me. I would've come and changed the damn thing for you."

"And if I were a man?" Trinity asked.

"Yeah, babe." Audra patted Dawson's cheek. "What's your response to that one?"

"Chivalry is different than misogyny," Hayes chimed in.

"If I didn't have flares, I wouldn't have done it alone, either. Not on that highway. I've seen too many people die like that," Dawson said. "Being a man has nothing to do with it. I would've called a buddy to have my back. That's what friends do."

"But you have no problem with me python hunting alone," Audra said with a sarcastic tone.

"I'd rather you didn't, but you don't like me doing it alone either. Sex has nothing to do with it. That's called caring about one another." Dawson lifted Audra's chin and gave her a kiss.

Trinity groaned. "Yeah, well, Keaton doesn't give a crap about me. The man hates me."

Everyone around the fire burst out laughing. Hard.

"I don't see why that's funny," Trinity mumbled.

"He wouldn't bother getting in your face if he didn't care," Dawson said with a more serious tone.

"Well, he's not coming back." Fletcher appeared. He snagged a beer and eased into a chair. "Of all the things you could've called him, you had to pick the one that pisses him off the most." He turned and pointed his finger. "And don't say the truth hurts."

"If it's not true, why does it bother him so much?" Trinity asked.

The three men glanced at each other.

"That's not our story to tell," Hayes said. "But I know that if any one of us was doing something he thought was reckless—and the key word is reckless, not dangerous—and for all the wrong reasons, he'd be up in our faces."

"Do you remember the fight he got into with me over crossing to the Bahamas a few months ago?" Hayes asked. "Thing was, he was right. It wasn't so much that I was being reckless. Just stupid. He was so pissed when he had to come out and save my sorry ass."

"We all were." Dawson cocked his head. "However, Keaton was over the top about it. But only because he cares."

"My brother could be a Class A misogynistic jerk," Baily said. She'd been incredibly quiet, but she often was around this crew. It seemed Dawson was the only one she'd begun opening up to, and that was only because of Audra. "He would push and push for me to leave Calusa Cove. He'd tell me the marina was no place for me. No place for the future wife of a Navy man."

Fletcher coughed, pounding his chest. "Damn, that was a thought from a long time ago, and I can't believe Ken said that to you. I mean, the plan wasn't for me to stay in the military forever. I hadn't thought about becoming a SEAL until four years in."

"Ken said a lot of weird stuff back then," Baily muttered. "It started with what went down the day Audra and her dad fought in town." She swiped at her cheeks. "I still can't believe he was involved at all with Benson and his dad, but his sudden departure and the way he left make more sense. However, I still don't understand why he was so hell-bent on me getting out. I get that he had this weird thing about the four of us— me, Fletcher, him, and Audra—being together forever. But in my mind, the plan was always for Fletch to get his education and to come home. When it became apparent that wasn't going to happen, and Ken moved on, got married, and our dad died, he pushed harder for me to sell. Once, he even spoke to an interested party on my behalf. I was so pissed at him that—"

"Wait. What?" Fletcher sat up taller. "I didn't know that. Why didn't you tell me?"

"We had broken up and hadn't gotten back to friendly terms just yet," Baily said. "Ken kept telling me that I needed to get my act together and get out of Calusa Cove—out of the marina business. That it was no place for a woman."

"I had no idea," Fletcher whispered. "Besides that not being true, it wasn't his decision to make."

"No, it wasn't. But he also wanted me to make things right with you." She shook her head. "The worst part about that conversation was that Ken told me no man wanted a chick who was as self-reliant, independent, and as stubborn as me, and that *you*..." She pointed to Fletcher. "...would only wait so long for me to change my ways."

"That was a dick thing to say," Fletcher muttered. "And that couldn't be further from the truth. Those qualities are a few of the many that made me fall in love with you." He leaned back, sipped his beer, and stared at the starry night.

All the men lifted their gazes, and quiet overtook the campfire as everyone absorbed that information.

Trinity resisted the urge to stand and run. She was still an outsider in this group—still an outsider in Calusa Cove. No matter how hard she tried, she'd probably never be *in the inner circle,* even though she was their friend.

It had been mostly her own fault. She'd always had her father's love. Her dad had adored her, cherished her, and showered her with love every day of his life. She'd never once doubted how much he'd cared, not even when he'd grounded her or taken away one of her many toys.

But her mom?

God, she felt as though that woman hated her very existence, and it had started before baby Gregory had been stillborn.

Trinity had done everything she could to please her mother, right down to trying to be a little version of Porsche Stevenson. She'd dressed like her mother, worn her hair like her mother, talked like her mom, and had even acted like her. It was that last one that had ostracized her from the community and from ever having a real friend in this town when she'd been a child.

Today, she knew people like Baily and even Audra were her friends. They showed it every day by their words and their actions. But to be part of the inner circle? No, that came from having strong bonds to the past.

That, Trinity would never have.

"It makes me wonder what else about Ken we don't

know, especially with some of the cryptic things Trevor has said," Dawson said softly. "I believed the slight distance in our friendship was because he'd had a wife and kids. I understood he had to put them first. I also respect why Julie doesn't want to speak to any of us and why she blames us for what happened."

Trinity swallowed. She knew the official story the Navy had given for Ken's death. But she also knew that wasn't the truth. She just didn't know the actual facts and probably never would. But by the looks of torment on everyone's faces, she suspected some really bad shit had gone down on that mission.

Baily looked away, wiping the tears. "She won't even talk to me or let me talk to the boys."

"That's terrible," Trinity found herself saying. "I'm so sorry. That has to be painful for you." She reached out and took Baily's hand, giving it a good squeeze.

"No offense, but I can understand why she struggles to talk to or see the guys. I did too for a long time. It's hard not to place blame. When someone dies the way Ken did, those left behind need someone to inflict their pain on. But she's being cruel. And not just to me, but to my nephews," Baily said.

Fletcher pushed himself to a standing position and made his way across the pit. He knelt in front of Baily, kissed her temple, and took her hands. "In no way will this make you feel better, but Julie never liked any of us. She merely tolerated us. We believed, over time, we'd grow on her and become a family, because that's what we do. Ken loved her. Therefore, she was part of us. However, it never happened."

"You're right. It doesn't make me feel better. I was his sister. I was his blood."

Fletcher wiped a tear that rolled down Baily's cheek.

While Trinity knew these two were still madly in love with each other, she also knew Baily carried so much of the past bundled up inside that, until she set it free, they had no chance.

It was too bad because what they had was pure gold.

It's what Trinity wanted. She wished she could have had it with Fenton. But he'd destroyed it when he'd shown her what kind of man he really was, and that had broken her heart.

"Once, when I was talking with Ken—more like arguing with him—I overheard her in the background telling him to force me to sell, that the marina was more his than mine. That he should flex his muscles and make it happen."

"What did Ken say?" Fletcher asked softly.

"The only thing he could," Baily said. "That it didn't work that way because when he made it clear he was staying in the Navy and not coming back, Daddy changed the will, leaving it all to me. Now, if I did sell, I had to share with Ken, but I got to make the decisions. It wasn't up to him. But he did tell her that he would continue to remind me of my place. I wanted to choke him."

Fletcher looked at Trinity and jerked his head.

She jumped to her feet and moved to an open seat.

"We didn't know any of this." Fletcher moved his new chair closer. "If we had, we would've confronted Ken."

"It wouldn't have changed anything," Baily said. "Certainly not what happened to Ken in the end." She held up her hand. "And honestly, I don't blame any of you for that. But I do still resent all of you for coming back and acting like I needed a savior." She cocked her head. "And now we're back to what is the difference between chivalry and misogyny."

"I'd say, not much. At least not from the woman's perspective." Trinity chuckled. "Like, why is it always women and children first? It should just be children first. We're not frail. We're not incompetent or incapable."

"Good Lord." Hayes shook his head. "Not a single man here—or even Keaton—is saying that. We served with some badass women. Some of them could've taken us down. Literally. Doesn't mean we wouldn't open the door for them or call them ma'am out of respect."

"Well, thank you, sir, for that." Trinity lifted her beer.

"We can't win this argument, so we might as well cut our losses." Dawson leaned over and tapped his beer against Trinity's.

"You could add that I'm right." Trinity smiled.

"Never gonna happen." Dawson took a big swig of his beer.

Trinity's phone buzzed. Twice.

She pulled it from her back pocket and glanced at the screen. Two texts. One from Keaton. Well, that was interesting. They had very few text conversations.

The second one was from Fenton.

Crap.

She decided she'd start with Fenton, hoping Keaton's would be the better of the two.

Fenton: *Hey. I'm going to be in Calusa Cove in the morning. I have a business meeting with your dad. I'd like to see you.*

That wasn't going to happen. For a split second, she thought about ignoring Fenton, but when she did that, he did things like showing up at her house unannounced. That was never fun.

Trinity: *Sorry, busy all day tomorrow.*

Fenton: *Working? I can bring by some coffee and a pastry before my meeting? Or maybe dinner after? A girl's gotta eat.*

She groaned. However, this time she would ignore him.

She brought up Keaton's text.

Keaton: *Sorry for being a jerk. Sorry for huffing out. I wanted to say that in person, so I'm sitting on your front porch and realized that makes me even a bigger dick for being that presumptuous. So, can I stay and wait for you to apologize properly? Or do you want me to leave? Apology stands no matter what. I'd like a chance to explain. However, my behavior was uncalled for, regardless.*

She blinked and reread the text. Twice.

Trinity: *That was long-winded.*

Crap. She hadn't meant to hit send. Her and her fat little fingers.

Bubbles appeared.

Keaton: *Took me ten minutes to write it, too.*

She chuckled.

"Who are you chatting with over there?" Audra asked.

Heat rose to Trinity's cheeks.

"Better not be that idiot, Fenton," Baily said. "Lilly told me he's still trying to win you back."

"He did text me, but no, it's not him, and he's got zero chance. I'm done with him." Trinity's fingers hovered over the screen as she contemplated her response.

"Are you going to tell us?" Dawson asked.

"Keaton. He's apologizing." She sucked in a deep breath, letting it out slowly. "His texting skills are... amusing."

Keaton: *Seriously. I am really sorry. Please don't leave me hanging.*

Trinity: *Sorry. Still at Dawson's and was in the middle of a convo. Apology accepted. No worries. I am curious about the explanation since you brought it up. So, yeah. I'm leaving here in five. See you at my place in fifteen."*

Keaton: *Thanks. See you then.*

Trinity tucked her phone in her back pocket. She stared at the fire, which was now more like gray ash with sparks.

"That was nice of him," Baily said.

Trinity nodded. Her stomach twisted and turned. From the moment she'd met Keaton, she'd been attracted to him. She'd see him in town or at the marina, and she'd find herself staring. It had gotten awkward when she'd been with Fenton, but only because her attraction hadn't gone unnoticed.

It had caused more than one fight, but that wasn't why they'd broken up.

Fenton had a fatal flaw. One that he'd accused her of, only she'd been faithful. Sure, she'd looked at Keaton, but she hadn't been interested. Keaton's personality—especially toward her—left something to be desired.

Fenton, on the other hand, had stuck his dick where it didn't belong.

Trinity had a few rules. They were simple. She didn't date liars. Cheaters. Or people who wanted her father's money.

It turned out that Fenton had ended up checking all those boxes.

"It's getting late." Trinity stood. "I better get going."

"Will you do me a favor?" Dawson arched a brow. "Make sure you check in with Baily at the marina tomorrow?" He raised his hand. "If you're going to be out after she closes up, will you kindly check in with one of us? It's not because we don't think you're not a seasoned pro, but because we know from experience what can happen down there."

"I can do that." She nodded. And she would because, while she hated Keaton's delivery of his message, she didn't disagree. Safety was always her number one priority.

CHAPTER 3

KEATON HAD SPENT the last year trying to shut down the demands of his body and mind. But no matter what he'd tried, Trinity's pull on him couldn't be stomped out—and he'd tried just about everything.

Women didn't affect him on this level. Contrary to popular belief, he did date.

He just didn't do long-term relationships.

The military and his career as a SEAL had made that really easy. He'd meet a woman, and if she didn't have crazy eyes and didn't seem to be the type of person looking for some guy to put a ring on it right away, he'd bite. Since he was constantly deployed and emotionally unavailable, those ladies walked away from him before he had to be the one putting the brakes on.

He knew that made him an asshole.

But he'd never lied about where he was in life. Or the fact that marriage and kids were not on his agenda and never would be, so there was that.

Moving to Calusa Cove had made dating a little

harder. For the first time in his adult life, he was grounded in one place. That certainly gave him the jitters. While he liked Calusa Cove, and leaving the Navy with his brothers-in-arms was a no-brainer, he no longer knew how to make a long-term home for himself.

Of all the guys, he'd thought Hayes would have understood, considering Hayes was a bit of a player. He was the only man on the team who had never been in love and planned to keep it that way. But he'd taken to this tiny little town like a duck to water.

Keaton glanced at the time flashing on the screen of his cell. It was the fifth time he'd checked it in the last ten minutes. It made him crazy. He didn't want to care. He wanted to drive off to a town a few hours away and pick up some girl in a bar.

But he couldn't even do that, and he had tried it a few times, but just couldn't bring himself to pull the trigger.

Ever since he'd laid eyes on the blond-haired beauty, she'd been all he could think about.

Headlights cut through the darkness, and her fancy little SUV rolled into the driveway. The hum of her garage door filled the air.

He stood and leaned against the railing. What the hell was he doing here? Did he really intend to explain to her why her actions mattered to him? Jesus, now that was nuts. They had such a competitive friendship—if one could even call it that—she'd probably toss him out on his ass.

But being called a misogynist, again, had a profound effect on him—one he couldn't ignore.

She climbed up the side steps, tucking her hair behind her ears as she tugged her hair out of her pony-tail, fingering the long strands. She smiled.

She was so goddamned gorgeous. Athletic build. Toned muscles. Killer blue eyes that could suck a person in with a twinkle—or cut them with a glare.

She had a quick wit—completely sarcastic, though often rooted in her desire to be seen and heard for who she was, not what the town perceived her to be. She was smart and tough as nails. Those last two qualities were the ones he admired most.

"Hey," she said. "I'm going to get a glass of wine. I love sitting out here on nights like this." She pointed to a storm lighting up the sky about five miles offshore. "Would you like a glass? Or a beer? Or a shot of whiskey? I might have some that burns going down. You know, the cheap stuff."

He laughed. They had once picked on her for always bringing the most expensive alcohol to their little gatherings. "A glass of whatever you're having is fine."

"Keaton Cole is going to drink wine?" She fanned her face. "I might fall over."

"How expensive is that wine going to be, because I will never understand anyone who drops a hundred dollars on a bottle. That just seems wasteful to me when you can get a decent one for twenty." He cringed. "Sorry. That was rude."

"I drink so much wine that I don't buy the stuff my dad does." She pointed to the chairs. "It's less than thirty dollars a bottle. But I'm not sure I've ever seen you drink the stuff."

He shrugged. "It's been a hot minute." Like ten freaking years, but he wasn't about to question his reasons for breaking that rule now.

"Come on in. You can help me carry a tray of snacks. I didn't even get a marshmallow tonight."

He stood behind her, inhaling the fresh scent of pears, and waited for her to finish tapping in her keycode to unlock the front door. Once inside, she went right for the alarm system and disarmed it. "I'm surprised you have an alarm system." Inwardly, he groaned. That was a dumb thing to say when he was trying to apologize for being a jerk.

She glanced over her shoulder while kicking off those damn wedge shoes. "When I moved back here a few years ago, it was after an incident where I used to live. Freaked my father out. Honestly, it freaked me out, too. When I bought this place, my dad insisted on the alarm in case what happened there followed me. I didn't argue because I worried about that, too."

"What does that mean?" He curled his fingers around her biceps. His heart pounded in his chest, pumping adrenaline—and not necessarily the good kind —through his system. "What happened? Are you okay? Is someone bothering you? Is this something Dawson should know about?"

She shifted her gaze from his face to his hand and back to his face. "It—or should I say, he—didn't follow me here. There has been no sign of my ex since I left St. Augustine. He doesn't call. He doesn't text. And he's never shown up. I don't think he ever will." She leaned closer. "He's kind of afraid of me."

"Okay. But you were sufficiently scared to put in an alarm system. Why?"

"It's not exactly what you think." She plucked his fingers off her body, turned, and marched down the hallway while his protective instincts suffocated him from the inside out.

"How about you ease my overactive mind and tell me what happened?"

"The short version is he lied to me, he stole from me, and then he hit me."

He growled. It was deep and hit his throat like a brick coming up. "That's—"

She turned, holding up her hand. "I called the police. I wouldn't be bullied. It didn't matter that, at the time, I was in love with the jerk. Lay a hand on me, and we're done. However, he didn't like my response. He didn't like that I wouldn't tell the cops it was a misunder-standing."

"I'm sure he didn't. Did you file an abuse report?"

"I did more than that." She pulled down two glasses and shoved a bottle of wine at him with a corkscrew before ducking her head into the fridge. "While he was spending a few hours in jail because he left a nasty bruise on my cheek and took a chunk of my hair in his hands—"

"That sounds like he more than hit you."

"I fought back," she said, "and then I packed up all his stuff—because it was my house—and had his mother come get it. I listed the house the next morning and sold it in two days. I filed a restraining order and came running home to Daddy."

"You say the last part as if it's a bad thing."

She sighed as she arranged a few blocks of cheese on the tray and opened a sleeve of crackers. She lifted the snacks and nodded toward the front of the house. "In the end, it wasn't. But my dad can be protective of his little princess. He hopped in his car and drove to St. Augustine so he could give that man a piece of his mind. Turns out, when I kicked him where it counts, I might've done a little damage, and he was in the hospital. My dad left it alone, but he made me promise that if he ever contacted me, I'd first call the cops and then call him."

"Well, now you can add me to the list of people to call." He tucked the recorked bottle under his arm and carried the two poured glasses out the front door. He set them on a small table and joined her on the plush sofa overlooking the beautiful waters of Calusa Cove.

"Now, why would I do that when you and I can't have a conversation without one of us calling the other a name?"

He chuckled. "Yeah, that one you hurled at me earlier was a little triggering."

"You know and understand that word?" She took the glass he offered and sighed. "I'm sorry. But ever since that night Jared died, you bring out the worst in me. I can't seem to help myself."

"I will admit, I can be rough, but that word has more meaning to me than you could know." He lifted the wine to his lips, stuck his nose inside, and sniffed. Not bad. He took a long, slow sip. "Damn, that's good."

"You appreciate wine?"

"I used to." He set his glass aside and tugged at his shirt collar, showing off his tattoo.

She leaned in and traced the infinity sign with her delicate, hot finger. It scorched his skin. "Who's Petra?"

"She's the reason I'm the way I am and why being called a misogynistic prick bothers me so much."

"Ex-girlfriend?"

"Dead fiancée." He leaned over, raised his glass, and downed his wine like it was a cheap shot of whiskey, but it didn't burn.

"Oh. I'm so sorry."

"It's not your fault. Not even my fault. But she called me that a few days before she died." He raked his fingers through his hair. It was longer than it had ever been since he'd been eighteen, and he still wasn't used to it. "It wasn't true, and I know she didn't mean it. They were words meant to hurt, and we had no idea that she'd die. But that's not even the worst part."

Trinity clutched her wineglass to her chest as if it were a rosary. "I can't even imagine anything could be more awful than that," she whispered.

"I was deployed when it happened, but because I was mad, I didn't say I love you when I left."

Trinity closed her eyes. Her chest rose and fell as she sucked in an audible breath. "I'm so sorry for your loss. That's gut-wrenching."

"You're not going to ask me how she died?" He reached out, taking a strand of hair between his thumb and forefinger and twisting it around. It was soft and smooth.

She blinked. "Does it matter? She's gone, and that was—is—painful for you."

"In this case." He waved his hand between himself and her. "With this conflict between us, I believe the entire context here is important."

She drew a deep breath. "Okay. How did Petra die?"

"Petra was an adrenaline junkie. We both were, but she was born and raised on it." He'd never intended to tell the whole story, to be this vulnerable, yet there was no stopping the word vomit about to tumble out of his mouth. "Her little brother was eleven months younger, and their dad pushed him to be an athlete. Water-skiing, snow-skiing, race car driving—you name it, he did it. He had to be the best of the best at everything, and father and son were as thick as thieves. But when it came to Petra, she was just a girl. She was too pretty, too petite, not strong enough—basically, not a man to do any of the things her little brother was doing and that just pissed her off. At the ripe old age of ten, she cut a deal with her dad. She could do whatever she wanted as long as she was the best. She became a world-class water-skier. She actually beat her little brother on the racetrack, and she flew planes. She became an aerialist. However, she never really got the respect of her father and brother that she thought she deserved."

"But she had yours," Trinity said softly.

He nodded. "She was an amazing woman. However, she could be reckless in her thirst for her father's attention. She pushed boundaries, and I did take issue with that." He raised his finger. "Because I loved her, not because I believed her place was in the kitchen."

"That's not what I said."

"I know, but when Petra and I spent two years engaged, I thought it was time for us to think about actually getting married. I wanted kids. I didn't want to wait. Of course, I'm not the one who would've carried them and given up a few months out of my crazy life, a fact that might've flown out of my brain the day we had our fight." For a second, he wondered if he was no better than Petra for leaving out key details and for not being completely honest about why he'd been so mad at Petra.

What she'd done had been her choice. He believed that with every fiber of his being. But he also thought that she'd owed him—owed their love—a conversation before making that decision without even discussing it.

"I don't believe most women think they're giving up anything by having children—if that's what they truly want," Trinity said. "But it's nice to have a partner who understands it's our bodies that become a human incubator for nine months."

"Trust me, I get that, and I never wanted Petra to stop being who she was. I just thought it was time for her to stop chasing the high—because that's all it was—a high. I know this because I enjoyed jumping from perfectly good airplanes for shits and giggles. I bungee jumped. I raced cars, too."

"You do all that stuff now?"

"No, not for fun anyway," he said flatly, pouring himself one very large glass of wine. "Petra was a

73

passionate woman—one of the many things I loved about her. The night of the fight, I was packing my things to go to the base for my briefing. I sat her down and told her I wanted her to set a date for the wedding while I was gone and that I wanted her to stop some of the activities. I wanted us to move forward with our lives." All that was true, but when he'd gotten frustrated, he'd stormed off into the bedroom to take a break before he really said something that would get him in the doghouse. That's when he'd found the medical records. That's when he'd learned the truth about the baby and the abortion.

"I shouldn't pry. This is your story."

"What do you want to ask me?" He took the opportunity to sip. And sip. Okay, he swallowed three large gulps.

"Was it a discussion? Or a demand?"

He laughed. "It started off as a conversation. I told her how proud I was of all her accomplishments, and that I believed it was time for something different. That it was time for us to start living our lives together. It ended with me telling her that I thought she was reckless and her calling me that dirty word." He lowered his chin. "I'm a lot of things. I can be controlling and opinionated. Sometimes, I can even be mean. I'll admit to my faults. But being misogynistic is not one of them. I respect the hell out of women and what any lady has to do to get where she is. I couldn't imagine being in her shoes. I'm a white dude who was born with a silver spoon in his mouth." He pressed his finger against her lips. "I don't care how privileged your life was, you've still had it harder than me. I do understand that. I've seen it with my own eyes. I just don't understand why you're trying to prove to anyone in this town that you're..." He sucked in a deep breath and sighed. "You've got nothing to prove to anyone."

"Easy for you to say. You're the golden boy. The most popular kid in school." She cocked a pretty little brow. "Yeah. I heard that about you. But do you know what I was? I was the rich girl who probably had a servant wipe my ass."

"Audra does have a way with words." He shook his head. "She's your friend and doesn't think that about you at all."

"Maybe not, but you think I'm reckless with a stick up my butt just because I back my boat into the dock."

"Backing your boat in doesn't make you reckless. It just makes you a show-off." He leaned closer. "You're reckless because you're emotionally charged about some of the things you do, like solo scuba diving for your friend."

"Oh my God. Really?" Her turn to chug. "Look, I do understand the difference between doing something dangerous and being stupid." This time, she covered his mouth. "I know all the dangers of scuba diving. I've been doing it my entire life. But I take all the necessary precautions each and every time I go out. *Because. I. Don't. Want. To. Die.* I go out there regularly because it brings me joy. It gives me peace and serenity from the insanity that is often my life. My mom is nuts, and while she doesn't live here anymore, it's hard being her daughter. Being underwater is the one place on earth I don't have to hear it. It's also the only place in the world where I feel free of judgment in a place that doesn't accept me for who I am." She waved her hand toward the big house. "I am a princess. While I've made adjustments in my adult life with not only how I treat people but how I behave, I will not apologize for enjoying the things I've earned or a little bit of Daddy's money. In this town, that makes me an outsider. People treat me differently. They look at me differently. Have you ever noticed that?"

"What are you talking about?"

"Everyone only expects two things from me. To be my mother's daughter and to screw up. It's like everyone is waiting for me to make a mistake. To fall on my face in my heels. To crash my boat into the dock." She waved her hand. "Like the night Jared died and the way Silas came at me. His utter disappointment in me. That wouldn't have happened to anyone else but me. And the way everyone stood out there, searching, scanning for my wreckage. It wasn't so much because they were all worried. But because I might have finally done it. I might've finally gone and gotten myself killed, and don't go and say that makes me reckless because that's the rub—I'm not. The only mistake I made was not radioing Baily and giving her my coordinates when I saw that boat. But everything else, I did perfectly right."

"Silas. Baily. Me. We were all scared for you," he said, his voice husky.

"Okay. Who else was *really* utterly terrified that something might have happened to me? And if you say

Dawson, Hayes, or Fletcher, I'll kick you where it counts."

He took a moment and pulled up that night. Plucked out the whispers and the chatter. It wasn't that people weren't concerned, because they had been—but she was right. Most had been gossiping about how her show-manship—weird choice of words—had finally bitten her in the ass.

However, that wasn't it at all.

Backing a boat in was commonplace. He did it all the time. He backed his truck into his garage.

All she was doing was what everyone else in this town did. Except, they saw a prissy little rich girl showing off daddy's toys.

He cringed. "I might have misjudged certain aspects of this."

"Ya think?"

"Jeez, you're a tough crowd." He took her glass, set it on the table, and traced her cheek with his thumb. "As crazy as this will sound coming from me, I like who you are."

"You have a weird way of showing it."

"Perhaps this is a better way." He cupped the back of her neck, drawing her closer. His heart tightened as he pressed his mouth to her sweet, plump lips.

A fire erupted deep in his belly. It spread over his skin like warm butter melting on top of a pancake. His tongue caught hers, twisting and turning, tasting the robust wine.

She grabbed his shoulders, and for a split second, he braced himself to be rejected. He wouldn't blame her.

He'd been an asshole. It didn't matter that, to him, he had justifiable reasons. She didn't know them any more than he'd taken the time to truly understand her. She fisted his shirt, deepening the kiss until it was wild and out of control.

They were both breathless, hanging on to each other as if for dear life under the blanket of stars, as the sweet sound of the ocean waves rolled across his ears.

He ran his hand down her collarbone and cupped her breast, forgetting they were sitting on her porch. He'd lost all touch with reality. Nothing mattered but her.

His thumb brushed over her nipple, eliciting a gasp from her parted lips. Emboldened, he let his fingers venture farther, tracing her contours with an artist's precision, a reverence that belied his previous disregard. Her grip on his shoulders tightened, her body melting into his touch like molten wax bleeding onto parchment. His heartbeat thrummed in his ears, a thrilling symphony underscored by the song of the sea and their ragged breaths.

"Wait," she gasped suddenly and pulled away sharply, breaking their connection. Confused at her reaction, he blinked. Her chest rose and fell heavily under the moonlit sky, eyes wide and filled with something indecipherable.

He feared he'd pushed too far, and his audacious move was unwelcome. But there was no anger in her eyes, no spurned offense or disapproval. Instead, there was an intensity that both intrigued and alarmed him.

"Listen," she said, quieter now but with a clear urgency in her voice.

The only sounds were the ocean waves rhythmically caressing the shoreline and the occasional faint laughter of some partygoers in the distance. And then it came, a gentle padding from around the corner of the house, growing louder until a dog appeared by their side.

The animal wagged its tail, completely oblivious to the precious moment it had interrupted.

Chuckling at the irony of it all—a man treading uncharted territory with an enchanting woman only to be halted by an excited pet—he dropped his forehead against hers and let out a relieved sigh. "Your dog?"

"No, the neighbor's down the street," she said, turning her head. "Sawyer, go home, now."

The dog whimpered but turned and trotted off, its tail happily wagging in the air.

"Shall we go inside?" she asked so softly he thought he might have been hearing things, but when she stood, collected the tray of food, and made her way toward the door, he knew he'd lost all ability to keep the emotions of the last year at bay.

He followed her into the house. This time, he noted the details. The decor was simpler than he'd anticipated. A seaside beach home. Teal-green, blues, and whites, decorated in a combination of new and old with a hint of nautical. So fitting.

He followed her to the kitchen, wine and glasses in hand. Without saying anything, he set everything down, watching her as she tossed the cheese back in the fridge.

She turned. "Inviting you up to my bedroom is crazy, isn't it?"

"I wouldn't go that far." He inched closer, wrapping his arms around her slender but muscular frame. "However, we can end things here." He kissed her tenderly. "For tonight, as long as I know you'll go out with me."

Resting her hands on his shoulders, she chuckled. "Would you think badly of me if I didn't want you to go?"

"No." He shook his head. "And for the record, this isn't a one-eighty. Whether I've behaved like it or not, I've been attracted to you since we met. You're all I can think about."

She smiled. "Don't take this the wrong way, but a part of me wishes I hadn't fantasized about you during the last year."

He groaned.

"I like that noise." She laced her fingers through his and before he could respond, they were at the top of the stairs, stumbling toward her bedroom, with their hands and lips all over each other as if they were about to experience sex for the very last time.

They practically tripped into her bedroom, a blur of lips and hands. Her room was decorated in the same theme as the rest of the house. The nautical blues gave way to soft pastels, walls adorned with seashells and paintings of mermaids. A large bed was nestled in the corner.

He tried to memorize the details, but she consumed every thought. She was intoxicating, a storm he had yearned for throughout the past year. Their clothes were discarded at the foot of the bed, their kisses growing more passionate and urgent. He could feel her heartbeat against his chest, and it echoed his own racing pulse.

He looked at her then—really looked at her.

Her tousled hair fell about her face, and her lips were slightly swollen from their previous bout of passionate kissing. "You're so beautiful," he murmured against her neck.

"You're not so bad yourself, sailor."

He chuckled, staring at her for a long moment with his pulse caught in his throat, suddenly, painfully aware of his tattoo. He covered it. He'd never done that before. It had always been a part of him. Of who he was.

She reached out, pushing his hand away and kissing his chest. "Don't ever do that again," she said sternly.

"Do what?"

"Try to erase your past." She glanced up. Her eyes glistened under the glow from the skylight.

Tears? But why? Petra wasn't her pain, but his.

"I wasn't...wasn't...it's just that... I don't know." He scratched the center of his chest. "It's never been an issue for me before. If anyone asked me about the tattoo, I shrugged and told them she was the...the..."

"Love of your life?"

"Something like that," he admitted.

Trinity stood before him naked and smiled.

God, she was amazingly gorgeous—a goddess.

"She's a part of what makes you...you. I would never take that from you, not even if this goes beyond tonight."

"I'm kind of hoping there's more."

"I'd be lying if I said I didn't want that, too, but let's see if we can go a week without fighting…about something." She tugged at him, and they tumbled onto the bed with her wrapped in his arms.

She was like nothing he'd ever experienced.

She was wild and gentle, ferocious and tender. A storm wrapped in tranquility. He ran his hands down the smooth column of her spine, soaking in the heat that radiated off her bare skin.

She lifted herself onto him, straddling with a grace that belonged to dancers and forest nymphs alike. Illuminated by moonlight coming through the skylight, it was a mesmerizing sight. A sense of surrealism enveloped him as he watched her move against him, their silhouettes painting an amorous tableau on her bedroom walls.

He cupped her waist, pulling her closer to intensify the connection—physical and emotional. Everything he had been averse to was now welcoming her in. He buried his face in the crook of her neck, inhaling the soft scent of pears that clung to her skin.

"Am I too much?" she whispered, her breath puffing against his spent nerves.

"Not nearly enough…" he replied through clenched teeth as sensations shot through him like wildfire. He looked at her, desperately willing his heart to communicate what words failed to express.

Her laughter echoed like a melodious hymn that breathed life into still air. She arched back, giving him access to an expanse of unblemished skin that begged for his touch. Every sigh that escaped her lips became a verse in the symphony they were composing together, each gasp a chorus in itself.

She tumbled into the sea of satin sheets beside him post-climax, gasping for breath with a contented smile dancing on her lips. She turned to face him, and her finger danced across a few of his scars. "Your body is covered in these."

"I know."

"Each one, like your tattoo, tells your story," she whispered. "Only, I don't know them."

"No, you don't, and honestly, some I might not ever talk about."

"I can only imagine what this one is from, and it's not painting a very nice narrative." She traced a dainty circle around the combination burn marks from being tortured by electrocution and knife wounds. His captors used to increase the pain, hoping to get him and his buddies to talk. It didn't work. However, Ken was dead and nothing they did would ever change that fact.

He brought her hand to his lips. "The only important thing about any of these scars is that I'm alive, I'm breathing, and I'm right here with you."

"Wow. I would not have expected such romantic words from you."

"Oh, I can get real mushy when I get going." He hadn't had a reason to get going in over ten years. Now, he did—and her name was Trinity.

"Do me a favor. If we last more than tonight, never buy me flowers."

He jerked his head. "Okay. Good to know, because I would've sent some in the morning. Can I ask why?"

She yawned. "Can I tell you that story another time?"

He nodded, kissing her temple. Something told him that as much as he suspected she wanted more, he was never getting that story.

And that meant there wasn't much of a future outside of a good time.

That shouldn't bother him, because he never thought about the future when it came to women. But tonight, knowing there wouldn't be, it crushed his soul.

CHAPTER 4

Trinity leaned back and guzzled half a bottle of water. The sun beat down on her face. A combination of exhaustion and frustration rippled across her muscles and needled her brain.

"I can't believe we haven't found it. I thought you marked where the boat was," Mallary said, frowning. She, too, was exhausted, and it showed, as well as her desperation.

"I marked the spot where my boat was anchored. I can't be exactly sure where I was under the water. It's two hundred feet down, and when I surfaced—"

"Yeah. Yeah. Yeah. I know. I get it. You were pretty far from the *Princess Afloat* and a hundred feet off the bow, not off the stern where you started, and you had been worried you were dragging your anchor anyway. It's just that we've been at this all day."

"And dragging anchor. We can't stay under for too long. You're getting tired, so one more dive, and then we'll have to call it a day."

Mallary bolted to her feet. "Are you kidding me? We have to keep going. My brother's boat is down there. I know it."

"Well, if it is, it's not going anywhere anytime soon. We can come back out." Trinity polished off the rest of the water. "Keaton and the guys have volunteered to come out, too."

"No way." Mallary shook like a wet dog. "He's best friends with the chief of police of Calusa Cove. All the cops think my brother's guilty. If they find anything, they'll pin it on Jared, and that will be the end of it."

"Dawson's not like that."

"Oh, really?" Mallary strolled to the stern of the boat with her back to Trinity. She raised her hand to her forehead. "Every cop believes Jared's a thief and a liar. I'm so tired of it. Even that sweet girl I helped him with turned on him." She glanced over her shoulder. "Are you going to turn on him, too?"

"No." Trinity jerked her head. "I know you're frustrated. But we can't even be sure of what I saw. I was at least twenty feet away. I was running out of oxygen and had to come up. Otherwise, I would've explored more."

"That's what you say," Mallary mumbled.

"I'm going to pretend you didn't just say that." Trinity could understand many things, but Mallary had come in hot today. She'd been snippy since they had met at the marina. "Okay, I'm sure I could talk the guys into having Dawson pass on the dive and just have Keaton, Hayes, and Fletcher do it."

"Since when do you trust any of them?" Mallary

turned, planting her hands on her hips. "Especially, Keaton. He's been nothing but a jerk to you."

"Yeah, well, we hashed out our differences last night."

"What does that mean?"

"It means we talked." Trinity sighed. She wasn't one to kiss and tell. It wasn't anyone's business, and she didn't think Keaton would appreciate it. She wouldn't like it if he went and blabbed it to all his buddies, though she figured, if asked, he wouldn't lie. Nor would she, but she didn't have to spell it out. "We understand each other better."

"That makes no sense." Mallary narrowed her stare. "He's always in your face, telling you how—"

"He didn't mean it exactly how I took it."

"Oh my God. You slept with him, didn't you?" Mallary's face hardened as if she'd swallowed cement. Or maybe Botox. Either way, it wasn't an attractive look.

Trinity said nothing.

"Have you no shame?"

"Now that's uncalled for," Trinity said. "I misjudged him as much as he did me. He's willing to help, and none of them have to. Nor do they believe what everyone is saying. They want the truth as much as we do."

"Or their version of it." Mallary leaned against the side of the boat. "I'm not going to tell you who to take as a bed partner, but mark my words, he's not good enough for you—and seriously, what about Fenton?"

"Fenton? Are you kidding me right now?"

"No, actually, I'm not," Mallary said. "He loves you and hasn't done anything wrong, but you're too stubborn to even listen."

"He cheated on me and only wants my father's money."

"You're letting your past experience rule your future," Mallary said. "Fenton is none of those things. He doesn't deserve this. Trust me when I say, Keaton doesn't care about you, and I can't believe you don't see that."

"Why are you so mad at me? And about this? About Fenton, of all things. Why does it matter to you?"

Mallary covered her face and sobbed. Her shoulders bobbed up and down, and she made ugly crying noises. The kind that made her sound like a dying sea cow.

Trinity loved Mallary. She really did. But this was the one part about Mallary's personality that grated on her nerves. The woman could go from zero to sixty with her emotions faster than Trinity could run in her heels. And Trinity could run a marathon in those suckers, if she had to.

"I'm sorry. I don't know. I'm just… I just…" Mallary waved her hand. "I got my hopes up. I really thought we'd find the boat and find that there were no jewels down there, so we could prove my brother did nothing wrong except for being a stupid idiot for being out here alone at night."

Ouch. Trinity had been out there alone. What did that say about her? She wasn't going to ask that question out loud.

"Come on. Let's start our safety check, and we can go down one more time," Trinity said.

"Do we really have to? I mean, we've done it twice already."

Trinity scowled. "Every time you go under, you do a safety check. Don't ever forget it. That's how mistakes are made, and people die."

Mallory sighed. "All right."

Trinity made her way to the cockpit and found her cell. Barely a signal. But she'd send a text to Keaton anyway. She'd promised, so she quickly shot one off and tucked her phone into the glove box.

The next fifteen minutes were pure hell. All Trinity did was listen to Mallary scoff. She honestly hoped Mallary would never go scuba diving again after all this. She wasn't cut out for it.

Trinity set her spare tank on the back seat. It was less than half full. She gave the thumbs-up to Mallary and fell back into the water with a splash. The second she hit the ocean, her world felt lighter. Freer. If she could live underwater, she would. It was the most intoxicating thing, next to sex with Keaton. *Where the hell did that come from?*

Once had been orgasmic. But the second time in the shower, when he'd brought her a mug of coffee? Well, that had been cosmic. He'd been so tender. So thoughtful. So sweet and romantic.

Not at all what she'd expected from a man like Keaton. She'd half expected him to bark out orders during their escapades, not ask if she liked what he was doing. As if her moaning and calling out his name hadn't given him enough of a hint.

She pushed those thoughts from her mind, flicked on her light, and waved to Mallary. She needed to keep that woman on a short leash.

Speaking of which, she tugged at the one attached to her diver's buoy. Every so often, she cleared her ears and reminded Mallary to do the same with a hand signal. The deeper they went, the darker it got.

The first few times she'd gone over a hundred feet, she'd thought for sure it would be pitch-black, but much to her surprise, it hadn't.

She pulled out her compass, checked the surface, and dove deeper. The ocean floor was a little over two hundred feet deep here. This was about five miles from where the Coast Guard had pinned where they believed the boat to have gone down. Seven miles from where she thought she'd seen it.

But the ocean did strange things to boats that sank.

It often took years, decades, even centuries for ships to be found.

She panned her light on the ocean floor. She swam in a twenty-foot zigzag, constantly checking her compass. She didn't want to get too far from her boat. That would suck.

Mallary swam like a banshee in front of her, looking over her shoulder and then pointing at something.

Slow down. You're wasting oxygen.

But Mallary did nothing of the sort. She kept on going. She was a faint dark spot in front of Trinity.

Trinity kicked harder, keeping her light pinned on

Mallary until she spotted a white and blue object...a boat.

Holy crap. Jackpot. That was it. Jared's boat. They'd found it.

Mallary twisted and turned and danced in the water. Massive air bubbles moved relentlessly above her head.

Their tanks were already low, and if Mallary wasn't careful, she'd have to surface before they were ready.

Trinity tried to signal to her to take it easy. They would need to be careful as they swam around the boat, poking around inside. Vessels did strange things while submerged underwater, even sitting on the bottom of the ocean floor. But Mallary wasn't having any of that. She was off to the races. Dodging in and out. Up and down. She opened the head, and the boat shifted.

Trinity kicked, swimming upward, panic seizing her heart for a moment. She shined the light, searching for her friend. Left. Right. Panning back and forth, and then finally, she found Mallary. Well, her fins anyway, sticking out of the head.

Quickly, she checked her tank. Five minutes, and then they'd have to head up.

Mallary jerked her body. The boat shifted again. A weird howl echoed under the murky water. The vessel might roll completely to its side if they weren't careful.

Trinity tugged on Mallary's fin. Thank God, Mallary swam backward. She held up a box. Her eyes were wide as if to say, *holy crap. What have I found?* Slowly, Mallary lifted the lid, and Trinity's heart dropped to her toes like an anchor pitching to the depths of the ocean floor.

The jewels from the *Flying Victoria*.

Gently, Trinity closed the box and pointed toward the surface. As her gaze shifted, she noted the oxygen level on Mallary's tank.

Crap. She didn't have enough to safely get back to the top.

Trinity tapped the gauge. She pointed to her own regulator. She'd done this during training but had never had to do it during an emergency. Mallary would likely panic. Trinity put the box in her bag. She held Mallary's gaze and slowly began to surface. She pointed to Mallary's tank. Then to her own regulator. Then to Mallary's mouth. Mallary nodded.

Hopefully, that meant she knew they would be sharing some oxygen at some point. But they needed to decompress. They needed to do it slowly and safely.

They got about seventy-five feet when Mallary's tank emptied.

Trinity pushed Mallary's regulator from her mouth and inserted hers. Trinity would have to be in control, and Mallary would have to follow instructions.

This should be fun. Not. Especially with the panic registering in Mallary's eyes.

Swiftly, Trinity snagged the regulator, and Mallary tried to make a beeline for the surface.

Trinity took in a few breaths, tugging at Mallary. She was a stronger swimmer than Trinity had expected, but she managed to bring Mallary back down to her level and gave her a few breaths before taking it back, ensuring she got the air she needed. She checked the oxygen. This was going to be a close call.

Keaton was going to have her head on a platter, and

she didn't blame him. But he'd have to read Mallary the Riot Act, too.

Trinity made her calculated stops, giving their bodies time to adjust. This was obviously hard for Mallary. It didn't matter that she was getting enough oxygen. Or that her body was doing what it needed. She was in panic mode and hyped up with adrenaline.

Once Trinity hit approximately sixty feet, she no longer needed to stop, but she continued to ascend slowly, just in case. She had no idea what Mallary's body could handle.

However, at about thirty feet, Mallary reached for the jewels. Her hands fumbled. Her eyes grew wide as the need for oxygen registered. She turned and hauled ass for the surface—without the box. It remained tucked safely in Trinity's bag.

Trinity could hold her breath for up to forty-four feet. That was a long-ass dive. It wasn't easy. Not something she wanted to do regularly, but she'd wanted to know her body's limits, so she'd tested it with a full oxygen tank. She knew other divers who could do fifty, but they were rock stars.

Taking only the oxygen she needed, she lazily made her way to the surface, clearing her mind of all the horrible things she wanted to say to her dear friend. A few of Keaton's well-placed angry retorts came to mind. She broke the ocean's surface and swam about fifty feet away toward the boat. Mallary was already climbing onboard.

She reached the vessel, and her annoyance grew when her friend wasn't on the back deck to give her a hand. Diving etiquette 101. She hoisted herself up, stood, and gasped, staring down at a masked man holding a shotgun at her chest. "What the hell?" she managed. "Where's my friend? What have you done with my friend?"

"She's right here." Another man shoved Mallary toward the stern. She was still in her wetsuit, her mask on top of her head, but no flippers.

"You have something we want," the man with the gun said.

"I don't know what you're talking about." Trinity swallowed, scanning left and right. There was no other boat in sight. But there had to be one somewhere. She lifted her gaze, but the man waved his weapon, forcing her focus back to him.

"Don't play dumb. It's not a good look," he said.

The other man gave Mallary a good push. She let out a little scream.

"Give me the box," the man with the gun said. "We know you found it."

"We have to give it to them." Mallary climbed onto the back deck. "I'm so sorry," she whispered, reaching for the bag. "They said they'd kill me."

"It's not your fault." If these men didn't shoot her first, Keaton was sure to for what she was about to do. "Swim under the boat," she whispered. She yanked off her tank and leaned over the back bench, holding her breath. With one hand, she grabbed the half-full tank she had as a spare and flung the empty one at the man with the gun.

Bang!

A sharp pain tore through her shoulder. She ignored it and shoved Mallary into the water, flopping in right after her. As quickly as she could manage, she strapped on the tank while swimming under the boat, searching for her friend.

Pop! Pop!

The sound was muffled. But she knew it was the rifle. Bullets tore through the open water, zipping only a few feet from her body.

She continued to search for Mallary, pausing briefly. No sign.

More bullets.

Her heart raced. Panic engulfed her entire being.

She shoved the regulator into her mouth and dove straight down, glancing up every few minutes, trying to gauge sixty feet.

A couple more bullets. Bubbles zipped by one foot from her head.

Shit. That was close.

A splash from above.

A diver.

She hit what she believed was sixty feet and went horizontal, leaving behind a trail of blood. She gave herself a few minutes to adjust, then dove deeper. She kept doing that until she found a cave at the bottom. She slinked inside and hid, checking her oxygen tank. Tears burned her eyes.

What had happened to Mallary? Had she resurfaced? Had they shot her? Pulled her onboard? Oh God, what had Trinity done?

Surely, if she'd stayed onboard, they both would've been dead. But that didn't make her feel any better.

She checked her tank, and that's when she realized that, unless those men had brought scuba equipment onboard, they weren't chasing her because all her other tanks were empty. Inching out of the cave with her shoulder throbbing, she made her way to the surface.

The sun smacked her face. She lifted her mask and spun herself in a circle. Her boat was gone. There was no sign of it—or anyone—in sight. She was miles from shore. It was close to dark.

She might as well be dead in the water.

CHAPTER 5

KEATON WIPED HIS EYES. They burned from the salty sea air. Or maybe the few tears he desperately tried not to shed. He panned the spotlight. Back and forth. Left and right.

Nothing but calm, dark water.

"We should head back," Fletcher said softly.

"No, not until we find her. She's out here. Somewhere." Only, he knew the chances that she'd actually be found were close to none. Her boat had been located fifteen miles out at sea. It had been stripped of all its navigational equipment, and not a single piece of scuba gear had been found.

Either she had resurfaced, and she was drifting somewhere, near dead, or the pirates had killed her and Mallary. Or worse.

It was the *worse* that he couldn't bring himself to even think about. Human trafficking was a huge thing in these parts, and you didn't have to be a young girl or boy for it to happen to you.

"It's nearly four in the morning." Fletcher put his hand on Keaton's shoulder. "We've been out here all night."

"I don't care." Keaton continued to scan the dark ocean. Miles and miles of pitch-black nothingness stared back. He dropped his hand to his side in defeat.

"Let's go check in with everyone else. Regroup. Rest. And then we can come back out."

Keaton nodded. He leaned back on the seat and pulled out his cell, reading the last text he'd received.

Trinity: *Doing safety checks and going down for one last dive. Mallary is beside herself. Not sure I want her out here with me again, but I'll fill you in on that tonight. I'll text when we surface and are heading in.*

He'd responded, letting her know he'd see her at the docks, but she'd never gotten his text, and her phone hadn't been recovered from the vessel.

"Why don't we head in from the north?" Keaton said. "Dawson and Hayes covered that area earlier but radioed saying they were heading in from the south."

"That's a reasonable request."

"Take it slow. Please."

Fletcher maneuvered the fishing boat toward the channel, and Keaton continued to use the spotlight, cutting through darkness barely illuminated by the glow of the moon. It would be a miracle...

"Over there." Keaton's heart slammed into his throat. "On the red channel buoy. Do you see that?" He held the light on the channel marker. A faint figure—a silhouette—illuminated under the bright light. Water, pushed by the current, swirled around the buoy.

"I see something. But I can't make out what it is." Fletcher swiveled the steering wheel to the starboard.

"Something...someone... Oh my God. That's a person holding on to that buoy." Keaton stepped to the side of the boat, clutching the spotlight in one hand and gripping the side rail with the other. He squinted, trying to take in the figure. "Blond hair. Jesus, that's her. That's Trinity." He glanced over his shoulder. "Radio it in." He shoved the spotlight at his buddy, then raced to the bow of the boat.

"What the hell are you doing?"

"Jumping in to save her. What does it look like?"

"Before you do that, why don't you let me get a little closer?" Fletcher said, giving the boat a little more gas.

"I can live with that." Keaton kept his eyes locked on that buoy and the body. She had to be alive. No way could she be clinging to that without breath in her lungs.

Once Fletcher was fifteen feet away, Keaton stepped up on the bow and dove into the water. The chilly ocean seeped into his clothing. He surfaced, and with his sight locked on Trinity, he swam as fast as possible.

He'd spent a lifetime as a sailor. He'd joined the Navy the second he'd turned eighteen. His parents had supported his decision, even though they had wanted him to at least entertain the offers that had rolled his way to play college football.

He hadn't given a crap about that. All that had done was put him at the center of attention as a star quarterback. Football had merely been something he'd done to exert energy. It hadn't been about having a passion for the sport but a passion to be part of something.

Nothing ever happened in a vacuum, but his coaches —even some of his teammates—had put him on a pedestal.

Not the Navy, especially not in boot camp. There, he'd just been a man.

The Navy—specifically, being a SEAL—had taught him that while he was a member of an elite team, that made him special, and humility mattered. What he'd done for his country—for his fellow man—hadn't deserved the spotlight. He'd always been good with that. Every medal he'd ever received, while important, had never been displayed. They were more reminders of lives lost. Battles forged. And the freedoms he'd fought for.

"Trinity," he choked on her name as he approached the buoy. Thank God the waters were calm. No wind. No rain. No weather to contend with. He grabbed the channel marker with one hand and wrapped his arm around Trinity's body with the other.

She moaned. Her limp body slithered into the water.

"I gotcha."

A badly tied tourniquet was wrapped around her left shoulder. Blood trickled from an open wound.

His pulse soared with panic and dread. But his body and mind remained sharp with the years of training, years of focus and dedication to his trade.

"Trinity? Can you hear me?" He floated her on her back, resting her head on his shoulder.

Her eyes fluttered but never opened. Her lips parted, and she gave a slight moan but no words.

"I'm going to need a hand getting her on the boat," he called to Fletcher. "She's going to need an ambulance."

"Already on that," Fletcher said. "One will meet us at the marina." He maneuvered the boat alongside Keaton, climbing on the stern. Together, they hoisted Trinity onto the back of the vessel.

Keaton dropped to his knees, cradling her head in his lap, pressing his fingers against her neck. "Pulse is weak," he said, forcing himself to take all the emotion out of his actions. However, it wasn't easy. All he saw was a woman he cared about.

One he cared too damn much for, and he'd been trying like hell not to. He hadn't wanted a woman in his life. He'd never wanted to feel that way again. It hurt too much.

"Here." Fletcher handed him a blanket. "Wrap her in this." He waved his hand over her shoulder. "Can you tell what the injury is?"

"No." Keaton shook his head. "But this tourniquet isn't doing shit." He untied it. A small amount of blood trickled through the wetsuit. Quickly, he unzipped it and pulled her arm through the sleeve. "Jesus. It looks like she's been shot." He lifted her upper body. "No exit wound." He retied the tourniquet, wrapped her up, applied pressure to the wound, and held her in his arms. "Haul ass." He tangled his fingers through her wet hair. "It's going to be all right. We've got you now."

A bag thudded to the floor as Fletcher hit the throttles.

He reached for it and undid the ties, pulling out a box. "Oh my God," he whispered as he peered inside. "The jewels." He set them aside, leaned forward, and kissed her temple. "What happened to you out there?"

A groan. Another flutter of her eyelids. A sharp intake of breath. A moan. No words.

"That's okay, babe. All that matters is I found you," he said. "I found you," he repeated. Wetness dribbled down his cheek. He swiped at it with the back of his hand.

Whoever had done this was going to fucking pay. Keaton would make sure of that.

KEATON PACED in the waiting room. He hated hospitals. They smelled like death. Felt like death. Nothing about them screamed anything other than death and sickness. Of course, his only experience in hospitals had been when he'd been injured during a mission.

He'd been shot, stabbed, and tortured—which had included electrocution.

Each time he'd awoken in one of these hellholes, he hadn't been sure what was worse, the experience that had brought him to the doctors in the first place or being stuck on the damn gurney.

He had nothing against doctors, nurses, or any of the staff. They were all wonderful people doing an excellent job, and honestly, he'd always gotten the best of care. It wasn't them. It was the environment and being told he couldn't do something. Sitting still wasn't his strong suit, even after he'd given up being an adrenaline junkie.

"Excuse me, son," Monty, Trinity's father, said. "All that pacing isn't doing anything but remind all of us that my daughter is in an operating room right now."

"Oh. Sorry." Keaton ran his fingers through his hair. He glanced around the small room. "I don't do hospitals well."

"No one does," Monty said.

"Just sit down." Audra shoved a paper mug of coffee at him. "You're making everyone in here nuts, and it's not going to bring the doctor out here any faster."

"We're all worried about her," Baily added. "She's our friend, too. But the doctor said he'd be out as soon as she was out of surgery and in recovery." She glanced around the waiting room. "Has anyone heard anything more about the search for Mallary?"

Dawson nodded. "Last update we all got was twenty minutes ago. They haven't found any signs of Mallary. They are discussing how to treat this because they don't know if they are looking for a body—dead or alive—or if this is a kidnapping. That changes the scope of the search and rescue."

Keaton tapped his Apple Watch. "It's been two hours since they rolled Trinity into surgery." He took a long breath and leaned against the wall, staring into the sliding doors leading to the recovery rooms. "I've had a dozen bullets carved out of my body. I don't think those surgeries took this long."

"We waited six hours when you took two to the gut,"

Dawson said. "She's in good hands. You heard what the doctor said. She's strong. Her vitals were good. The bullet wasn't in a difficult place. I'm sure—"

Dawson's words were cut off by the doors swishing open.

"Hey, Doc." Keaton raced toward the woman who had headed up the team taking care of Trinity during the operation. "Did the surgery go as planned?" His mouth suddenly grew dry. He couldn't swallow. Hell, he could barely suck in a breath.

Dawson flanked his left, Fletcher and Hayes his right. These men were as much his family as his blood relatives. He'd be lost without them.

Audra and Baily inched closer.

Her father jumped in front of all of them. "How's my little princess?"

"She's a fighter," Doctor Emily Sprouse said. "We were able to remove the bullet."

"I'm going to need that for evidence." Dawson looped his fingers in his belt as if he were standing there in his uniform—which he wasn't.

"It's been bagged, and we'll need your signature." Emily nodded. "Trinity has been taken to the recovery room. There was some damage done to the shoulder joint, and she's going to need rest and lots of rehab. Her body temperature is back to normal. Her vitals are strong. I suspect she'll be awake soon."

"When can we see her?" Monty asked before Keaton could untie his tongue.

"I don't want to overwhelm her," Emily said. "We have no idea what happened to her out there since she never regained consciousness before surgery, except to utter a couple of words. So—"

"She spoke?" Keaton's heart throbbed in the center of his chest. Mindlessly, he rubbed it as if to make the odd sensation go away. "What did she say?"

"Not much. She muttered 'Mallary,'" Emily said.

"That's her friend who was out on the boat with her that we believe was either taken by pirates or lost at sea," Dawson said somberly, glancing at his wristwatch. "I need to head out soon to meet with the Coast Guard."

"That's terrible." Emily lowered her head for a brief second. "The second name was Keaton." She gave him a weak smile. "She repeated your name when we were rolling her to recovery, along with something about her jewelry."

Keaton shot Dawson a glance.

"What about seeing her?" Monty asked again.

"Two at a time and not for long periods, especially while she's sleeping. She needs her rest."

"Most of us can come back later," Baily said. "We're just glad she's going to be okay."

"Monty, you should go see your daughter." Keaton ran a hand over his unshaven face. His legs had turned to putty. It was as if he'd been underwater for hours, and they could barely hold his weight a second longer. He found a chair and eased into it.

"Before I do, I'd like a word with you and the chief," Monty said. "Thank you, Doc. I appreciate everything you've done for my little girl."

"My pleasure. We'll keep her here overnight. But if

all goes well, she'll be able to go home sometime tomorrow."

"Thanks." Monty squeezed Emily's biceps.

"I've got to get back to the marina," Baily said.

"I'll drive you." Fletcher rested his hand on Keaton's shoulder. "Stay and visit with Trinity. We'll check in on you later."

Keaton lifted his head and watched Audra, Baily, Fletcher, and Hayes disappear down the hallway.

Monty stepped away from the sliding doors and put his hands on his hips. "I don't pretend to know what the hell is going on between you and my daughter." He pointed his finger at Keaton. "But I know whatever that is, it's too early in the game for a ring." He arched his brow.

"Sir, I—"

"Don't ever call me that. The name's Monty." He let out a puff of air. "While my child doesn't need to tell me everything she's up to, I do know she was hell-bent on helping Mallary. I know what Mallary's half-brother was accused of. So, I'm guessing she found something down there yesterday, and either we're all just finding out about it, or you didn't think I should know."

"Mr. Stevenson—" Dawson began.

"It's Monty."

"Okay." Dawson nodded. "Monty, my time is limited. I need your word that this conversation stays right here. It's not only because we're dealing with two different active investigations, but because I haven't had the chance to interview Trinity, and until I know exactly what happened to her, I'm not telling anyone about what Keaton found when he located Trinity clinging to that buoy."

"My daughter and her big heart," Monty muttered, pulling up a chair and sitting down. "When she was a little girl and we first moved back here, she saw it as one big adventure. Of course, her mother hated it here. It wasn't posh enough for that woman. But Trinity loved it, at first. I think deep down she always loved it here, even when she was acting like her mom."

Keaton sat up a little taller, leaned in a little closer, and hung on to every word. Anything to know her better, because fear still gripped his heart like a disease. He resented that feeling. He wanted to brush it under the rug and ignore it, to somehow make it go away.

But he couldn't. And there was a part of him—even if he wanted to deny it—that didn't want to. For the first time since Petra had died, he felt alive. Not that he'd felt dead inside for all these years. It wasn't that. He'd lived his life. He'd enjoyed his career, his friends, and his family.

He'd cared about all those things with every fiber of his heart. But his soul? That had belonged to the woman he'd buried. And now, it had come to life, and he had no idea how he'd managed these ten years with his feet firmly planted in the past.

"Trinity could be such a little brat." Monty chuckled. "She knew how to boss people around, just like her mother. But there were always subtle differences. If anyone bothered to take a closer look, they'd see it. They'd see a young woman who left a twenty-dollar tip when five was plenty. Or a girl who went out of her way to put lunch money on a wild redheaded girl's school card."

"Audra always wondered who'd done that." Dawson laughed. "We were talking about that a couple of months ago. Everyone assumed it was Silas."

"I'm sure he did, too." Monty smiled. "Another misunderstood soul of Calusa Cove. But Trinity was so hell-bent on her mother's approval, she wouldn't dare get caught doing a good deed."

"No offense, sir—"

"I get your former military, and that stuff is ingrained in your psyche or something, but please, I beg of you, stop it," Monty said, interrupting Keaton.

"I'll try." Keaton rubbed his hands on his jeans. "I mean no disrespect to your family, but wouldn't doing that kind of stuff make you proud?"

"Me? Hell yes." Monty nodded. "But sadly, not Porsche. That woman, and I get what a bastard it makes me to say it that way, but if you ever meet her, you'll agree, she believes there are stations in life." He lifted his hand over his head. "She's up here, and everyone in Calusa Cove is down here." He lowered it to his ankle. "Porsche treats most people like they were put on this earth to serve her. If she gets what she believes is poor service, she'll leave you a penny tip because she believes that will teach you a lesson. Writing negative reviews is one of her favorite pastimes. So, my lovely little daughter spent from the age of ten to eighteen trying to please her mother. It never happened, and Trinity finally figured out that it wasn't worth the effort. But it all came at a cost."

Monty tapped his chest. "I take ownership of some of it, because I spoiled that child."

"She's not that bad," Keaton found himself saying.

"Trust me, she's a princess. Date her long enough, and you'll learn."

Dawson chuckled.

Keaton pounded his chest. He wasn't even sure they were a thing. One night doesn't make for a relationship. The fact they hadn't fought for twenty-four hours was a big deal, but still, caring didn't mean two people could make it work.

"Monty, is there a point to all this?" Dawson asked. "Because I still need your word that the word 'jewels' will not come out of your mouth and I really need to head out. Mallary is still missing."

Monty lifted his gaze. "You have my word, but Mallary's family has already called me five times since they learned Trinity was found."

"I'm not surprised by that," Keaton said. "They were close friends and I'm sure they are worried sick. I wish we had more information to give them."

"I'm afraid the Coast Guard might be suspending the dive portion of the rescue," Dawson said. "State's getting involved now."

"Is that typical?" Monty asked.

"It depends on a variety of things and right now, I don't have enough information to speculate why," Dawson said.

Monty nodded. "Mallary's parents have been incredibly kind and very concerned for Trinity. However, with each phone call, they have asked me the same question, and that's if the jewels from the *Flying Victoria* were found, which I suppose I don't find all that odd, since it's one of the things Trinity asked about when she woke up."

"These jewels have been at the heart of the search ever since Jared's boat went down last year." Dawson rested his hand on Monty's shoulder. "While Trinity didn't go around blabbing to the world what she was doing—as a matter of fact, she kept it to just us—we all know that Mallary told everyone who would listen."

"I know, and that's one of the reasons this is so hard." Monty let out a long breath. "I don't like blaming a missing girl, who might be dead, but her actions are probably what set this in motion. Pirates were probably watching Trinity for weeks, maybe longer.

That thought burned through Keaton's body like a wildfire.

"Pure speculation," Dawson said calmly. He was always the voice of reason.

"All Trinity wanted to do was help. It's all she's ever wanted to do, but she never wants to take credit for it. While she wants this town to see her, she doesn't want to own much of what she does," Monty said softly. "Like when she asked me to help her buy that boat. I thought she should keep it at the big marina. But no, she had to do it at Mitchell's, which is fine. Baily is a great person. But when I bought the thing, the marina gave us a year of free docking." Monty shrugged.

"Don't ever let Baily know that," Dawson said.

"Never." Monty waved his hands. "I shouldn't have even told you, but that's Trinity." He laughed, shaking his head. "The house she bought? It was owned by a couple who had to move up north for family reasons. They were also upside down and had to sell fast. She came in, offered them over the asking price without batting an eye, and she did that without daddy's help."

There was a lot about Trinity that Keaton didn't know. Money didn't necessarily buy respect, and Trinity felt as though she needed to earn it. Except, she kept doing it the ass-backward way.

"You raised a lovely girl." Keaton stretched out his hand. "For the record, I'm not sure we're dating, but I'm hoping to change that."

"Trinity has spoken of you many times." Monty stood. "She's used some interesting superlatives to describe you."

"I can only imagine." Keaton chuckled.

"A father knows when his child cares about another human, and she likes you or she wouldn't bother calling you the biggest royal pain in her pretty little ass. Her words, not mine."

"Sounds like Trinity." Dawson jerked his thumb over his shoulder. "I'd better get going. I need to find out what the Coast Guard wants, and then head home for a quick meal with Audra, or she'll serve me to the gators because she can."

"You two make for a great couple. I'm looking forward to attending that wedding." Monty laughed. "I just have to wonder if Audra will have a python or an alligator as her maid of honor."

"With my luck, she'll have an owl witch." Dawson

waved his hand over his head and strolled out of the room.

"Interesting." Keaton scratched the back of his neck.

"What is?"

"He didn't get all weird and tell you that it was too soon to be talking about a wedding."

Monty slapped Keaton on the back. "You didn't hear this from me, but I saw him at Casey's."

"As in the Casey's Fine Gems? The one that sells engagement rings?"

Monty shrugged. "Give me a few moments alone with my daughter, and then the little princess is all yours." The doors opened, and Monty paused, glancing over his shoulder. "Thank you for not giving up. Most men would have."

"I was just doing what the Navy trained me to."

"No." Monty tapped his chest. "Whether you believe it or not, you did what your heart commanded. My daughter's just lucky that you're a retired SEAL." With that statement, he disappeared through the doors, leaving Keaton alone with his thoughts. He didn't have many. They mostly consisted of confused emotions that made him vulnerable.

He'd always thought that if he ever opened his heart again, he'd feel massive guilt. That he'd somehow be betraying his love for Petra, but that's not what happened.

Sure, there was a tinge of something. A hint of...of... maybe fear of the fact he didn't feel guilt.

And that scared him more than anything.

CHAPTER 6

Gasp. Gurgle.

Trinity opened her mouth to scream, but instead, she got a throat full of salty water.

Mallary? Where's Mallary?

Oh God. She remembered. She'd never made it under the boat. She was gone. Just like Jared. Lost to the sea. Or murdered by pirates. Pirates who wanted the jewels of the Flying Victoria.

Trinity wrapped her arms around...around...something. It was big. Hard. Cold. And it bobbed gently up and down.

Water rushed by as if it were in a hurry to get somewhere. All she wanted to do was go home, curl up in bed, and sleep. Her body ached, and part of her soul had died today.

She sucked in a shallow breath. Her chest burned. Her shoulder throbbed. Her head was in a daze of confusion as she tried to piece together the events that jumbled her mind. She blinked, straining to see something. Anything.

But all she saw was utter darkness.

She did her best to adjust the tie around her shoulder, but it slipped off, and she was so weak. So tired. And cold. She shivered. Glancing over her shoulder, she checked for fins. However, it was too dark to notice anything, even with the moon dancing in the black sky.

Her eyelids grew heavy. She rested her head on the hard object. "I'm sorry, Daddy," she whispered. "Oh, Keaton. You were right about me." She let herself drift off...and the nightmare started all over again.

"No!" Trinity jerked. She winced, grabbing her shoulder as a gut-wrenching pain tore through her limbs. It started out as if someone had thrust a knife into her body, and then it danced across her skin. "Oh God."

"Hey. It's okay. You're okay," Keaton's voice cut through the fog. He took her hand, ran his fingers over her knuckles, and leaned in, pressing his lips on her forehead. "You're safe now." He dotted her cheek and temple with more tender kisses.

"Mallary? The jewels?" Trinity grabbed Keaton's wrist. "Did you find them? My boat? What happened to my boat?" Panic clutched her chest like an elephant had taken a seat on it.

"Babe, slow down. You literally just woke up after being lost at sea for close to nine hours. You've had surgery on your shoulder. You need to rest. Your dad went to eat, and if he comes back and I'm sitting here talking about all this crap, he won't be happy."

"Please, Keaton. What I need are answers." She stared into his brown eyes, pleading. Begging. Everything that had happened replayed like a bad dream over and over again. She couldn't stop it. It didn't matter that she was awake because all she could see was a gun… pointing at her. Her pushing Mallary into the water… Bullets racing through the darkness…

He sat on the side of the bed, holding her hand and staring at her fingers. He lifted his gaze. "I guess I would, too, if I were you." He nodded. "The search for Mallary at sea was called off."

Trinity yanked her hand away, covered her mouth, and gasped. "No," she managed in a mangled cry.

"I'm sorry. I didn't say that well. The Coast Guard found your boat stripped of anything of value. It appears it was the work of pirates. Dawson called that FBI agent, Chloe, and reported Mallary as missing. She's going to work that angle."

"What about the je—"

Keaton pressed his lips against her mouth. He kissed her cheek. Then he whispered, "Don't bring that up. Not in front of anyone. Certainly not here. We decided not to tell anyone that we have them. Not until after Dawson has had the chance to speak with you. Someone tried to kill you, and until we know more, no one needs to know what you found." He kissed her softly one more time.

She stared at him for a long moment.

"I need you to trust me on this. Okay?" he said. "You can't talk to anyone but us about it. At least for now."

"Okay," she said softly.

The machine's beeping grew louder and faster, as did her pulse. The nightmare snapped into view, but it wasn't a nightmare. It had been her reality. It had been what she had survived.

"I floated and swam for hours in the dark," she managed. "A few boats hummed right on by. They didn't see or hear me." Tears trickled down her cheeks. No one ever liked crying, and she was no different.

The sweet man snagged a tissue and swiped under her eyes, all while gazing into them with a mixture of sadness, kindness, caring, and a hint of rage. It was that last emotion that Trinity knew she'd have to tether. At least this time, she believed she hadn't caused it. Or she hoped she hadn't been the one to put it there.

"I thought I was going to die out there. I tried not to close my eyes because I knew what would happen, but I managed to grab hold of something, and now I'm here. How did that happen?"

"When I didn't hear from you, and Baily said you never radioed before she closed, we all came looking. We spent the night and morning out there. Fletcher and I were coming down the channel from the north and spotted you on a channel marker." Gingerly, he ran his hand over her arm, which was in a sling. "I don't want to think about what would've happened if even another half hour had passed. You were completely uncon-scious, barely hanging on, and you'd lost a lot of blood."

She pushed out a hard breath through her nose and closed her eyes. "Two men boarded my boat. They were masked. One shot me when I tried to disarm him with my empty tank. I managed to grab another tank with a little bit of oxygen before I dove back in."

"You did what?" Keaton ran his thumb across her cheek.

She blinked. "It wasn't my brightest moment, but I

had to do something. He was going to kill us both. Instead, I saved myself, and Mallary is probably dead." She turned her head. "It's all my fault." Tears flowed down her face. Hot. Hard. And fast.

He gently wiped them away. "Sweetheart, I don't see how that's possible."

"Maybe she wouldn't have been taken. Or lost at sea if I hadn't tried that stupid stunt."

"Oh, babe." He cupped her chin. "I wasn't there, so I can't assess whether it was the right thing to do or not. But based on what you just told me, it appears it was the only logical course of action. And truth be told, I would've done the same thing in hopes of saving my friend."

"You're just trying to make me feel better."

"I think you know me better than that." He cocked a brow. "If I believed you were in the wrong, I'd say so." He smoothed down her hair. "I'm just so grateful you're alive."

She scrunched her face. "But Mallary isn't."

"We don't know that, and we're going to pull out all the stops to look for her." Keaton yanked his cell from his back pocket and tapped at the screen.

"What are you doing?"

"Letting your dad know you're awake. I'm also texting Dawson. He needs to take your statement." Keaton glanced up. "I should go get the doctor."

"You have my father's cell number?"

Keaton chuckled. "I spent the last few hours in the waiting room with him. It's been… interesting."

"I'm going to need more information." She pointed

toward the cup on the tray. "Am I allowed to have water?"

He lifted the straw to her lips. "Let's just say your dad wanted to know my...intentions."

She coughed, and a little water dripped down her chin. "How awkward for you."

"Not really." Keaton smiled. "I like your dad. He's cool."

"Yeah, he is." She glanced around the room. Cards and flowers lined the windowsill. She pointed.

"None of those are from me." He arched a brow. "Though I have half a mind to toss out that bouquet."

"Why?"

"Because they came from Fenton."

She rolled her eyes. "You have my blessing to burn them."

Keaton frowned. "Is he the reason you don't like it when a man gives you flowers?"

"No." She sighed. "I've never really been a flowers girl—partly because my mom demanded them from my dad for every single occasion. But mostly because the guys who gave them to me did so because they had done something they needed to apologize for. Usually lying or cheating or both."

"Ah, I see." He strolled over to the window, snagged the largest arrangement, and stuffed it in the garbage. "Well, if I ever get you flowers, it won't be for those reasons, that's for sure."

"They're kind of a waste of money."

"Maybe someday I can change your mind about

that." He eased back on the side of the bed. "Do you need anything? Are you in pain?"

"I honestly don't know what I am."

A tap at the door filled the room, and a young man pushing a tray strolled in. "Oh, good. We're awake. That will make my job easier," the man said. "I just need to check your blood pressure, temperature, change out your IV, give you some more IV antibiotics, and escort you down for some X-rays." He nodded to Keaton.

"She needs more? Why?" Keaton asked.

"It's standard procedure with a surgery like hers," the man said.

"The doctor didn't say anything about that." Keaton furrowed his brow.

"I'm not sure what to tell you, but it was in her orders this morning." The man shrugged. "I'm sure the doc just wants to make sure there are no complications from surgery before she sends her home. It's going to be a little while. Why don't you grab yourself a fresh cup of coffee? Or better yet, some food. I hear you've been here all night and day." He lifted the chart at the end of the bed. "Unfortunately, Trinity missed dinner. You could grab her something from the cafeteria. Nothing too heavy on the stomach. Soup would be good. Or some ice cream. Something like that."

"Are you hungry?" Keaton asked, glancing at Trinity.

"Even if she isn't," the man said before she could even open her mouth. "She should have something. The chicken noodle soup isn't horrible."

"I could eat that." Trinity let out a long breath. "And maybe some hot tea."

"I'm on it." He squeezed her hand. "I won't be too long."

"Thank you."

"Anything for my princess."

She cocked her head. "I might be one, but I don't belong to anyone, and the only person who can call me that is my dad."

He chuckled. "I couldn't help myself." He leaned over and brushed his lips over her mouth. His tongue snagged hers in a possessive swirl, letting her know that while he might not own her, he certainly didn't want her accepting any other suitors.

Not that she would. Wow. Was Keaton her man? Were they dating? Exclusively?

That was enlightening.

Keaton slipped off the bed. "Before I go, mind if I check your hospital badge?" He waved his finger at the young man.

Oh, my. "Is that necessary?" She glared, though, when she glanced at the man and didn't see a badge, which was standard hospital practice, it did give her pause.

"It is." Keaton rested his hands on his hips and looked the poor man up and down.

Trinity groaned. This was an aspect about Keaton that if they were going to have a go at it, he would have to tame. Not the action, because she appreciated that, but how he went about it.

"No problem. I understand." The man patted his chest. Then his waist and hips. "Crap. I must've left it at the nurses' station when we had a changeover meeting."

He hung the chart on the bed and reached for the near-empty IV bag. "This needs to be changed out, and she's already late for her antibiotics. That's important. Let me do that first, and then I'll go grab my badge."

"Nope. I'm sorry. I need that before I—"

"Mr. Cole, there are bubbles in this line, and infection after surgery is a real thing." He pulled out a vial. "If you'd like, you can snag my badge from the station around the corner." The man turned and took a bag from the tray he'd pushed into the room. He reached up and hung it on the metal hook, untangling the line.

"Please stop what you're doing," Keaton said with a harsh, dark tone. "I know enough about IVs to know she's got a couple of minutes. I want to see that hospital ID before you do anything else." He pointed toward the door. "Don't make me put my hands on you."

"Keaton, that's uncalled for." Trinity narrowed her stare.

"Really? Then why is he making it such a big deal, and how does a man I've never met know my name?" Keaton asked.

"Mr. Cole." The man let out an exaggerated sigh. "Calusa Cove is a small town, and everyone on the floor has been talking about you and how you found this one." He jerked his thumb over his shoulder in an angry shake.

Trinity didn't blame the poor guy.

However, considering the recent events, she could also see Keaton's point. He was simply trying to protect her, and she appreciated that. Her father would be grateful. The reality was that if she were in his shoes, she would have pushed for him to find his badge. She might have been a little less aggressive, but she would have wanted to see it, too.

If she'd thought to look for it, and that was the part that scared her more than anything.

* * *

"RIGHT NOW, TALK IS CHEAP," Keaton said. "I'm sorry if you think this is all one big inconvenience, but if the whole floor is gossiping, you know what she went through and why I might be a little overprotective of my girlfriend."

The word girlfriend rolled off his tongue quickly and easily. Perhaps a little too easily.

But it felt right, and that was strange.

"All right. All right." The man ruffled something on the portable tray. He stuffed his hands in his pockets. "I'll be right back with that badge." The man stared at Keaton as he strolled by the edge of the bed.

"Why don't I walk with you?" Keaton said.

"Now, that's really overkill, dude." The man lunged toward Keaton, pulling something sharp and shiny from his pocket.

The small scalpel nailed him in the biceps. "Motherfucker," Keaton mumbled with a groan.

Trinity gasped.

Keaton slammed the asshole up against the wall, but the jerk managed to yank the knife from Keaton's flesh and stab him higher in the shoulder. He gritted his teeth, jerked his arm, and kicked the man's ankle, sending him crashing to the floor. "You fucked with the wrong man." He held him by the throat. Not too hard. Not enough to cut off all the oxygen, but enough to put pressure on the windpipe and make it incredibly uncomfortable for this idiot. He pressed his knee into his chest before gripping the knife and giving it a good yank. He glanced up. "Are you okay?"

Trinity nodded. "But you're not."

"I'll be fine. Just a few scratches."

"What the heck is going on in here?" Doctor Emily Sprouse skidded to a stop at the door, followed by one of the female nurses. "Why are you holding that man down? You're going to hurt him."

"Please call the chief of police, Dawson Ridge. Tell him that someone tried to attack—"

"I'm here." Dawson sidestepped the two people at the door. "Jesus, man. I leave you unattended for five minutes, and this happens."

"He doesn't have a hospital badge, gave me shit for asking for one, and then stabbed me. Twice."

"Let him go." Dawson took over, restraining the man. "What's your name, son?"

He got nothing but a stare down.

Keaton raced to Trinity's side, ignoring the pain registering in his brain. It wasn't horrible, but his muscles burned every time he flexed his biceps. When he shifted his shoulder, it was the same thing. It was a minor inconvenience, but it still put him in a major sour mood.

Had he not been diligent, or if he'd stepped away for

even a moment, he shuddered to think what would have happened to Trinity. And on his watch.

"Are you going to give me your side of the story? Or are you going with the one where you were going to do something to Trinity when Keaton left the room? Maybe give her something to make her sleepy? Kidnap her? Kill her? You tell me," Dawson said.

The man said nothing.

"Okay. I'm guessing you attacked him instead when that didn't happen?" Dawson asked.

More silence. Nothing like taking the fifth to new heights.

Emily lifted Keaton's shirt. He winced as he jerked his arm away. He didn't need attention. He needed to give his attention to Trinity. He took her hand and pressed his lips to her palm.

"Let her look at it," Trinity whispered.

Keaton sighed and sat on the edge of the bed while Dawson continued to try to get information from that little asshole. He asked questions like, *Were you acting alone? Did someone hire you? Was your goal to hurt or kill?*

But the jerk wasn't saying shit.

"Hey, Doc, do you know that guy? Does he work at the hospital?" Keaton asked softly while the good doc poured antiseptic on his wounds.

"I don't think I've ever seen him, and I pretty much know everyone on this floor," Emily said. "Lulu, do you know that man?"

Lulu nodded. "His name is Warren Harley. He works nights as a janitor in the ER. I've seen him down there when I've filled in a couple of times, but never up here."

"If he worked in the hospital, why wouldn't he have his credentials?" With his good hand, Keaton squeezed Trinity's thigh. His pulse had yet to calm down, and he wasn't sure if it would until whoever was behind this was caught. "Wouldn't he have needed them to get the supplies he rolled in here with?"

"Yeah, care to explain that one?" Dawson asked.

Warren huffed out air, but not an answer.

"If I might wager a guess here," Emily said. "That cart was left in the hallway. He'd need a special keycode that only the doctors and charge nurses have, so he wouldn't have been able to do anything."

"What about the IV bag?" Keaton asked.

"It's fluid," the nurse said. "It was on the tray because I was making my rounds and knew Trinity needed a flush." Lulu unclipped her badge and tucked it in her pocket. She then pulled it out and waved it. "I've been known to start my day with this sucker tucked neatly away. When I start my shift, it's always easier to pull it out of my pocket to run it across the door for meds and supplies. But when entering a patient's room, I always have it clipped." She waved her hand toward Warren. "Any hospital staff member should have it when they enter a patient's room, and Warren knows that, especially working in the ER. That place is a zoo, and security is tight down there, even though we're a small town."

"Good to know," Keaton said.

Dawson read Warren his rights, but he still refused to speak. He stood rigid, lips pursed, and glared at

Keaton, as if Keaton had personally ruined his day, instead of the other way around.

"Who do you work for, you piece of shit?" Keaton said. "Because no way could you have pulled off something like this all by your little self. You're not smart enough."

Warren's eye twitched, and he snarled, but he didn't cave.

"You know, whoever sent you is going to let you rot." Keaton sneered. "They'll let you take the blame. They aren't going to bail you out or even send you a lawyer. Nope. They're going to let you hang for attempted murder."

"I did no such thing," Warren said with his nostrils flaring.

"Oh, really?" Dawson let out a sigh. "Because those two stab wounds in my buddy over there paint a different picture." He cocked his head. "And even if your intent with my friend wasn't to kill, what the hell were you doing with this vial?" Dawson waved the small glass object he'd taken from Warren's pocket. "Hey, Doc. Can you tell me what this is? Without touching it?"

"Sure." Emily leaned over, glancing at the vial. "Jesus. That's fentanyl." She glanced between Dawson and Warren. "Where'd you get that? Only certain medical professionals have access to that."

"I want a lawyer," Warren said.

"Thanks for making more work for me today." Dawson curled his fingers around Warren's elbow. "I'm going to radio Remy and have him come get this guy.

Once that happens, I'll be back to take both your statements."

Keaton nodded, doing his best not to wince as the doctor glued his wounds together. At least it wouldn't be traditional stitches. Those sucked. "When can I take Trinity home?" He met the doctor's gaze.

"I'd like to keep her overnight for observation."

"Is that necessary or for precaution?" Keaton cracked his neck.

"If all Trinity underwent was surgery, we would have sent her home as soon as she woke up." Emily held up her hand. "But that's not the case, and to be safe—"

"She'll be safer where I can protect her from whatever that was." Keaton stretched his arm. "Someone tried to kill her yesterday, and it seems they just tried to do it again. I mean no disrespect to you and your ability as a doctor."

"None taken, but if I release her, it will have to be against medical advice, and I'm going to send you two home with some strict guidelines."

"That's fine." Keaton nodded.

"Um, excuse me." Trinity poked his good arm. "Both of you are talking as though the patient isn't even in the room or incapable of making her own decisions."

"Are you seriously going to fight me on this after you watched that jerkoff stab me? He was going to dope you full of a drug that could have killed you." Keaton held her gaze. He tried not to glare. He tried to be soft, kind, and caring. But he doubted that's how he came off.

"No, but I'd at least like to be treated like I have a brain and know how to use it."

"Never said you didn't." He shook his head. "Doc, can we get those walking papers?"

"I'm sure you're familiar with how red tape works. It'll take some time, but I'll get the ball rolling." Emily patted his good shoulder. "Just promise me you'll try not to be a repeat customer. Either one of you."

"We'll work on it." He laced his fingers through Trinity's. "Thanks."

"Get out of my way," her father's voice bellowed through the hallway. "What on earth happened?" Monty asked as he rounded the corner. "Princess, are you okay?"

"Once again, thanks to Keaton, I'm fine."

"I shouldn't have left you." Monty yanked Keaton off the side of the bed and shoved him to the side. "I'll never leave your side again."

"I'm a grown woman, Daddy. That's going to be kind of hard," Trinity said.

"You're going to move home until we know for sure whoever tried to kill you yesterday is the same man Dawson just dragged into the elevator." Monty tugged at the comforter, lifting it higher over Trinity's body.

If Keaton ever had the chance to be a father, and he had a daughter, he suspected he might go a little overboard, too. Not that Monty was being overboard at all. He cleared his throat. "To be honest, I don't think—and I'm sure Dawson will agree—that Warren Harley isn't the mastermind behind what's happening."

"I have other patients. I'll get the discharge paperwork started. Good luck having any say over what happens next." Emily laughed, patting Keaton's good shoulder. "You're gonna need it. No one will ever be good enough for her or be able to protect her. No one. Not even someone like you."

Keaton had waged that war before with Petra's father. Talk about a high-strung dad with control issues. "Sir," Keaton started.

"Do not call me that." Monty fluffed Trinity's pillow. "If you want to stand guard at my front door, feel free. But my daughter is staying with me. I have the best state-of-the-art security—"

"I'm sure you do, but you're not a trained Navy SEAL. I am." Keaton rarely puffed out his chest or used his career to get what he wanted. It was even rarer that he ever needed to do it. "And while what is available on the open market is good, really good, what I have access to is ten times better. It's been tested by the FBI, the DEA, the ATF, and the highest levels in the Department of Defense. You've never seen anything like it. My place might not be a mansion, but it'll keep you and Trinity safe. I can guarantee that."

"You're inviting me to come stay with you?" Monty folded his arms across his chest.

"I know that where she goes, you plan on being at her side, so yeah." Keaton nodded, holding Monty's painful glare. "My place has two bedrooms. We'll manage."

Monty chuckled. "You don't know my child very well if you think a two-bedroom home is going to serve—"

"Daddy, stop it," Trinity said. "Keaton, does it have to be your place? Can't we make my house safe?"

"I'm sorry, but no. It's too big, with too many weak spots—too many exits and entrances. If I had more time to set something up, maybe, but right now, it's got to be my house. I know it's small, but—"

"We'll make it work." She took his hand and squeezed before shifting her gaze. "Dad, please stop giving Keaton a hard time. He's only trying to help, and he's a lot more qualified than either of us."

Monty glanced toward the ceiling. "How concerned do I need to be for my own safety?"

"I don't know," Keaton answered honestly. "But I don't think it's a good idea for you to stay alone in your house. I suspect whoever is after Trinity, and what they think she may have found, won't think twice about coming after you to get to her. Considering what happened, I wouldn't put it past whoever came after her to do that."

"Why not announce that Dawson has the *Flying Victoria* jewels?" Monty asked. "Wouldn't that stop them from coming after my little girl?"

"Now that she's awake, and we know what happened, Dawson may want to do that." Keaton nodded. "Lord knows I want to do whatever will ensure hers and your safety. But that doesn't mean they won't stop trying to kill her for what they think she knows."

"But I don't know anything," she said with a tremble in her voice.

God, he hated that her normally confident self had taken a back seat to this scared person. He understood trauma. He'd had his own battles with PTSD over the years. Those demons didn't vanish. They didn't disappear. They lurked in the shadows of his mind and occasionally reared their ugly heads. It would take time for her to work through what had happened. To feel safe again. To regain that confidence she'd carried around like a badge of honor.

But he had no doubt she'd get there. She was strong. Stronger than most.

"I didn't see them. They both wore masks. I can't even remember what they sounded like. It all happened so fast." Tears sprang from her eyes like a raging river.

Her father wiped them away, holding her tight.

"That's just it." Keaton rolled his neck. A million things raced through his brain, and he resented where they went. He knew Dawson was thinking the same thing. "They have no idea what you know or don't know."

"They know Mallary and I found the jewels," Trinity said.

"But they don't know for sure you have them." Keaton arched a brow. "Knowing Dawson the way I do, he might want to keep a lid on things to draw the bad guys out."

"You mean use my little girl as bait?" Monty stood. He inched closer.

Keaton wasn't afraid of most men, but Monty scared the shit out of him. "Not her, the jewels."

"That's semantics, son. And you know it." Monty glared.

He sure did, and just saying it left a bitter taste in his

mouth. "That may be true. However, it's also not my call."

"But you'll stand by your friend, even though you claim to care about my daughter." Monty folded his arms. His eyes turned into narrow slits that shot spiked daggers right at Keaton's heart.

"I do care about her, and I will protect her." He held up a hand, hoping it didn't tremble. "Based on every-thing I know so far about what happened, and the fact they sent some asshole in here to kill her, I wouldn't be surprised if they have Mallary and—"

"You think Mallary is still alive?" Trinity bolted to a sitting position. She groaned, clutching her shoulder.

Her father rushed to her side.

Keaton raced to the other side of the bed, leaning his hip on the mattress. Gently, he rested his hand on her thigh and held her gaze. "I don't know. But it's possible. Again, she could be used as leverage to get to you and the jewels. Our first order of business needs to be to get you to a safe place. Then, Dawson and the rest of us will devise the best plan to catch the bad guys. It's not our first rodeo."

"No offense, but you're not a cop," Monty said. "I respect the hell out of your previous profession, and I will gladly take your help protecting my child, but going after these guys? Seriously?"

Ripping his gaze from Trinity, he shifted it to her father. "We helped Dawson take down Paul Massey and his special band of idiots. I don't say this to be cocky, but that operation wouldn't have gone down the way it did without us. Besides, Dawson won't do anything without careful consideration. He has not only Trinity and Mallary to think about but also all of Calusa Cove. If it makes sense to act as if the jewels of the *Flying Victoria* were once again lost to the sea, then that's what we will do."

"Daddy," Trinity said softly.

"Yeah, princess?" Monty brushed her cheek much like he used to when she'd been a little girl.

"While sometimes Keaton's delivery is god-awful, and he acts like a chest-pounding gorilla, Dawson's an excellent chief of police. We need to do whatever he and his friends think is best."

Keaton ran his fingers through his hair. "I'm not that bad," he muttered.

"Yes, you are," both father and daughter said simultaneously.

"I wouldn't want to get in the way of police business." Monty crooked his finger. "But I'm going to be in your face every step of the way."

"I would expect nothing less." Keaton swallowed. When he became a parent... no, if... no... What the hell? He couldn't think straight when he was around Trinity. There was no if—or when—but he could appreciate how much Monty wanted to protect his daughter.

Keaton would die before he let anything happen to her...again.

CHAPTER 7

"You're worse than my father," Trinity muttered as Keaton pushed her down the corridor. "You don't have to do everything."

She understood she needed to be in a wheelchair. She didn't have a problem with that. Not one bit. Not only was it hospital policy, but she didn't have the energy to walk. Her legs couldn't have carried her very far.

However, Keaton didn't have to be the pain-in-the-ass boyfriend and practically shove the nice orderly out of the way and do it himself.

Boyfriend.

It was odd to think of him that way. They'd shared a night. One night. And while it had been amazing, and she more than appreciated everything he had done to help—no, save her—that didn't make him her boyfriend.

Yet he behaved like one, and honestly, she'd been fantasizing about him for far too long.

She glanced up at the man in scrubs strolling alongside them, his hospital ID proudly displayed. Keaton had checked it three times. She had done the same thing. Every time someone walked into her hospital room, her heart rate increased, and she nearly had a panic attack when a new nurse came in to take out her IV.

She hated feeling this way. She hated the idea that someone was lurking in the shadows, waiting, watching. The closer she got to the door that opened to the outside of the hospital, the more fear bubbled in her throat. Her chest tightened. Her lungs burned. She'd been frightened before—terrified, actually.

But she hadn't wanted to jump out of her own skin when Charlie had hit her. She'd been stunned. Temporarily paralyzed. However, as soon as her brain had registered the danger that could've been her future if she hadn't acted, she hadn't hesitated.

"I know that," Keaton said. "I want to."

"But that's what this nice man here is for," Trinity said.

"It's no problem, ma'am." The orderly smiled and nodded. "I've had more than one fine gentleman do this. If it were my wife, I might do exactly the same thing."

"I'm glad you understand." Keaton slowed as he neared the door. "I am going to have to pull my truck around, and I don't like leaving you here alone."

"She's not alone." The orderly rolled up his sleeve and tapped his biceps, showing off a tattoo. "Former Marine. Combat medic." The man lowered his chin. "Fletcher made sure it was me who walked her out. He was supposed to let you know."

"I haven't checked my cell in the last twenty minutes," Keaton said as he pulled it from his back pocket, fumbling with it.

"We can sit in here or outside. Whatever makes you comfortable, sir," the orderly said.

"Fletcher sang your praises. Semper Fi." Keaton stretched out his arm and shook the orderly's hand. "Sorry, I was harsh."

The orderly nodded. "Not a problem."

The sound of the doors in front of her swishing open startled her, and the warm Florida air mixed with the cold air-conditioning made her shiver. She wrapped her good arm around her middle as a silhouette of a tall person shuffled through the opening. She couldn't see the person's face—only the hurried body movements as the person rushed into the hospital as if on a mission. They took a couple of long strides toward the information desk to her left.

She hadn't realized her heart had been beating in the center of her throat until she tried to swallow and failed. Inhaling sharply, she tried to release the lingering horror. Having a healthy dose of fear because someone had tried to kill her twice was normal. She knew that. There would be something wrong with her if she weren't scared. But this?

It was the worst thing she'd ever experienced.

"Oh my God, Trinity," a familiar male voice bombarded her ears.

She stiffened.

Fenton was the last person she wanted to see. The last person she wanted to deal with.

ELLE JAMES & JEN TALTY

"Sweetheart, I'm so glad you're okay." He dropped to a knee in front of her wheelchair.

Keaton made a noise that could only be described as a deep, low growl. The two men had met several times, and Keaton hadn't been impressed. Once, he'd told her that she could do better.

She'd told him to mind his own business. Only, he'd been right.

"What are you doing here?" she managed to choke out.

"Are you kidding me?" Fenton stared at her with wide eyes. "I came as soon as I could manage to leave the dealership. You must've been so terrified. Did you get my flowers?" He raised his hand and touched her cheek.

She jerked back. It wasn't just that it was Fenton's touch. It could have been anyone. After Warren's failed attempt to kidnap or kill her, any man—or woman—putting their hands on her made her flinch. Even if Keaton were to come up behind her without warning, she figured she'd do one of two things.

Clock him.

Or curl up in a ball and cry like a baby.

"What can I do for you? What do you need? Do you want to come stay with me?" Fenton asked with a smile. He did have a nice smile. That's what had initially attracted her to him. "I have plenty of room. It would be no problem, and it might be exactly what you need."

She opened her mouth, but no words tumbled out.

Keaton pressed his hand on her good shoulder. "She

won't be staying with you," he said in a gruff voice. "Now, if you will excuse us."

Fenton rose.

He was a tall man. Maybe six-one, which gave him at least one, if not two, inches on Keaton. But Fenton didn't have the muscles Keaton had. Nor did he have that badass, don't mess with me look. It was a subtle look, and Keaton didn't give off that vibe very often.

When he did, even a rock would shudder.

Fenton didn't quake in his boots. All he did was look Keaton up and down. "I'm pretty sure Trinity knows how to speak for herself."

Keaton laughed. "Oh, I know." He squeezed her shoulder, rubbing his thumb on her exposed skin near her neck. It was soft, tender, kind...loving even. He turned, catching her gaze. "Babe, can I tell him to go screw himself, or shall you?"

Why the hell had she ever told him about Fenton's extracurricular activities?

"Who the hell do you think you are?" Fenton inched closer.

So did the orderly.

Her heart continued to pound in her throat. But she couldn't let them beat the crap out of each other, and while she knew Keaton deep down was a sweet man, he'd toss the first punch. She'd seen that at Massey's one night when some asshole had relentlessly put his hands on a young girl.

"I will be your worst nightmare if you don't leave," Keaton said.

She cleared her throat, finding her voice. "Please stop arguing," she said softly.

"Sweetheart, I'm so sorry." Fenton didn't shift his gaze.

But Keaton did, and he gave her an apologetic smile, but then he shifted back to Fenton and widened his stance.

Wonderful.

"Fenton," she whispered. "Go home. I'm fine."

"I will not go home, and you are not fine." Fenton planted his hands on his hips and glared at her with daggers shooting from his eyes. "Who is going to take care of you?"

"I am," Keaton said.

The orderly leaned in. "Shall I call security, sir?"

"Not yet," Keaton grumbled.

Trinity rubbed her temple. She didn't have the bandwidth to deal with this crap. Fenton was a royal pain in her ass. He'd never wanted to break up. He denied he'd been cheating. Of course, it had been difficult to prove simply because she'd never caught him. All she had were a few strange texts. Some sexual emails from an address she hadn't recognized, a couple of weird, random voice messages, and an odd earring in his vehicle. But nothing concrete, and he'd explained it all away.

However, once she'd overheard him talking to a buddy about how he'd been banging the boss's daughter, how he was close to being the heir to it all. Well, that had been the end of them.

Audra, Baily, and the guys were right. She'd been too

nice to Fenton when she'd dumped him, which was why he kept coming around.

Her chest heaved up and down. Her breath came in short pants. Her blood roared in her ears. It had been a long time since she'd feared telling anyone what she thought. It was as if she were transported back to being sixteen, when all she'd cared about was being accepted.

She still wanted that, but today, it was different, and she wouldn't sit there and be silenced.

"I doubt Trinity wants to go home with the likes of you," Fenton said.

"Shut up." Trinity lifted her chin. "Don't speak to my boyfriend that way."

"Boyfriend? Seriously?" Fenton laughed. "You're slumming it with this guy?"

Keaton unfolded his arms, clenched his fists, and took one small step forward.

She reached out with her good hand and grabbed his forearm.

He didn't flinch. That was a good sign.

"No, I was slumming it with you." Crap. That wasn't too smart, but it flew from her mouth and gave her power. It felt good. As if she were taking back parts of her life that had been snatched from her at sea. "Now, leave us alone, and never call or text me again."

Fenton pursed his lips. His nostrils flared.

She wasn't sure she'd ever seen that look—not even when they'd broken up. Then again, he'd told her he'd never believe they were through, that she'd be crawling back to him within weeks.

That had never happened.

"You're making a big mistake." He leaned a little closer.

Keaton stepped between her and Fenton.

She held her breath.

Fenton raised his hands. "Trust me when I say, this asshole isn't who he says he is. You can't trust him. Mark my words, he's going to hurt you." He dared to smile. "But because I still care and always will, I'll be there to pick up the pieces. I promise you that." He turned on his heel and marched out the door.

The panic that had momentarily been held at bay gripped her muscles once again. She breathed slowly in through her nose, out through her mouth.

Keaton kneeled in front of her, taking her hands, staring into her eyes, and breathing with her as if this were normal.

But it wasn't, and she hated it.

"I'm right here, babe. It's okay."

"I hate that guy," she managed.

"He's not my favorite person, either." Keaton leaned in, kissing her forehead. "I'm going to have Chloe run a deeper background check on him, just to be safe."

"I'm not going to stop you, but I'm sure you'll just find he's a two-timing asshole who's looking for a sugar mama."

Keaton chuckled.

"It's not funny. I felt like an idiot after I broke up with him."

"Babe, you're no fool. Even I could fall for his charm. And he's not bad-looking."

"Now you're being an asshole." She couldn't help it. She smiled.

"Are you going to be okay while I get my truck? It's not far. It's in the main parking lot, so if you sit outside, you can see me the entire time."

"I shouldn't do this," the orderly said. "But Fletcher's a good man. He's done a lot for me since I've come back. I can walk both of you to your truck."

Keaton nodded. "Thanks, man. I appreciate that."

Trinity let out a long breath. All she wanted to do was sit out on the back patio at Keaton's place, sip some tea, put her feet up, and try to forget.

Only, she knew that would be impossible.

CHAPTER 8

KEATON QUIETLY CLOSED the door to his bedroom, grateful that Trinity had finally fallen asleep. He walked through the small family room and into the kitchen, ducking his head into the fridge and snagging a beer before stepping out on the back patio. He had two access points to his home—one from the front door and the second through the glass sliders in the back.

His house sat on the same street as the marina. He had his own dock, which had given him pause about safety in this situation. But he had the best security money could buy. He'd also tweaked it, thanks to having more than a basic understanding of technology. Fletcher might be the comms guy with a better-than-average working knowledge of how these things worked, but Keaton had an odd aptitude for it. In the field, he'd been the intelligence officer. He and Fletcher had often worked in tandem because what Keaton didn't know, Fletcher did—and vice versa.

The thing with Keaton, though, was that he tinkered

with this stuff because, if he didn't, he got the itch to do those things that he'd given Petra shit for and the last thing he needed to do was start racecar driving again.

He glanced at the time. He'd argued with Monty about his plans to return to one of his dealerships, but he couldn't stop the man if he tried. He'd promised to check in, which he had. Monty also had no problems with spending the night here.

Now, that was going to be strange.

Keaton had no idea where everyone was going to sleep. He supposed he'd be stuck on the sofa, even though he wanted to lie next to Trinity.

But not with her father resting his head in the guest room.

Thank God, he'd put a bed in there. His siblings had promised to visit. So had his parents. That hadn't happened yet.

They were all busy in Colorado, and he understood that. His little brother was married with kids, and his sister was the same. His dad refused to retire, and his mom was busy being a grandma.

However, what he really wanted was his cousin, Foster, to visit.

It had been a while since they'd seen each other, and Foster had been through the wringer. The last time he'd seen him was after a mission had gone sideways. That was an understatement, and Keaton couldn't keep his distance. Not since a few months before that Foster had lost his parents.

He eased into the lounge chair and fired up his computer to see the front of the house, making sure no one came near it, including Fenton. Keaton tapped his cell. It would be around six on the West Coast.

Freaking Oregon. Keaton had only lived there for a short time when he was young, and what he remembered, he hated. It was always gray, rainy, and cold. There were only two things to like about Oregon. First were the storms. God, Keaton had loved sitting in that damn stupid tree fort that Foster had built and watching the lightning flash in the sky while the thunder rumbled the ground, shaking the tree with all its might.

And, of course, Foster.

Back then, his older cousin had been larger than life —a freaking superhero.

Keaton sighed. To say Foster was just a man wasn't something Keaton was capable of saying. Foster might be mortal, but he wasn't simply...a human.

Foster picked up on the second ring. "Hey, cuz. How's Florida?"

"Never a dull moment." Keaton took a hearty swig.

"That doesn't sound like things have calmed down since the shit hit the fan with that case your buddy Dawson was working on."

"It was quiet for about five minutes," he admitted. "How's Oregon?"

"Barely settled, but so far, no complaints."

Keaton knew Foster had a ton to complain about. He'd left the Air Force, something he'd loved —something he'd excelled at—and Keaton understood the demons that lurked in Foster's mind, reminding him of that mission, of all the things that had gone wrong—all the choices he'd made or hadn't made.

Keaton knew the drill, and he knew it would take some time for Foster to get that poison out of his brain. However, some would linger, and it would spike like blood sugar when he least expected it.

Keaton closed his eyes momentarily and allowed his childhood memories to flood his brain. There was so much he hadn't understood about his mom's relationship with her sister, Foster's mom. Things he might never know. While his parents had attended the funeral, it had been years since the two sisters had been close. They spoke occasionally, but it was strained.

The car crash that had taken Foster's parents had been tragic. It had hit Keaton in ways he hadn't been prepared for, and Foster understood that better than anyone.

His aunt and uncle hadn't been doing anything dangerous. Nothing reckless. But still, it had brought to mind Petra's death and crushed his spirit all over again.

Foster's mom had been his favorite aunt. She'd been the coolest, sweetest woman ever, and Keaton missed her dearly.

Miles and years had separated them. So had some weird family feud that neither Keaton nor Foster had ever understood or cared about. They weren't grudge holders, but they'd been kids when Keaton's parents had packed them up and moved them to Colorado.

They hadn't spoken to each other for a few years. Not because they didn't like each other, or because they were involved in the bullshit, but Foster was older. He'd been doing his thing, and Keaton had been busy trying not to shine and be the star of everything.

They had reconnected when Keaton had joined the Navy. Foster had been there for him when Petra died. He'd been his rock. The least Keaton could do was be there for him when his parents had died and he'd been deployed on some supersecret mission, in an undisclosed area, unable to do jack shit.

Keaton had stepped in. He'd taken care of the details and made sure Foster got what he'd needed for his parents.

But those emotions were still so raw for Foster. It was evident when Keaton had visited after Foster had returned Stateside, right before he'd retired. Right after that messed-up mission. Both men had become slightly broken—slightly left of center—but they were vertical.

"How's the house coming?" Keaton asked, needing his brain to rattle with nothing but cobwebs, but he wasn't sure that was possible.

"You didn't call me to bullshit about my DIY projects," Foster said. "I suspect one of the reasons is you're going to tell me you're going to cancel your visit next week."

"That's one of the reasons," Keaton admitted.

"What's the rest of them?"

Keaton set his beer aside and pinched the bridge of his nose. Usually, he went to Dawson, Hayes, and Fletcher for anything that demanded advice. It didn't happen often, but those men were family as much as Foster. And while they'd all been there when Petra had died, they hadn't seen him lose his shit quite the same way Foster had.

Sure, those three—well, four, because Ken had still been alive—had held him while he'd cried. Stood next to him when he'd buried her. They'd also had to work with him and help him deal with those demons, day in and day out, until he was close to being a whole man again.

Keaton would have surely drunk himself to death had it not been for any of those men. But Foster had become a different kind of lifeline.

"It's twofold," Keaton started. "First, I met a girl."

"One you're serious about?" Foster asked with a voice that made him sound like a small child. It screeched and was high-pitched.

Keaton chuckled at the noise. "I'm not sure."

"Only you wouldn't know how you feel about a woman."

"It's complicated," Keaton said. "And someone tried to kill her."

"Jesus. Why?"

"That's a long story, and I'll send you the details. A second set of trained eyes on what's going on there can only help," Keaton said. "If you don't mind giving me your take on the situation."

"Not at all. Don't think twice about that. You'd do the same for me."

"Thanks." Keaton lifted his beer and chugged half. He checked the computer screen, tapping on a few keystrokes and checking every angle he could.

Silas drove down the canal in one of his boats, waving.

Keaton nodded.

"So," Foster said with a long draw. "You called me to get advice regarding a woman. Why?"

"She has this habit of trying to gain people's respect, and sometimes when she does it, she ends up being reckless. It's how she managed to get herself in this situation."

"Cuz, someone trying to kill her is not her fault," Foster reminded him with a dark tone.

"I'm not saying she's to blame." Keaton often fumbled over his words when he had to deal with emotional things. He'd been worried when he'd spoken at his aunt and uncle's funerals. He'd been terrified he'd trip over his tongue. He'd managed not to botch it up, but this was different. This was about him. "And to be fair, for a full year, I've been harsh. It's amazing we ended up in the same room alone together and didn't kill each other."

"How long have you been dating?"

Keaton laughed. "I'm not even sure we can call it that, but if we are, a couple of days."

"And she's got you this crazy? Jeez, Cuz, what's in the water in the Everglades besides gators and pythons?"

"Like I said, she's been under my skin for a lot longer, but I kept my distance because all I saw was a girl doing crazy things to get the respect of others. The thing was, I got some of it wrong. Hell, I got a lot of it wrong. But that's not even the point. I keep kind of fucking up. I keep acting like some raging, overly aggressive, controlling boyfriend. I'm a hundred times worse than I was with Petra. I mean, I feel like I'm becoming that thing she called me, and what's even worse, Trinity called me that, too."

"Man, we both know you are not that word," Foster said. "But between the way Petra was—and let's face it, she was out to prove something—and how you were raised, it's always going to be hard for you to put that genie in a bottle."

"I'm not even sure what that means." God, his head hurt. He hadn't slept much in the last two days. Nor had he eaten. He'd fed Trinity, and he'd nibbled, but he hadn't had a meal.

"My dad always described Uncle Oliver as old school. The kind of man who didn't believe women belonged in the kitchen but liked that his wife didn't work. That her career was raising her kids, and he's super proud that your sister is doing the same thing."

Keaton chuckled. "Yeah, he says some stupid stuff sometimes around my little brother's wife. It's not bad, but it comes out sideways about their kids being in daycare or her career. She makes more money than Joe. I don't know what difference it makes. I won't deny I enjoyed having my mom home, but it didn't make or break me. Joe's kids won't be any better or worse than Tilly's. I don't think your argument works here," Keaton said. "I've always believed women can do anything a man can, that her gender shouldn't be what holds her back, and you know I hate it when people treat women that way."

"I know, and I get that," Foster said. "But I've seen how you flip. You did it with Petra anytime she got hurt.

Or with Tilly when she broke her leg. Even with your mom. That protective instinct in you would be strong without your dad telling you that it's your job to take care of the women in your life, and I want to state for the record, this isn't about women not being able to do something. It's about you coming in full throttle and taking over once something bad happens."

Keaton opened his mouth to protest. But what was he going to say to that? He could hear his father's words. See his old man's face when he'd lecture him on how important it was to care for his little sister and mother. He never came out and said women were weak, but it was implied that he was strong physically and that his role was different than his sisters.

The difference between his father and Petra's father was that when Tilly had wanted to play a sport, his father hadn't said no, and he'd supported his child. It wasn't about girls not being able to do the same things. It all came down to roles in marriage, roles in the family, and roles when raising children.

"Add in the military training, and you're one bark away from being an asshole," Foster said.

"I'm not that bad," he said for the second or third time that day.

"If you're calling me for advice about a woman I don't even know, yeah, you are," Foster said with a laugh, but he quickly cleared his throat. "Is it the fact she has a free spirit that reminds you of Petra, or is it that you find yourself being vulnerable again for the first time since Petra died?"

"How about it's a little bit of both of those things,

and that I don't feel guilty about it. Not one freaking bit, and I should. I loved—still love—Petra. She meant everything to me. A piece of me died with her."

"I know that, cuz. Any woman who happens to fall in love with you now will have to understand that about you," Foster said. "Does this Trinity know about Petra?"

"Yes."

"And?"

Keaton closed his eyes, remembering how Trinity had told him not to cover up his past. Not with her and what that had done to his heart. "It's like she understands me. All of me. Every broken piece of me."

"That's not a bad thing, man."

"That's easier for you to say since it's me we're talking about."

That made Foster burst out laughing. "Because that's never going to happen. Now, why don't you enjoy living for a change? You've been half-dead for too long."

He wanted to tell his cousin it was like the kettle calling the pot black, but he wouldn't dare. Things were just too...raw. "I'd like to do that, but now I have to figure out who's trying to kill her. I know the why. But I don't know the who, and there are way too many possibilities."

"Send me the file. My buddies and I will look it over and give you our thoughts, if your buddy Dawson doesn't mind."

"He'll be glad for the help." Keaton's computer lit up. Two vehicles. One was Dawson's patrol car. The other was Monty.

"Talk to you later, and I promise, when this is all over, I'll be out there to visit."

"You better, and bring this Trinity. I'd like to meet her."

"We'll see." He hung up the phone and made his way back into the house, locking the doors. He set the computer on the small table in the kitchen before racing to open the front door before anyone rang the bell and woke up Trinity.

"Brought you dinner since I know you probably haven't eaten." Dawson held up a bag full of something that smelled like burgers, bacon, and onion rings.

He had never liked onion rings until he'd met Audra.

Now, he loved them. The big ones from Massey's. They were fried and crunchy on the outside, and he smelled like an onion for days after, but he didn't care. They were so freaking good.

Hayes stood behind him, sucking on a straw. The man had become addicted to milkshakes. Chocolate. Vanilla. Oreo. It didn't matter. He loved them. He drank at least one day, sometimes two. Everyone was starting to call him Ken since he loved the things, but Audra and Baily got ornery about the comment, so they'd stopped. But still, Hayes had never even been an ice cream kind of man, so they had no idea where this had come from.

"I'm not going to say no to food from Massey's." He choked on the last word. "Someone needs to change the name of that pub. I know his wife still owns it, but it's on the market, and whoever buys it needs to change the name. I can't say it without wanting to vomit."

"You and the rest of this town." Monty slapped him

on the shoulder. "But some people blow through town just to stop there because it's kind of famous thanks to Paul and his drug and arms business that landed him in prison."

"Some of that food in there is for the rest of us." Hayes waved his beverage. "I ordered tots and a burger, and we brought that wrap that Trinity loves."

"Relax. No one is going to eat your food," Dawson said with a chuckle. "Are you going to invite us all in?"

"How about we go around back? I don't want to wake Trinity." Keaton waved everyone toward the back of the house.

"I'm so glad she's sleeping," Dawson said. "We can save her wrap for when she wakes up in the middle of the night because she does that a lot."

Keaton might have only spent one night with her, but he'd watched her eat a sandwich and an entire piece of chocolate cake at two in the morning.

"Or she can eat it tomorrow. The girl's a human garbage bin," Monty said. "Do you have any wine in this place?"

"I stopped and bought some for Trinity on the way home, but it's not the expensive stuff." He pointed toward the kitchen.

"Don't care." Monty tapped his temple. "Got any whiskey? I don't usually drink that, but I seriously need to take the edge off."

"It's all in that cabinet in the kitchen. Feel free to pick your poison." Keaton waved his hand toward the front door. "Anyone else want a beer?"

"I can't." Dawson tapped his badge. "Might not be in uniform, but I'm still technically on duty."

"As soon as I finish this shake, I'll kick one back. But I'll get it. You set that up on the table in the back." Hayes lifted his fingers to his lips and spoke softly. He was always good at respecting and reading the situation, but all the guys were.

Keaton and Dawson slipped out the back with the bag of food, utensils, and paper plates.

"I need to ask you a question and tell you something," Keaton said, staring at the dark channel of water that led into the depths of the Everglades. Keaton had spent the bulk of his childhood living in Colorado. He loved it there. He loved the mountains. The hiking trails. The snow. Skiing. There wasn't anything not to like about that state.

When Fletcher had proposed that they all start an airboat touring company in Florida, well, Keaton had balked. Florida was flat and hot and sticky, especially in the summer. He didn't give a crap about the gators or the snakes. He could deal with those creatures. However, after traveling the globe and seeing the world, he couldn't imagine what a state like Florida could offer.

There were times when he still struggled, but it had nothing to do with his surroundings and everything to do with grounding himself in one place—making a home for his unsettled spirit.

However, this tiny town had given him something unexpected. It had eased some of his pain. Even he could admit that.

"I'm listening." Dawson sat at the table, resting his elbows on the wood.

Keaton joined his longtime friend. Dawson was like an older brother, filled with the voice of reason. He was the calm during the storm, and the man had a heart of gold. He'd lost his parents when he'd been young and had been raised by his nana, who had died shortly after he'd joined the Navy.

The military had shaped Dawson. The friendships he'd forged as a SEAL had become the only family he knew, and Keaton was honored to be part of that.

"I called Foster and asked him if he and his team would look at what we know about Trinity's case," Keaton said, holding Dawson's gaze.

Dawson arched a brow. "Foster's a good man. He's smart, and I certainly value his opinion, but that's sensitive police business."

"Are you telling me you don't want someone who has no ties to Calusa Cove and all the rumors circulating about what happened to Jared, Trinity, and Mallary, to see if they can find an angle we might have overlooked?"

"Not saying that at all." Dawson shook his head. "I just need to be careful what I let come out of my office, and what concerns me the most is if anyone finds out we have the jewels."

"That's fair, but I've already emailed him what I know using the same code language that Foster and I have always used when dealing with sensitive intel. He knows the drill."

"Of course you have, and I honestly have no prob-

lem, but anything he gets didn't come from me."
Dawson waggled his finger. "That few degrees of sepa-
ration is definitely needed, not just because I don't want
to lose my job, but for Trinity's protection. The chatter
on this is loud. There is a lot of speculation and too
many calls into the station. We're following every lead,
but all of them are coming up as duds."

"Whoever is after those jewels will come again. I'd be
a fool to think they won't come at me just because I'm a
former SEAL. It makes me wonder if holding off on that
announcement, that she did find the jewels, is the
wrong move."

Dawson shook his head. "That takes the hunt away
from her because then either the jewels go back to
Ralph's family or stay in police custody. If we want to
catch these assholes, we need to give them a reason to
come, and I need to consider the idea that Mallary is
alive. That they might use her as leverage. You know
how this works." He held up his hand. "Chloe's thinking
we should put out there that we have a lead on Mallary.
I have my reservations about doing that, but it could
bring these bastards out of the woodwork."

Keaton nodded. "That brings me to Monty and my
question."

"Because that last bit wasn't an actual question?"
Dawson chuckled.

"Monty's going to be a houseguest of mine." Keaton
pinched the bridge of his nose. "I have no intention of
keeping anything from Trinity, not unless I believe it's
for her own safety, but since knowledge is power and—"

"I don't expect you to keep things from her," Dawson

said. "We're asking a lot of her by keeping this close to the cuff, and I know that's not easy for you."

"I want to be able to keep Monty informed. I get that there will be things you don't want the public to know about this case, but that's his daughter." He rubbed one of his stab wounds. It still ached, but the pain was dull and barely registered, until he thought about what could have happened. Then it coursed through his body as if someone had carved out his heart. "I'm not sure I can lie to him."

"I won't ask you to."

"Does that mean you'll keep things from me?" Keaton asked.

"No," Dawson said firmly, lifting his index finger. "If there is something I feel no one should know, including him or Trinity, I'll tell you, and as always, we can discuss the pros and cons, and you can bitch me out if you think I'm wrong."

Hayes meandered through the glass sliders, carrying two beers—no milkshake—and Monty was nowhere to be found.

"Where's Trinity's dad?" Keaton asked.

"After taking two double shots." Hayes wiggled his fingers. "He went to go peek at Trinity. Then he was going to open one of those 'less than stellar bottles of wine'—his words, not mine—before joining us."

Keaton laughed. Trinity had commented how her dad would stick his nose up in the air over her choices, but she didn't care. She liked the brand, and she was going to continue to drink it. Besides, she'd realized that his spending habits on wine were as bad as when she used to drop a few grand on one handbag.

"Monty said we should start eating before it gets cold." Hayes sat down and dug in.

So did Keaton and Dawson.

"I'm so glad they decided to get rid of that special sauce altogether," Keaton said. "It was gross anyway."

"Pissed off Audra. If you put that goop in a cup, she'd drink it." Dawson scrunched up his nose.

"I might have vomited a little in my mouth." Hayes lifted his burger. His was plain, nothing but lettuce and one tomato and nothing else. No ketchup. No mustard. Not even a freaking pickle. The man was weird.

"Why didn't Fletcher come?" Keaton asked.

"He's doing a few things around the marina for Baily." Dawson shook his head. "Audra said a few superlatives were coming from Baily's mouth when she pulled in from the sunset airboat tour tonight."

"Baily gives Fletcher a lot of crap for coming around and doing stuff, but she never says no." Hayes waved a fry in the air before he plopped it in his mouth, with nothing on it. Freaking sacrilegious.

"And how are things with you and Chloe?" Dawson lifted his beer and lowered his chin. "And before you go denying anything, I saw you chatting her up when she was in town last."

"Chatting, yeah. But that's all it is." Hayes shrugged. But if Keaton wasn't mistaken, his lips twitched. He might have even cracked a smile. And his eyes darted away from him and Dawson.

That dirty dog. He was keeping secrets.

Well, Keaton would let him have his secret love life —because that's all Hayes ever did. He'd date a woman —if one could call it that—and then the next thing the guys would know it was already over. Keaton had once asked Hayes why he was like that. Why didn't he bring the girls around that he took out? No one cared that he wasn't interested in a long-term relationship. They just didn't understand.

All Hayes did was shrug and say, most of the time, things were over before they got off the ground.

For the longest time, the guys wondered if Hayes was ashamed of them. Or maybe the women. But it wasn't that.

And there were a few ladies he did bring around. The ones who lasted longer than a few weeks. But it wasn't often. And the guys, well, they didn't push. They had each other, and no one would mess with that dynamic.

It's what made Audra so flipping perfect.

Dawson didn't have to constantly race home to the little woman. He didn't need her permission to go out with guys. Of course, he was respectful and checked in, but she loved the guys and wanted nothing in their bond to change. And it hadn't. Nor would it.

Honestly, Trinity had been the same way for the last year. She was always there, always hanging out with them, like Baily, who was madly in love with Fletcher, and vice versa, even if the two of them were being idiots.

But Trinity, she just fit. Sadly, she didn't know it. Nor did she accept it.

Keaton glanced over his shoulder as Monty nearly tripped over the track on the sliders.

"Crap. Sorry," Monty mumbled, holding a full glass of wine in one hand and the open bottle in the other.

"You okay?" Keaton asked.

"Just ducky, and before you ask, Trinity is still sound asleep." He set the wine on the table. "I put my stuff in your guest room. I assumed that's where I'll be staying."

"Yeah. I'll take the couch." Keaton nodded.

Monty laughed. "I doubt that, and she's going to need you. When my daughter had troubles with Charlie, her ex, she had nightmares. While the situations are vastly different, and in so many ways this is worse, what she went through because of that asshole was traumatizing."

Keaton cocked his head. "She told me what he did and how she fought back. How he never bothered her again. But I'm starting to wonder if she downplayed it."

"I doubt that. But I also doubt she told you the whole story, and that, young man, isn't a confidence I'm willing to break." He brought the wine to his lips and chugged like it was whiskey. Then he made a funny face.

"Speaking of Charlie," Dawson said. "I've requested the police files. They might be sitting on my desk by now. I am looking at him as a possible suspect." He held up his hand. "It doesn't matter she's had no contact with him for three years. He could've been stalking her. Watching and waiting. I've seen that shit before."

"Wonderful. One more pissant to deal with." Monty sipped, this time more slowly.

This was not a side of Trinity's father that Keaton

was used to. While the man could be a little rough around the edges for a rich dude, this man was on edge. And not just because someone had tried to kill his princess—twice.

"Monty, what's going on with you tonight?" Keaton asked, making sure he used the man's first name. He didn't want to cause more conflict, even though "sir" still rolled off his tongue easier.

"Fenton has been up my ass since he left the hospital today. The man has been relentless." Monty pointed his index finger at Keaton. "And boy, does he dislike you. He thinks you're nothing but trouble. He told me I needed to talk some sense into Trinity. Tell her to go home to my place or stay with him—that no way was she safe with you." He let out a long, exasperated breath. "I've known Fenton for eight years. That's how long he's worked for me. He started as a salesman at my dealership over in Orlando. I brought him to the Marco Island one three years ago as a manager. He's good. Real good. But things have been weird ever since he got involved with my kid."

Keaton did not want to have this conversation.

Fenton was an arrogant prick with an ego that did nothing but make him look like an asshole.

"Weird how?" Dawson asked, shoving aside his food and clasping his hands together.

Monty shrugged. "For as long as I've known Fenton, he's been a driven man. Hardworking. Always wanting to please me. He worked his way from being in sales, to finance, to service manager, to finance manager, and finally, running one of my most prestigious dealerships.

I always thought I'd lose him one day to opening up his own dealership. I can't blame the guy, but it's a tough gig. Then he started dating Trinity."

"I've got a dumb question," Keaton interjected. "Who initiated that relationship?"

"He did," Monty said. "But I know she wasn't uninterested."

"They didn't last very long," Hayes added.

Keaton squeezed his beer. He'd heard all about Fenton and what Trinity suspected he'd done. He knew Fenton had denied cheating and, technically, Trinity couldn't prove anything, but still, there was some pretty damning evidence.

"I don't know what she told you about that, but my daughter tends to tell me everything about her life." Monty stared at Keaton.

More like, he chuckled with his eyes as if he found humor in what he thought he might know. Then he glared. More like, hosed him down with fire instead of water. Again, as if he knew, but this time, he didn't find it so amusing.

Keaton swallowed. Hard.

"So, I know that she believes that little shit cheated on her and only wanted to be with her so that he could have access to my money." Monty polished off his wine and poured more.

The man hadn't slurred a single word—yet. But soon, he would if he kept drinking like that.

"She begged me not to say a word to Fenton, and well, I couldn't fire him because unless he laid a hand on my girl, which he didn't, I don't have cause, so I've acted like nothing happened other than my kid doesn't want to be with him anymore." Monty waved his hand in the air.

"She doesn't," Keaton said under his breath. "But she's too nice in her delivery." He chuckled. "Though she did tell him to shut up today."

"Good for her." Monty nodded. "When it comes to Fenton's employment, I can't complain. Not one bit. But I don't like him sniffing around my daughter. Not even when they first started dating. But she's a grown woman, and I learned a long time ago not to butt in where I don't belong." He lowered his gaze. "Unless I think she's going to get into serious trouble, but even Charlie the creep didn't come off that way at first."

"Most guys like that don't," Dawson said. "They 'love bomb' to get what they want."

"Yeah. Unlike Keaton, who acts like a Neanderthal for a year." Hayes leaned back, folded his arms, and smiled.

Keaton ignored him, but it was hard not to ignore Monty's laugh.

"Oh, I heard all about it," Monty said. "I tried to tell her he was just like little Tony on the playground."

"Who's Tony?" Keaton asked.

"This boy back in California, from when she was four. He'd tease her and pull on her ponytail. But that kid loved her. Had a big four-year-old crush on her. Kind of like you for this last year."

"I don't crush on anyone," Keaton grumbled.

"And I'm not halfway to drunk." Monty lifted his wine and lowered his chin.

"Well, just to be safe, I'm going to do a full background check on Fenton." Dawson stood. "I need to stop by the office for a little police work before heading home to Audra."

"I'm on your six, boss." Hayes hopped to his feet with a grimace. "That sounded like I'm a sad, pathetic puppy."

"Because sometimes that's exactly what you are." Dawson reached out and patted Hayes on the head.

"Jerk," Hayes mumbled.

Keaton smiled. Not much had changed since they'd left the Navy, other than that, technically, Dawson wasn't their team leader.

But in some ways, that title would always be his.

Keaton's mood turned somber, remembering Ken. The whole reason they'd left the Navy in the first place and landed in this perfect little town. "I'll talk to you both tomorrow."

"Call if you need anything." Dawson waved his hand over his head. Instead of walking through the house, he and Hayes strolled around the side.

"Those two are good men. You're lucky to have them as friends," Monty said.

"I sure am." Keaton nodded. "I'd be lost without them."

"I appreciate Dawson checking into Fenton, but other than being the male version of a gold digger and a cheater, I doubt he had anything to do with this. Same with Charlie, though that man still scares me."

"Better safe than sorry." Keaton sipped his beer. "Any thoughts on who else, outside of random pirates, because that's about our best guess. The Coast Guard had reports of them being in the area that day, and with Trinity's boat being stripped of her expensive nav system and them coming after the jewels, we're at a loss."

"Pirates have always been a big thing around here." Monty shoved his wine aside. "We have so many legends built around the idea. Some are special to the Everglades, and some are specifically related to the ships that have sunk in nearby waters, like the *Flying Victoria*." Monty leaned closer. "Did you know that some say the jewels from that ship are cursed?"

"I've heard that before." Keaton nodded. "That anyone who touches them will have bad luck both in this life and the afterlife."

"It's more than that." Monty ran his hand across his mouth and glanced toward the water. "When the *Flying Victoria* was first found, no one would even scuba near it. It was believed it went down because of the jewels. There are stories about Edgar Watson and his ghosts going after the jewels, and that's why they were cursed."

"Now that's one I hadn't heard."

"Not well known, but there are many versions of each story," Monty said. "However, the documented story is that the jewels being found didn't end so well. The family, well, they were excited. A year later, their house burned down. The man who found them survived, but his wife, his children, and even his grand-children all died."

"Jesus."

"It was terrible," Monty said. "The only thing to survive, besides him, were those jewels. This was in the early fifties. The headline was something like: *Man Survives House Fire, Clutching Jewels from Sunken Ship, while Family Perishes*. It was harsh. Everyone believes, months later, he tried to put the jewels back."

"And did he?"

"At first, no one knew what had happened. He was considered a missing person. People thought he went up in the Everglades and killed himself, but no one could find the jewels." Monty shrugged. "Two years later, the mystery was solved." Monty sighed. "His body was found in the wreckage—decorated with the jewels. He'd been tied to something. It's believed he was murdered."

"Now that's weird. Why murder him and not take the jewels?"

"The legend is that someone did, but the jewels caused them great suffering, and they brought them back and put them on the bones as an offering to the sea gods."

"How long did Ralph's family have the jewels? And did it cause them any pain?" Keaton found himself asking.

"Not that anyone knows of. But here's the interesting part." Monty raised his finger. "The jewels disappeared again after they were recovered the second time. Ralph's dad and his buddies went diving one day, and they found them. That was about six months before Jared was lost to the sea. The legend is that, for those who find them, bad things will happen, and then the jewels will compel you to return them."

"That's a clusterfuck if I ever heard one."

Monty tossed his head back and laughed. "Trinity did say you had a way with words."

"Sorry. That was—"

"No, son. That was fine," Monty said. "You forget. I grew up in this town." He motioned across the water and up toward Manatee Island, where Keaton knew Audra had been born and raised. "My family was dirt-poor, and when I say that, I'm not exaggerating. The only family who had less than us would've been the McCains. I went off to California on a scholarship with no money, nothing but a dream, and a big fucking chip on my shoulder. I thought I was too good for this place. Too good for the great legends this place was built on, or the good people who've lived here for centuries. I had no intention of coming back until I had Trinity. She made me realize there's more to life than making millions and proving to people that I wasn't some dirt-poor, barefoot kid from backward Florida." Monty shook his head, laughing. "Somehow, I managed not to screw up her life too bad, but she'll never understand what it's like to wonder if you're going to have breakfast the next morning."

"Trinity's a good person. I wish she'd stop trying to prove to this town she's cut out for its way of life."

Monty chuckled. "That's a combination of her desire to be liked for who she is, not what she represents, and her need to be seen as a capable human. The former, well, she has friends, and that's all she needs. Anyone else can go screw themselves—a lesson she could learn from Audra," Monty said. "The latter will only happen if she stops being so flashy and showing off just because she can."

"That's what I told her."

Monty leaned forward. "Telling my child anything like that is like asking you to ignore your instincts." He tapped his knuckles on the table. "I have a feeling you're going to be really good for my kid. Don't mess it up." With that, Monty disappeared inside, leaving Keaton alone with his thoughts. They comprised only a few.

Monty wasn't exactly who he'd thought he was—and that was a pleasant surprise.

His feelings for Trinity ran way too deep. A thought that didn't shock him but totally petrified him on all sorts of levels, but he wasn't going to spend any time contemplating them.

But it was the final thought that he was going to do something about, and that was to learn more about the Legend of the *Flying Victoria*. Not that he believed any of that crap, because he didn't.

But he wanted to learn more about Ralph and his family. They might have missed something, and it was time to find out.

CHAPTER 9

Trinity sat on the back patio with Baily, Audra, and Chloe, the FBI agent, of all people.

She'd seen Chloe around town several times over the last year, but lately, she seemed to be coming around more often—and hanging out with Hayes. Trinity had seen them once at the coffee shop together and a second time milling about the marina.

She hadn't thought too much about it, but now she wondered if there wasn't something to it. Not that it was any of her business.

"Thanks for letting me join you tonight," Chloe said. "While I'm used to eating alone in hotels, it gets old after a while."

"How long are you staying in Calusa Cove?" Trinity asked, staring out at the canal, unable to make eye contact. While she was glad Chloe had stayed, she knew one of the reasons Chloe stuck around was because she was a federal agent, and Keaton didn't want Trinity and the rest of the ladies to be without the protection of someone who held a badge or who had served.

"Just tonight," Chloe said. "I met with Dawson about a case I've been working on this past year. Tomorrow, I need to head over to Tampa."

"Did your meeting with Dawson have anything to do with my friend Mallary?" Trinity held up her hand. "I understand if you can't get into the details. It's just that I feel responsible for what happened out there, and not knowing anything makes me crazy."

Chloe set her wineglass on the table and leaned forward. "I've spoken with Dawson and Keaton about what happened out there, and you are not responsible. You did what any normal person would have done in that situation."

Trinity let out a long breath. Tears welled in her eyes. "I don't know about that. I keep replaying my actions, and I can't help but wonder if I shouldn't have given them the jewels. Maybe they would've let us both go."

"No." Chloe shook her head. "While I don't work cases like that, I've been at this job too long and seen too much. Criminals like that don't leave witnesses behind."

A guttural sob caught in Trinity's throat.

"I'm sorry." Chloe reached across the table. "I didn't mean to imply your friend was dead."

"But that's most likely what happened." Trinity swiped at her cheeks.

"I won't lie to you," Chloe said. "It's possible. However, because they don't have the jewels from the

Flying Victoria, it's quite probable they're keeping her alive to use her as leverage to get them."

"Then why haven't we or her family heard from them yet?" Trinity asked. "Why haven't they reached out asking for the jewels in exchange for her?"

"I don't know." Chloe leaned back. "There could be a dozen reasons why. One reason could be that they're watching you, checking out where and who you're with while assessing the situation and waiting for the right time. They could even be using her to deep dive in the area."

"But I have the jewels and Mallary knows that," Trinity said.

"That's true. However, we haven't released to the news that we found the jewels. For all the pirates know, you dropped them when you dove off your boat during the fight, and they sank to the ocean floor. That's why Agent Ballard has requested the Coast Guard keep an eye on the area. He's the agent in charge of Mallary's case. I'm just helping out where I can."

"Thank you," Trinity whispered. "I appreciate all your efforts."

"I'm happy to help." Chloe nodded. "Ballard and I do a lot of work together since we're both part of the violent crimes unit."

"Are you working on that woman who went missing twenty miles from Calusa Cove?" Baily asked.

"I can't get into that." Chloe reached for her long ponytail and twisted it.

"I understand. However, we all know you've been

asking questions about missing people for a while now," Baily said. "Should we be concerned?"

"It never hurts to be vigilant about your surroundings," Chloe said.

"As if I don't have enough to worry about with someone trying to kill me." Trinity raised her glass. "I don't know what I'd do if it weren't for Keaton and the rest of the gang."

"You and Keaton have certainly turned the corner." Baily lifted her wine and clanked it against Trinity's. "It's nice to see the two of you get along because, you know, all that sexual tension was starting to grate on the rest of us."

Trinity rolled her eyes. "Right, because you and Fletcher don't have any of that."

"What Fletcher and I had was a long time ago, and the tension between us now isn't sexual in nature," Baily said with a defensive tone and a wave of her hand. "At least not on my part."

"And I've got a bridge for sale." Audra shook her head.

"You don't know what you're talking about." Baily turned and stared at the water.

"How are things going with you and Keaton?" Audra asked, bringing her wineglass to her lips and changing the subject before an argument ensued, because that's what always happened when anyone brought up Baily's feelings for Fletcher.

"I'm not even sure how to answer that question amid everything that has happened to me in the last couple of days," Trinity said.

"I get that." Audra nodded. "Things with me and Dawson went from zero to sixty in seconds." She laughed, shaking her head. "He thinks I'm clueless about what he has planned, but he forgets who I am."

"What are you talking about?" Chloe asked. She smoothed her hands over her slacks. She always wore a dark suit with a white button-down shirt, and her hair pulled back in a tight ponytail at the nape of her neck. It wasn't just her FBI persona that made it hard for Trinity to figure her out, but it was the fact that the few times they had spoken, outside of official federal business, Chloe pretty much kept to herself.

Trinity was happy to have the chance to get to know Chloe. Partly because of her involvement in Mallary's case, and partly because of her interest in Hayes. Trinity enjoyed Hayes's company. Heck, she liked all the guys. They were fun and energetic. They all made her laugh, making her feel like she was part of this special group, as if she'd finally found a place inside Calusa Cove where she belonged.

It hadn't happened overnight, and for a long time, she hadn't believed it would ever happen. It wasn't until she'd been in the hospital that she realized just how much she mattered to them. It warmed her heart to know they cared as much as she did. And that it was genuine. She felt that to her core.

"My darling boyfriend has been ring shopping, and he thinks I don't have any idea." Audra smacked her forehead. "The worst part is the other day he asked me weird questions and then showed me a couple of pictures of engagement rings, wondering which ones I liked. He got all tongue-tied and tried to act as if he were just flipping through some magazine and making small talk. We don't do small talk. Not like that."

"Aw, that's sweet," Trinity said. "When do you think he's going to propose, and are you going to say yes?"

"Of course, I'll say yes." Audra giggled. It was a strange noise coming from her, but it was nice, and Trinity loved that Audra and Dawson had found each other. "But that man should know me well enough by now to know I don't want flashy. He could just blurt it out without a ring and march me down to the judge so we can get on with it. He's not the most romantic human in the world, and we know I suck at it. So, if he drops to a knee and opens some box with some big diamond, I'll probably laugh at him, and then it'll cause a fight."

"I doubt that," Chloe said. "He just wants to do it right."

"The right way with Audra would be to have a gator or python present it." Trinity laughed

"I could be down with that." Audra raised her glass. "I just wish he wouldn't get his underwear in a twist over it, like he did when it took him a week to figure out how to tell me he loved me. All he had to do was say it. I have half a mind to ask him to marry me to get it over with."

"Oh no." Chloe shook her head. "I might not know any of you very well, and I can't say I've had good luck with relationships, but I don't think any man would like that."

"I doubt Dawson would care," Trinity said. "Keaton,

on the other hand, would take offense. He might not be that word he hates, but he does like to be a *man*." Trinity lifted her fingers and made air quotes. "He's a walking contradiction about it."

"What do you mean by that?" Baily asked.

"He's all about equity and equality." Trinity laughed. "He truly does believe that a woman should and can do pretty much anything a man can. He doesn't believe that her sex should hold her back or that a man should be the thing that stops her. But in that same breath, he's all about opening doors, chivalry, and, in a weird way, gender roles. And I don't say that in a bad way. Nor am I saying he thinks a woman's place is in the home once a relationship changes. It's just that he's one hell of a protective, chest-pounding man when he gets the chance." She pointed her index finger over her head. "And all I've done since we got together is give him reasons to flex his muscles and grunt out commands."

"Dawson once told me that he was always the kind of team member who took charge in the field. That, as team leader, he loved and hated that about Keaton. He loved it because he knew that no matter what, Keaton would always be the first to think on his feet and make decisions. He hated it because sometimes he didn't consider the chain of command."

"I can say I've honestly seen that firsthand," Chloe said. "The boys helped me and Ballard with a case six months ago, and while Keaton's take-charge attitude didn't bother me, it grated on my boss's nerves, especially since he was a civilian who technically had no business doing what I had asked."

"He does come on strong at times," Audra agreed. "But only when he's passionate about something or feels like there has been a major wrong in the world or he cares deeply." She held Trinity's gaze. "Dawson will be pissed at me for saying this, but it's not like we all don't know that Keaton fought his feelings for you for an entire year. He stumbled around, acting like an idiot because, for whatever reason, he wouldn't act on the fact that he wanted to be with you."

"If you had said that to me even a couple of weeks ago, I would have laughed in your face," Trinity said. "The way he treated me—the things he said to me— didn't seem like a man who was remotely interested in me. And I was totally into him, so it was a bit of a shock. But once we talked, I understood where he was coming from. Understanding his history put it in perspective."

"He doesn't talk much about his past." Baily lifted the wine bottle and filled her glass. "I was still on and off with Fletcher when Keaton got engaged to Petra, so I know some of it, and she did shape a lot of who Keaton is today."

"I know almost nothing about Petra," Audra said. "Dawson always tells me it's not his story to tell."

"It's not," Trinity interjected, feeling as though she needed to stop the conversation. As if she were breaking Keaton's trust somehow.

"I have no idea what or who you ladies are talking about." Chloe sipped her wine.

"I'd rather we not continue discussing it," Trinity added. "And for the record, it's not because the topic upsets me, it doesn't. The only reason I want to end this right here is because Dawson is right, and no offense, Chloe, but for me to go into detail about who and what Petra meant to Keaton would be me breaking a confidence."

Chloe nodded. "I'm totally fine with that."

A quiet silence filled the evening air. The only noise was an owl in the background and an engine humming down the canal. A few minutes ticked by with no words.

"I want to ask you girls something, and it's okay if you don't want to answer, but I'm going to ask it anyway," Chloe said, shifting in her seat. "I'm very much out of my element. I'm married to my career, and for now, I like my life that way. Settling down, getting married, or having children is not on my radar anytime soon. I became an FBI agent because I've always wanted to work in law enforcement, and there are things in my career I want to do. Before I achieve them, a husband or long-term relationship is out of the question. When I date, it's with the understanding that I'm not sticking around. That makes me a bitch. I get that."

"Stop right there," Audra said. "I hate that. A career woman who knows what she wants and where she's going isn't a bitch because she doesn't want what the world thinks she should want. So please don't say that."

"I appreciate you, but it doesn't change my world." Chloe laughed. "I grew up in a conservative family. While my parents are proud of me and what I do, they want me to get married and have kids, and they don't believe I'll find a husband in the FBI."

"My late brother Ken didn't want me to snag a husband here in Calusa Cove." Baily laughed. "Of course, he thought the only person out there for me was Fletcher." She raised her hand. "And if any of you try to tell me he was right, I'll put a python in your bed."

Audra laughed. "Right, because that's going to scare us."

"It would freak me out." Chloe sat up taller, squaring her shoulders.

"What was your question?" Trinity asked, bringing them back on task.

Chloe fingered her ponytail. "I'm sure you all know that Hayes and I have been...talking."

"Is that all you're doing?" Audra asked with a wide smile. "We're not blind, and I'm not judging."

"Nothing is going on. He's asked me out a million times, and I've always said no. But we've had coffee. We shared lunch a couple of times. The flirting is a bit intense. There's definitely an attraction there. It's just that I'm not in a place where a solid relationship can form. Hayes is a good man, one of the truly nice guys out there. I've always said no because I wouldn't want to hurt him when I do what I always do and say thanks for the good time, but we're done because I'm too involved with my current caseload."

"I don't know how to say this without it coming across the wrong way," Audra started. "And also, without sounding like a gossip."

"Well, then I'll say it." Baily sighed. "I've known all the guys longer. I met them all before my brother died. I know them, but Hayes, well, he's just different."

"What does that even mean?" Trinity asked.

"Hayes doesn't do relationships. He never has. At

least not that I've ever known." Baily shrugged. "I can't tell you the why because that I don't know. But I can tell you that he's never had a long-time girlfriend. Ken, Julie, Fletcher, Keaton, Petra, Dawson, and some chick he was dating came for the holidays one year. Hayes came, too. But he came solo. Hayes always came solo. I once asked him, and he flat-out told me that unless he lasted more than a couple of months, he didn't see the point. I pressed Fletcher on it, and he told me that Hayes never went that long. And he didn't bring the girls he dated around them all that often. He's just not interested in marriage or kids."

"And now we are gossiping." Audra laughed. "But Hayes is a good man. The best."

Chloe leaned back. "I like Hayes. He's funny, smart, and sexy. I just don't want to lead him on, and whatever this is, it can't go anywhere."

"Looks like you both share the same dating philosophy. All you have to do is be honest," Trinity said.

Chloe stared out at the water with a furrowed brow as if their words hadn't registered.

"Is something else bothering you about getting involved with Hayes?" Trinity asked.

"It's me," Chloe said. "I don't usually allow myself something like this when I'm knee-deep in such a big case. I'm conflicted, and I don't like being conflicted. While I'm good at compartmentalizing, I'm finding myself in a place I've never been before."

"Wait a second." Baily leaned forward. "Are you saying it's *your* feelings you're worried about and not Hayes's?"

"No," Chloe said quickly. Too quickly. She lifted her glass. "I might have had too much booze." She chuckled. "That's another thing I don't do when working a case, but it's been a long day."

The sound of big tires over the pavement caught Trinity's attention. She glanced over her shoulder. Keaton and the guys were back with pizza.

"Finally, the food's here." Audra jumped to her feet. "I'm starving."

"Me, too." Baily pushed her chair back. "And we need another bottle of wine."

Trinity adjusted her sling. The throbbing in her shoulder had become part of her new normal. A reminder of what had happened. She shivered.

"Hey, babe." Keaton appeared at her side. He leaned over and kissed her temple. "Did you ladies have a nice chat?"

"We did." She nodded.

"I noticed there were flowers in the trash." He arched a brow.

"Fenton," she whispered. "They came shortly after you left to pick up food. Remy signed for them and tossed them out for me."

"I seriously don't like that man." Keaton eased into the chair beside her while Baily and Audra helped Dawson and Fletcher with the pizza and paper plates.

Chloe and Hayes had taken a stroll down toward the docks and stood there, staring at the water...talking.

"Fenton's a harmless asshole." She pointed toward the canal. "What do you make of those two?"

"I'm not sure," Keaton said. "Hayes is acting all weird

about it. I've never seen him pursue a woman like he is with Chloe. I get it. I mean, she's an attractive woman. She's smart. But she's unlike any girl I've ever seen him date."

"And how many women has that been?" She cocked a brow.

He laughed. "Very few. But none of them were badass Feds. They were all quiet, which I guess Chloe is, but they were more..." He glanced toward the sky. "... how do I put this? They weren't career-minded women."

"That doesn't sound like a man looking to avoid relationships."

"Oh, Hayes has always been a bit of a player." Keaton raised his index finger. "I don't mean that in the sense that he was a dick about it. More like he dated one girl, then it ended, he took a break, and then he dated someone else. Anyone we ever saw him with, he treated them like a princess." Keaton sighed. "I get the impression he really likes Chloe, but I worry it's the hunt that has him going full throttle, and that wouldn't be fair to her."

Trinity bit down on her lower lip and groaned.

"What?"

"Nothing," she mumbled.

"No. It's something." He leaned over and kissed her. "What do you know that I don't?"

"I can't say. It would be breaking girl code."

"Ahhh. I see." He chuckled. "Well, as long as it isn't bad or something Hayes needs to know about, you and your girlfriends can have your private talk."

She smiled. Never in her life had she been with a man like Keaton. His sweetness often outweighed his chest-pounding. "And what did you and the guys talk about while you were out getting us dinner?"

"Now that would be breaking bro code." He tapped her nose, then shifted his gaze back to the canal. "They are an interesting pair, though."

"I bet that's what your friends say about us."

He burst out laughing.

"I don't see what's so funny."

"We are an odd couple, but that makes it fun." He patted her thigh. "We spent all of last year fighting this, arguing over...I have no idea... and now, well, look at us. We get along just fine."

"I wouldn't go that far. I've had to talk you off the ledge a few times and remind you that I can speak for myself." She arched a brow.

He sighed. "I won't let you pick a fight with me tonight. I'm in too good of a mood."

She rested her head on his shoulder. She could honestly get used to this banter.

CHAPTER 10

THE FOLLOWING MORNING, Keaton opened the door to
the coffee shop. He hated leaving Trinity. It didn't
matter that Dawson had made his deputies available,
and one of them was standing guard at the house. Or
that her father was still there. Or that he was only going
to be gone for a short period of time.

Someone had tried to kidnap and kill her, and they
would do it again.

But he had promised her he would get up early and
bring back her favorite coffee and a freshly baked
chocolate croissant. He'd learned a long time ago that
the little things mattered, and if this was what it took to
make her comfortable, then he'd be happy to do it.

Besides, Hayes and Dawson were meeting him with
the latest update.

Not that it would be much since he'd been with
them until eleven last night.

He'd watched Hayes drive away with Chloe tucked
in the front seat of his truck. She'd had too much to

drink and drive. When he'd left to get coffee this morning, Chloe's vehicle had already been gone. Hayes had texted to say they were picking it up at around five. He suspected they had spent the night together.

Good for Hayes.

But Keaton still worried about his buddy. He wasn't exactly sure why. Hayes had never been afflicted with the love bug. Women didn't get under his skin. He liked women, dated them, but he could honestly take them or leave them. He'd always stated he liked being alone too much. He'd never elaborated much past the fact that being one of twelve siblings had made his childhood crowded, and the idea of living with someone gave him the jitters.

He did understand the idea of wanting space. After Petra had died, Keaton had no longer wanted to be attached. He hadn't wanted to love again. He'd needed to close himself off from that pain to heal.

He no longer felt that way. It frightened him how quickly that had all changed, how utterly vulnerable he had become, and how Trinity consumed his daily thoughts. He tried to tell himself that it was because of what surrounded them, that it was because of the danger.

But he knew better. He knew what was happening to him, and he couldn't stop it if he tried. Love wasn't something you controlled. It was something that happened. It didn't discriminate.

He pushed that thought right out of his mind. It was too soon. He wasn't falling that hard. He pounded his chest and coughed as he approached the counter. A young girl smiled and took his single coffee and bagel order. He'd return to the counter to get Trinity's after he sat down with Hayes and Dawson. He wanted to make sure it was hot and fresh when he brought it back.

Again, the little things.

He waited at the far end of the counter, scanning the room, taking in all the people. Old habits died hard, and this one was never going to change.

Dawson and Hayes entered the coffee shop. They waved as they stepped up to the counter and placed their orders.

Keaton snagged his coffee and bagel before finding a table in the back. He sat with his back to the wall, knowing that would piss off both his buddies. It was a running joke between him and all his friends. They all wanted that spot. Well, today it belonged to him.

Dawson and Hayes strolled through the growing crowd. Dawson was decked out in his uniform. He wore it well and proudly. Becoming a cop had been good for Dawson. His contract had been the first to end in the Navy, and he'd gone right into the Police Academy. Plans had already been made for the Everglades Over-watch airboat touring company, and Dawson had been the first to arrive at Calusa Cove.

Dawson loved this town. It was as if he'd been born and raised here, not Upstate New York.

Hayes had taken to it much the same. But Hayes was like a chameleon. He'd fit in anywhere he went.

Calusa Cove was Fletcher's hometown, and he'd been welcomed back with mostly open arms. The local hero. The man who'd escaped the town had made them proud with an honorable career serving his country, and then he'd returned to a quiet life. He had the respect of everyone—except maybe Baily—though it wasn't so much that she didn't respect him as much as she resented their past and what had happened.

Keaton, however, struggled to ground his feet in this sleepy little town. What he'd loved about the Navy was that, even though he was always stationed somewhere and had a home base, he'd never really had a home. Not since Petra had died. Being in Calusa Cove had forced him to calm that inner restlessness, and it hadn't been easy until he'd allowed his heart to open.

And now, all he could think about was what his future might look like. Something that had never once crossed his mind. Not even when he'd agreed to come here with his friends.

"I've got to step outside and make a phone call." Dawson placed his cup on the table. "Trevor is being interviewed again today, and Anna thinks Trevor might have some insight regarding where Trip's notebook was hidden."

"What do you think is in that thing?" Keaton asked.

Dawson arched a brow. "For starters, Trip's personal thoughts on what happened to Audra's dad."

"But Paul and his son confessed to you," Keaton said.

"His lawyer is trying to say he didn't. He's painting quite a different picture of the events that happened when I arrested them." Dawson ran a hand over his mouth. "While we have them on the drugs and guns, they're doing their best to cut a deal. Anything to shorten their prison time, gain protection, or get into the witness protection program if they turn completely. I can't have the latter. They can't ever be set free. If they are, Audra and I will constantly be looking over our shoulders, wondering if they're gunning for us." He sucked in a breath. "But there are other things Anna believes might be in that notebook, and that has my hackles up." He shook his head. "I get keeping side notes. I do it. But to hide it like Trip did, that I don't understand. It's putting people in danger, and technically, it could be criminal." He waved his cell. "I'll be back in a couple of minutes."

"Take your time." Hayes eased into one of the chairs and unwrapped his bagel sandwich. "I'll fill Keaton in on what we know so far."

Dawson nodded and slipped out the back door.

"There's news?" Keaton lifted his coffee and took a long, slow sip of the bitter brew. He needed the caffeine. He'd tossed and turned all night. Besides it being difficult to sleep with Trinity by his side and keep his hands to himself, he'd constantly woken to check his computer and his security cameras. He'd needed to ensure they were safe and that no one was lurking in the shadows. He believed without a shadow of a doubt that whoever sent Warren Harley would send someone else soon.

"Not sure I'd call it news." Hayes took a massive bite. He chewed and chewed while Keaton sat there, crawling out of skin, waiting for his buddy to finally swallow. Hayes lifted a napkin and wiped his lips. "At a little after four thirty in the morning, Chloe got a call from a friend of hers with the Coast Guard. They boarded a vessel that was moving slowly around the area where Trinity and Mallary were diving. They were suspicious because the boat was using a spotlight, and they circled twice."

"And what happened?"

"Nothing. The Coast Guard didn't find anything out of the ordinary, and the captain—a guy by the name of Riggs Oppenheimer—said they had lost a cushion and were looking for it."

"Seriously?"

Hayes nodded. "When pressed, they showed the Coast Guard where the missing cushion would go, and sure enough, one was gone."

"Who else was aboard that boat?"

"Two other people, one by the name of Eddy Ives, and the other, Willie Avery. Chloe is going to run the names in every database she can, and she'll let us know what she finds out."

"None of those names rings a bell." Keaton picked at his bagel. His stomach had suddenly soured. "Their story's lame. Where were they headed? Why were they out there at four in the morning?"

"They said they were anchored north of Marco Island and wanted an early start for crossing to the Bahamas. The seas are expected to kick up later in the day, and they wanted to ensure they missed that." Hayes raised his hand. "We checked the weather, and that was all true. Not to mention, the Coast Guard followed them for a good distance. They did continue in that direction. They gave Chloe the registration numbers for the vessel. She gave them to me, and now Dawson has them. He's going to check in with immigration for when they hit the Bahamas as well as when they land back in US waters."

"If they even make that call." Keaton leaned back. "Do you know how many boaters don't bother since there isn't a port that requires small vessels to report into the States? The guys from the Aegis Network are always telling me that they see boats coming in from a crossing through the Jupiter Inlet, and they know damn well they never did a customs clearance."

"That's a major fine if you get caught," Hayes said. "Either way, Dawson's got the information, and if they don't make it to the Bahamas, he'll know it. Same if they don't call in with the US Customs. If that happens, we'll have Chloe call in another favor with the Coast Guard."

"I'm glad your girlfriend has those kinds of connections." Keaton raised his coffee and smirked.

"She's not my girlfriend." Hayes stuffed his mouth with another large bite of his breakfast sandwich and glared.

"Oh, really?" Keaton chuckled. "How is it that you know she got a call at four thirty in the morning?" He arched a brow. "And shortly after that, you drove her to my place to get her standard-issue FBI vehicle."

Hayes took a gulp of his drink. "I'm not going to answer that question."

"Did you spend the night at the cabin she rented from Dawson? Or did she stay at your place?"

"This coming from the man who took an entire year to finally get his shit together and ask out the woman he'd been drooling over." Hayes cocked his head—as if that was going to divert Keaton from the third degree of his buddy's current love life.

The back door opened, and Dawson zigzagged through the few people milling about, either waiting for their morning jolt or for a table. "I take it Hayes filled you in?"

"He did." Keaton nodded. "But now he won't give me the scoop on where he and Chloe slept last night."

Dawson sat down, tossed his head back, and laughed. "I can answer that."

"Shut up," Hayes mumbled.

"I don't see what the big deal is." Dawson set his phone on the table. "It's not like we all don't know you've got the hots for her. So what if you crashed at the cabin? We're not judging you for that. Just the fact that you're being unusually coy about it—even for you."

Hayes narrowed his eyes. "Maybe she doesn't want all of you—or this town—gossiping about her. She is a federal agent, and she has a job to do. The last thing she needs is people spreading rumors." It was rare that Hayes ever got defensive about a girl. The last time had been about eight years ago when he'd dated someone a little bit on the older side. She'd been only ten years his senior, but since they were all ballbusters, they'd enjoyed giving him shit about it. They probably shouldn't have and realized too late just how much Hayes had liked that one.

But it was never going to last.

She'd had a kid, and that was breaking a major cardinal rule in Hayes's book. He didn't do kids. He liked them. He had lots of nieces and nephews, and that was one of the reasons—probably the only one so far as the boys could tell—that had him going home to visit his family. When he showed any pictures of his family, it was of those cute little buggers. Not of his siblings. Or of his parents. Just the youngsters and their activities.

Dawson rested his forearms on the table. "No one is gossiping," he said in that kind, soft, older brother tone he got when he was trying to diffuse a potential argument. Not that this was where the conversation was headed. But Dawson had always been the man on the team who spoke the voice of reason. The one who kept them on task. Fletcher was always right behind him. While Keaton, Hayes, and Ken had tended to rush to action, those two were more thoughtful. More likely to pause and assess.

It's what made their team so special. So unique. They had a good balance, and most importantly, they trusted each other.

"What you fail to understand is how different you are about Chloe," Dawson said.

"I can't figure out if it was the challenge of her constantly turning you down or if she's the first woman to actually get under your skin." Keaton studied Hayes's facial expressions. The man generally had two modes. The happy-go-lucky guy or the guy who sprang into action when the shit hit the fan. Becoming a firefighter had been an interesting choice, but also an obvious one. He got to serve—and run into danger.

Plus, he got to take time off, kick back, relax, and do absolutely nothing for a few days. He'd always enjoyed his time off, whereas Keaton wasn't built that way.

Keaton was still struggling to learn to be a turtle, as Fletcher put it.

"Chloe's not a challenge." Hayes's face hardened. His brow furrowed. His lips drew into a tight line.

Well, crap.

Keaton hadn't meant to insult his friend, but now he had his answer. He held up his hand. "All I meant was that you're the kind of man who generally takes rejection well. When it happens, you move on."

Hayes sighed, leaning back in the chair. "For the record, she never flat-out rejected me. Her life is her career. I respect that. And no, she hasn't gotten under my skin. Not like you think. But yeah, I do like her, and there's nothing wrong with that. I just hate it when you all start psychoanalyzing my love life."

"Can I ask you a question about all this without you jumping down my throat?" Dawson didn't wait for a response. "We've been best friends for a long time. We've been through a lot together—botched missions, injuries, and the deaths of more than one brother-in-arms. We were captured and tortured—together—and our lives were forever changed when Ken died."

"Get to the question," Hayes interjected.

"We have never pushed. Never judged. Never questioned. But in all the years I've known you, I've never seen you this preoccupied about a woman. Not even Betsy, whom we all know you really liked. Outside of the fact that your family is massive, with religious beliefs that you don't share, and the fact that you don't want kids, which is fair, what is your aversion to being in a committed relationship?"

"Do I have to have a big, profound reason?" Hayes folded his arms.

"No, but most people have one." Keaton certainly carried an emotional trauma that had closed him off from being able to make connections with the opposite sex.

"It's not very complicated." Hayes uncrossed his arms and rubbed his thighs.

Keaton held his breath, hanging on every word.

"You know, I was six when my twin died." Hayes ran his fingers through his hair. He didn't talk about his twin often. It had been something that had shaped his childhood and his relationship with his family.

But Keaton would have never guessed it could have been something that would have shaped his relationships with women.

"My parents didn't believe in vaccines. My family still doesn't. It's all part of their crazy religion. My brother died of a disease that a shot could've prevented. I got sick with the same thing, but I survived."

Keaton had heard this all before. However, he wasn't about to stop his friend. If he needed to retell it to get to the root of his issues, he'd listen.

"My folks didn't even take us to the hospital. They had the neighbors come over to pray at our bedsides. I watched my twin die, and all my folks had to say about that was two things." He wiggled his fingers. "That God had called for him. That God loved him so much that he wanted him in heaven. And that I didn't pray hard enough for my twin. That I must've prayed only for myself."

That last part, Keaton had never heard. "Jesus, I'm sorry, man. That's a horrible thing to say to a child."

"When Max died, it was as if my better half died right along with him," Hayes said softly. "For years, I was told that the devil must've slithered its way inside me. I would have random people pray over me in the streets. It was so messed up, and it screwed with my head for a long time. To be honest, sometimes, it still does because during those prayer sessions, someone inevitably reminds me that Max was the good twin, and I was the bad twin." He raised his hand. "Logically, I know that's not true. But the little boy in me will never be able to erase those memories."

"I can't even imagine what that was like for you," Dawson agreed.

"I'm not done yet," Hayes said. "When I was seventeen, there was this girl at school. She was so pretty and so sweet, and she had eyes for me. I thought I was the luckiest boy in school. We started dating—if you could call it that. I'd go to her house and sit on her porch, with her father watching, because in that crazy, backward town, if you even kissed, you were going to hell. But I followed the rules. We were finally given permission to go on unsupervised walks. I got to steal my first kiss."

Keaton expected Hayes to smile at the memory, but he didn't. Instead, he looked as if he'd swallowed a lemon.

"I was falling in love with that girl, and I thought she felt the same," Hayes said softly. "I told her all about my plans to leave and join the Navy and how I wanted her to come with me. I had already secretly gotten all my vaccines. I had done so much without my parents' knowledge, and you know what she did?"

"Told your folks?" Keaton asked.

Hayes nodded. "What a shit show that became. But I turned eighteen the next month. I left that place, and I didn't look back. I didn't speak to my parents for two years. The only reason I do now is that some of my siblings have a more tolerant viewpoint. I see my nieces and nephews on some holidays. I forgive them for their insanity. My parents were born into that church. They don't know any different. And to be fair, they're trying, but they're getting up there in years, and I doubt they'll change their ways now."

"I get those years were messed up and how hard that was for you," Dawson said. "But that girl, she was a long time ago. I don't understand why her betrayal is keeping you from finding love. It's not a horrible thing, you know."

"Never said it was." Hayes lifted his chin. "And it wasn't just her. Shortly after boot camp, I got involved with another girl. She lied to me. She told me she was pregnant when she wasn't." Hayes shrugged. "After that, I decided to make the Navy my focus. I went right into SEAL training. I met all of you. Ken and Julie's relationship always seemed so weird to me. Something wasn't quite right with that."

"You've said that before, and outside of her not really fitting in with us and being possessive over him, I'm not sure I saw the same thing," Dawson said.

"Maybe it was simply the possessiveness. I don't like that. It's why I adore Audra. She's a strong, confident woman, and you have mutual respect and trust," Hayes said. "Julie treated Ken like a puppet, and she was his master sometimes. I didn't much care for how controlling her family was of them." He crooked his finger. "I loved Petra. She was great. However, I don't want you to get pissed at me for saying this because I always thought the two of you had a great relationship, but her dad meddled in it, and you let him."

"I know I did." Keaton nodded. "It was hard not to. He was such a huge part of why she was the way she was, and there wasn't much I could do about it."

"Trinity's good for you," Hayes said. "If you can get your head out of your ass and stop barking orders at her."

Keaton chuckled, shaking his head. "You are so good at taking the focus off yourself and putting it on others."

Hayes nodded. "My point is that when I decided to focus solely on my career, women didn't fit into my life. I didn't want the ties that went with them. I didn't want to think about them when I was deployed. I didn't want a picture in my wallet or someone to worry about if I didn't make it home. It's hard enough to have a big family that doesn't care all that much about what happens to me." He lowered his chin. "I'm not bitter. I'm not lonely. I have everything I need in the family I chose. The Navy—being a SEAL—gave me more purpose than anything my previous life could've ever offered me. It also allowed me to accept the death of my twin in a meaningful way so that survivor's guilt didn't eat me alive. But now that I'm out and living here in Calusa Cove with you misfits, life is very different. It's slower, and that's not necessarily a bad thing because I love it here. However, I'm not blind as to what's going on around me." He pointed to Dawson. "You're going to get married soon, and don't say you're not." He turned his attention to Keaton. "You're falling hard for Trinity, and if you deny it, I'll kick your ass. And Fletcher, well, we came back in part so he could win back the love of his life."

"What are you trying to say?" Dawson asked. "Because you're rambling like I've never heard before."

"I've been thinking a lot about Max lately. We were only six when he died, but he and I were everything to each other. I do know he's part of why I've chosen to live my life this way, and I'm okay with that. It's just hard when everything is changing around me," Hayes said. "But you're right. I do like Chloe. She's smart, sexy, fun, and, believe it or not, she has a wicked sense of humor. This might make me sound like a total asshole, but because she doesn't live in Calusa Cove, that makes a relationship even more appealing. We're ships passing in the night. We can see each other without massive strings attached."

"That doesn't make you sound like a dick," Keaton said. "But it does make you sound a lot like the old me." He laughed. "One of my many tricks to not fall in love, get attached, and have some perfectly worthy girl steal my heart."

"Anyone ever tell you you're a romantic sap?" Hayes chuckled. "Are you boys satisfied now? Can we drop the subject of my love life? Will you stop picking on me and leave Chloe alone?"

"Absolutely not," Dawson said. "What fun would that be? Besides, have you stopped busting my ass about Audra?"

"Speaking of her… Were you ever going to tell us about ring shopping?" Keaton shifted his gaze. "Seriously, dude. When do you plan on popping the question?"

Dawson smiled like a big kid. "Last night."

"You dirty dog." Hayes crumpled up his napkin and tossed it at Dawson. "Why didn't you say anything when I saw you this morning?"

"Because we got talking about other things, but I'm telling you now." Dawson puffed out his chest.

"I have to know," Keaton said. "How'd you do it? Did you fumble it all up? Or did you do it right?"

Dawson smacked his hand on his forehead. "She found the ring in the glove box on the ride home. She slipped it on her finger and informed me that she wasn't wearing a white dress. That she wasn't wearing a dress at all. That she wanted to have a small ceremony, just friends, with the justice of the peace, maybe at Mitchell's Marina."

"That sounds like Audra." Keaton slapped Dawson on the back. "Congratulations, man. That's awesome, even if it's the worst proposal I've ever heard." He glanced at his watch. "I better get going. I don't like leaving Trinity this long." He stood. "I'll see you all later. Thanks for everything."

"Watch your back, and call if you need anything," Dawson said.

"I will." He approached the counter to order Trinity's

coffee and food. For the first time in a long while, Keaton had someone other than his friends and Foster to care about. Someone else to think about. To consider.

It added a little spring to his step. It supercharged the blood in his veins.

And it utterly terrified him.

CHAPTER 11

THREE FULL DAYS had passed since Trinity had woken in the hospital. Three full days of being waited on by Keaton and her dad. Three full days of going stark raving mad. If she didn't get out of the house, she was going to lose it and fast.

Keaton rarely left her side. If he did, one of his buddies was at the house. Or one of Dawson's deputies. But soon, he would have to go back to work since he was head of Fish and Wildlife for Calusa Cove. That made him grumpy. Not the job. Just that he'd have to return when not a single solid lead had come their way.

Dawson was working tirelessly around the clock. He'd been on the phone with the FBI and in constant contact with the police chief over on Marco Island. But they'd learned absolutely nothing. Not one clue.

Charlie had an alibi, though Keaton still wanted to keep a close eye on him, and he kept asking her weird questions.

Trinity wondered if he knew she'd been pregnant.

Her father swore he hadn't told him, and she believed her dad. Still, something had triggered Keaton's desire to know about that relationship.

Fenton texted her at least three times a day and had sent flowers two more times. She didn't respond, which spurred him to accuse Keaton of controlling her actions. Ridiculously, Fenton had begged her to hide in the bathroom and give him proof of life.

Her dad had finally told Fenton that she was just dandy, healing nicely, and that Keaton was taking good care of her.

She was sure that hadn't gone over well, but she didn't care.

Honestly, right now, all she cared about was that, while she enjoyed sleeping in Keaton's bed and waking up next to him each morning, the man hadn't laid a finger on her.

Granted, it had to be weird for him that her dad was sleeping a couple of rooms away, but if it wasn't odd for her, it shouldn't bother him.

Obviously, it did because he'd get all weirded out if they were kissing and her dad walked into the room.

Keaton Cole had some issues she hadn't anticipated. Everything about him had been unexpected. Besides being romantic, sweet, gentle, and tender, he had his own brand of insecurities. He had trust and intimacy issues, something she had figured out the moment they'd met.

Only, she didn't completely understand why.

Losing Petra had crushed him. That had destroyed

him in ways she couldn't even imagine. But there was more, and she wanted the whole story.

She leaned back on the lounge chair, lifted her tea, and sipped. The sun had begun to settle behind the horizon. She loved nights like these. His little slice of waterfront was vastly different from hers, but she didn't care. She loved this tiny lot of land. Being able to watch boaters as they returned from a long day of fishing or simply enjoying the ocean was so different from how she sat on her porch and stared at the open ocean.

She wondered how many times Keaton had watched her pull her boat down this stretch of water. He could see the marina in the distance and the canal mouth opening into the bay.

"Hey," he said as he approached from the dock. He'd been tinkering with his small boat for the last half hour. The man struggled to sit still. He'd remodeled his cabin by himself, and there wasn't much left to do. If he wasn't working, he was giving airboat tours. If he wasn't doing that, he was bothering Baily at the marina or helping Audra and Dawson at Harvey's Cabins and B&B.

Hayes had a few projects that needed to be done around his place, so Keaton could often be found helping him with that as well.

The only time she ever saw him idle was when they all sat around the campfire. She lived for those nights.

"Hey, yourself," she responded. "Have fun playing grease monkey?"

He laughed, wiping his hands on a rag. "It was something to do while you had your nose in that book."

She lifted it and waved it in the air. "All done. The ending was so predictable."

"It's a romance. Aren't they all?"

"Well, that part, yes," she said. "I mean, we expect the hero and heroine to fall in love and live happily ever after. But sadly, the plot of this one didn't have many twists and turns and not enough emotional baggage to make me care. I like to either sit on the edge of my seat because it's so suspenseful or cry like a baby because everyone is so fucking broken."

"You've been swearing like a truck driver lately."

"You're rubbing off on me," she teased. "Or maybe it's the lack of sex." She waggled her brows.

He glanced at his watch, then at the door, and then at his watch again. But he didn't say one flipping word.

"Um, Keaton. That was a hint. Or perhaps, a direct proposition. Either way, my dad's working late. He won't be back for at least two hours. We've got plenty of time."

He waved his hand over his arm. "What about your shoulder? I don't want to hurt you."

"Are you going to make me beg? Because I'm not past begging, though you're giving me a complex. I mean, I walked right out of your bathroom naked, and you didn't even blink."

"Oh, I blinked," he said with a throaty growl. "Your father was in the kitchen eating breakfast. If I had acted on the thoughts going through my brain at the time, I wouldn't have performed well because all I would've thought about was your dad…a bowl of oatmeal…and the fact my gun was only four feet from his fingertips."

As gracefully as she could, she rose. "Are you seriously afraid of my dad?"

"One hundred percent terrified." He looped his arms around her waist.

She rested her good hand on his shoulder, fingering the hair that landed on the back of his neck. "Why?"

"Because he's fiercely protective of you. Much like my old man is with my sister Tilly, and if I thought my dad was bad, well, I'm worse. If anyone had ever even looked at my sister cross-eyed, I'd have decked them."

"Are you telling me that you beat up Tilly's boyfriends?"

"Unfortunately, I did. She wasn't always happy with that." He chuckled. "Nine out of ten times, she was downright pissed off."

"Wait. You actually hit them?"

"No." He shook his head. "But Joe and I, we'd scare them. We'd let them know if they ever hurt our baby sister, there would be hell to pay. And let's just say we weren't subtle about it."

"I'm so glad I didn't have brothers." She patted his chest, laced her fingers through his, and tugged him into the house and toward the bedroom. "While it's honorable how you looked out for Tilly, women don't always need protection."

"I know that," he said grimly. "And please don't start with the whole women aren't weak or frail or any of that business, because I never said that." He closed the bedroom door and pushed her back up against the wall, shoved his knee between her legs and tangled his fingers through her hair. "It's just that some men can be assholes—you know, like your ex, Charlie. Or worse. And I've seen that firsthand." Gently, he ran his thumb across her cheek. "I had a friend in high school. She was just a friend. A good one. A guy she was dating raped her."

Trinity gasped, covering her mouth. "That's horrible."

"She trusted him, and he took advantage. It was years before she could reassemble her life."

"Where is she now?"

He smiled. "She's a counselor back in Colorado. She's friends with Tilly. She works with young girls who have gone through what she did. She turned a shitty situation into a positive one. But not everyone can do that. So, trust me when I say I'm not like this because I don't think you're incapable or incompetent. It's just that I know men, and most of us are jerks."

She palmed his face. It was scruffy from not shaving for the last three days, and she relished in it. "You're not."

"That's not what you said for the first year we knew each other," he mumbled.

"Yeah, well, neither one of us made a good first impression, now did we?"

"I always thought you were special. You just... scared me."

"Because I was reckless," she whispered.

"That was the reason I made myself believe. It was the only thing I could grab hold of that allowed me to make sense of the fact that I not only found you attractive, but that I cared about you."

She opened her mouth to respond, but he didn't let her. He ravished her mouth with a passionate kiss.

His lips bruised hers, and his tongue twisted and twirled around hers as a deep guttural moan filled her throat.

She tucked her free hand under his shirt. The first time they had been together had been raw. It had been pure sex. Pure gutted pent-up desire. Sure, they had shared some deep emotions. They had run the gamut with them and come to one simple conclusion.

They wanted each other. Needed each other. But this was different.

It wasn't just about sex. Or purging misunderstood emotions and intentions. This went deep.

It wasn't love. She couldn't describe it as that...could she? It was too soon for that.

His breathing hitched as she moved her hand up, tracing the contours of his muscular back and the scars that lined his skin. His touch was like fire, igniting a sensation that caused a gasp to escape from her lips. The heat between them was like an ember, a spark that intensified with every flickering second.

He pulled back, his gaze holding hers. The intensity in his midnight-blue eyes told her more than a thousand words ever could. He ran his fingers through her tangled hair, gently tucking a strand behind her ear.

"You do scare me," he confessed, his voice a mere whisper as if he were divulging a secret that had been locked away for centuries. "You scare me because I feel things for you that I haven't allowed myself to feel in a very long time. Things that I thought I never wanted to feel again. It's why I kept my distance this past year. It's why I've been so reserved."

His revelation both shocked and humbled her, but she could understand. She could relate.

"And you frighten me because I've discovered parts of myself with you that I didn't even know existed," she admitted.

His smile was half-wistful, half-amused, yet fully disarming. "I guess that makes us equally frightening then."

And as passion flared anew between them, they relinquished themselves to this fresh terrain of affection. One that demanded exploration—no stone unturned, no emotion unconveyed, naked and bared in every sense of the word.

Carefully and gently, he undressed her as he pressed his lips over every inch of her body. He left no speck of skin untouched by his mouth. And when he was done, he laid her on the bed, standing before her, and removed his clothes.

God, he was beautiful, scars and all.

In her eyes, each scar etched upon his skin was not a mark of detriment but rather a testament to his resilience, an ode to survival. Her fingers traced the path of each battle wound, soothing and adoring. His body trembled under her touch, his heart pounding against his chest like a wild drum echoing her own racing heartbeat.

He rolled to his back, making it easier for her arm to remain in the sling.

Straddling him, she pressed her hands on the center

of his chest. She clung to him as if he were the oxygen she breathed. She'd never wanted anyone as badly as she wanted him. She took his length as if she were made only for him.

Not that she'd ever thought of herself as a possession, but she wanted to belong to Keaton. For him to belong only to her. It made no sense at all. She felt a fierce protectiveness of what they had. Of who he was. Of what they could be together.

The world outside his cabin was in chaos. Someone had tried to kill her, and one of her best friends was missing.

It felt so utterly selfish to be with him like this right now, but it's exactly what she needed.

Keaton touched her as if trying to commit every inch of her skin to memory. His fingertips danced across her body like finely tuned instruments playing their favorite melody. Her response was visceral, every nerve ending coming alive. They moved together—two bodies in perfect sync—in an unspoken understanding that no one but them would ever comprehend.

His fingers tightened on her hips momentarily before loosening again, a silent promise that he wasn't going anywhere. She knew then that she wasn't alone in this sentiment—that this strange mix of lust and affection wasn't just one-sided. She felt it in his fingers as they roamed her body and heard it in his gasps as she touched him in return.

Her climax came hard and fast, and she hadn't expected it when it slammed into her body. She cried out his name so loudly that she was sure she woke the alligators deep in the Everglades.

He gripped her thighs. His body tensed, and he thrust deep into her, spilling his orgasm.

He curled his fingers around her neck, pulled her lips to his, and kissed her like a delicate flower.

Or perhaps, his princess.

He broke off the kiss, palming her face. "You're so beautiful." He smiled. "And wicked."

"Wait until I'm out of this sling." She winked. "You don't know how wicked I can get."

"If I wasn't scared before, I'm utterly terrified now."

She stared at him for a long moment, soaking in his sexy gaze. She loved the way he looked at her and how he wasn't so quick to want to get out of bed. Or stop cuddling. How he genuinely enjoyed the lazy part of being intimate.

She traced his cheekbone. His jaw. His lips. His chin and neck.

Then she fingered the tattoo. The reminder of his lost love. Immediately, her hand went to her midsection. He'd lost someone special. Something she vowed never to ask him to forget.

Tears stung her eyes. It was strange to think she'd lost a child. She'd miscarried during the fifteenth week. It had been hard, and what she mourned was the idea of a child, not her child.

He glanced at her hand over her belly, and then his gaze smacked hers like the sun's warmth.

"Oh, Trinity," he whispered with so much emotion. Too much. "I'm so sorry. I didn't know." He cradled her in his arms, bringing them both to a sitting position. He ran his hands up and down her back. Her arms. He kissed her temple and stared into her eyes with...love.

"Know what?" She blinked. Her world turned upside down in a flash. This perfect moment was tainted with the thick memories of a fist to her face. A boot to her gut. A visit to the ER. "What are you talking about?" Her body grew rigid, and she could hear the defensiveness in her voice.

This was not something she talked about.

Occasionally, her father could get her to muster the courage. But he'd been there. He'd picked her up at that hospital. He'd brought her home. And he would have killed Charlie if given the chance. Now, all her dad wanted was for her to be whole. For her to live her life and love again.

"Trinity?" Keaton lifted her chin with his thumb. "Open your eyes and talk to me."

She had no idea she'd even closed them. Tears rolled down her face.

He brushed them away.

"I'm sorry. It's just that when you placed your hand on your stomach, well, I know what that means," he whispered.

"How on earth could you know that?"

"My sister lost two babies," he said softly. "I know the gesture, and there's another reason. But we'll get into that one in a second."

"No, tell me." God, anything to not have to tell him what happened. "I want to know."

"All right." He lifted her from his lap and set her on

the other side of the bed, covering her body. He swung his feet over the side, found his jeans, and hiked them over his hips. Standing tall, he walked across the room and leaned against the wall, staring at her with a strange look. One that she hadn't seen before.

All she knew was that in that moment, she felt like he was anywhere but in that room with her, and there was nothing she could do about it.

"When I told you about the fight Petra and I had, I didn't tell you everything." He stared at his feet and stuffed his hands in his pockets. "I left something out."

"Okay," she said softly.

"Petra lied to me." He blew out a puff of air. "During our argument, I left the room because I was afraid I would say something I might regret. I do that sometimes."

"Everyone—"

"If you want to hear this, you've got to be quiet." He lifted his gaze, and it bored into her like a freezing iceberg.

She nodded.

"I wanted kids. I mean, so did she, but we weren't exactly on the same timetable. So, when I stormed off to the bedroom to pack, I stumbled onto something she'd been keeping from me for a few months."

A million things ran through Trinity's mind. Like, were they trying, and she was secretly taking birth control? But instead of asking, she kept her mouth shut. Only that thought reminded her of something incredibly important. Really important.

Her pills.

They were still back at her place. Keaton hadn't brought them over when he'd picked up her stuff. She'd asked him to grab the packet in the bathroom, but he'd forgotten, and now they'd just had unprotected sex. Well, crap.

She pushed that thought from her brain and focused on Keaton.

"When I pulled the document from the drawer, I wasn't sure I was reading it correctly. But sure enough, Petra had an abortion and didn't tell me."

"Oh my God," Trinity whispered. "I'm so sorry." What else was she supposed to say? That bitch? No, she couldn't say that. It was Petra's body, and she still didn't know the entire story. Didn't know Petra's side. Didn't even really know his side.

Keaton ran his fingers through his hair. "I was pissed. Not that she'd had one, though I wasn't happy she had. However, to this day, I'm not sure what angered me more in that moment—that she had the abortion or that she hadn't trusted our relationship— our love—enough to tell me she wasn't ready to be a mother." He lifted his gaze. "Or was it that she hadn't believed I was ready to be a father? And I'll never know the answer."

Oh boy. That was a lot to unpack. She needed to choose her words carefully, and the only thing she had was her own experience, which wasn't anything like his, but it was something.

"An unplanned pregnancy isn't easy to deal with for anyone," Trinity said. "And I was in a shitty relationship."

Keaton sighed, nodding. "The bottom line is, I never got to tell her that I loved her. And that I forgave her, even though, to this day, I still struggle with why she couldn't tell me, and for me, that will always be the rub. It always sends me down a path of wondering if maybe I loved her more than she loved me. Or if I didn't understand her. What if—"

"Keaton, you need to stop doing that." She patted the bed. She wasn't sure if telling him about what happened with her mother, with her miscarriage, or both would be the right thing. But she needed to do something. The poor man was torturing himself for something he had no control over.

"It's kind of hard when I can't have a conversation with her."

"Well, imagine being able to have that conversation and still not getting an answer." She tilted her head. "My turn to talk. Your turn to listen. Now sit."

"Yes, ma'am." He sat on the side of the bed, but the distance between them couldn't have been greater. Well, she'd forced him to tell her all because she hadn't wanted to face her demons.

"I'm going to tell you two stories—"

"Two?" He stared at her with wide eyes.

She nodded. "I'll do my best to make them brief." She tucked her hair behind her ears. "My mom got pregnant shortly after my dad moved us back to Calusa Cove. My dad was thrilled. Another kid to spoil. My mom thought a second child might make this town bearable. She also thought it might be the thing that got my dad to leave.

Anyway, the pregnancy wasn't easy, and my mom had a stillbirth."

"That's terrible. I'm so sorry."

"It was god-awful," Trinity agreed. "We were all heartbroken. But my mom was devastated, and she took it out on me. Still does."

"Excuse me?" Keaton blinked. "I don't understand."

"The way my mother sees it is, if I had never been born, my dad would never have moved back here, and she would never have lost her second child." Trinity pursed her lips. Her heart still broke for her mom, her dad, and for that child. But it was hard to feel more than apathy for a woman who didn't care about her own daughter's well-being.

"But you had nothing to do with it. You didn't cause it. No one can honestly hold you accountable."

"I know that." Trinity nodded. "However, my mother can't even look at me and not think I'm the reason her life blew up, her marriage fell apart, and her other child isn't here. I'm the bane of that woman's existence."

"I don't even know what to say to that." He took her hand and kissed the inside of her palm.

"For a long time, I tried to gain her approval. I wanted her to love me. Maybe she does. I don't know. I've stopped trying." Trinity let out a short laugh. "I guess I haven't learned my lesson, though, since I'm still trying to make everyone in this town respect me."

"Those that matter, do."

"So you and my dad keep telling me." She smiled weakly, taking his hand and pressing it over her stomach. She inhaled sharply and let it out slowly. "I wasn't honest with you about everything that happened with Charlie."

"I know," he whispered. "I had no idea what you left out, but I think I do now."

"He hit me. He kicked me. I fought back. I told you all that. But what I didn't tell you was that I was pregnant. I hadn't told him yet because I had learned he'd lied to me, and I wasn't sure I wanted to be with him anyway. I didn't know what I wanted to do, but I was past the point where I could have an abortion."

"That's a tough spot to be in."

"I had a second-trimester miscarriage, and it didn't happen that night. I started spotting that evening, but it wasn't until the next day that I realized what was happening."

He inched closer, wrapping his arm around her and tugging her close. "Did Charlie ever know?"

"I didn't tell him. Neither did my dad. I wouldn't have wanted his support, but that's vastly different from you and Petra." She glanced up, catching his gaze. "I told these stories because, sometimes, things aren't about you. Whatever Petra's reasons for not telling you might have had nothing to do with you, your love, or your relationship. There could have been something wrong, and she was trying to protect you. I didn't see the paperwork, but I had to have what's called a D&C, which is essentially the same as an abortion. You could have read the paperwork wrong." She cringed. "No offense."

"None taken. But when I confronted her, she didn't deny it."

"Lord knows I'm not defending her. But again, for all you know, her father might've had something to say about it. You were young and did say he was judgmental and controlling."

"Very much so, and while he liked me, he had issues with me." Keaton leaned back. "I need to accept I will never know." He kissed her temple. "I'm sorry about what happened to you. Since you were past the point of no return, would you have kept the baby?"

"I honestly don't know." She rested her head on his shoulder. "Keaton?"

"Yeah."

"Why did you need to leave the bed, separate from me, to tell that story?"

"If I tell you the truth, do you promise not to freak out and run away?"

"I promise I'll tell you if I'm freaked out."

He chuckled, turning his head. He tilted her chin with his thumb. "By telling it while lying naked in bed with you, it felt like a betrayal to...us. To what we're building together. Whatever that is, and trust me when I say, I'm both terrified of what's happening as much as I am of being insanely excited about it."

Her lips parted. Her throat dried up. Her heart hammered in her chest. Her eyes blinked wildly. She tried to speak, but instead, all that came out was something that sounded like what people described as an owl witch.

"You want to run," he said.

"No," she managed. "I just expected you to say it was a betrayal to her, not me." She traced the infinity tattoo with Petra's name. "She meant the world to you."

"She did, and I did love her. I won't deny that." He brushed his lips over Trinity's mouth in a hot, tender kiss. "I also won't deny that I have very strong feelings for you. That I lo—"

Ding-dong.

"Who the hell could that be?" Keaton growled.

"You won't know until you answer it." She patted his chest.

"We're not done with this conversation." He jumped from the bed and padded across the room.

There was no way that man had been about to say he loved her. She'd simply been mesmerized by the moment. By his intense eyes. By bonding through painful stuff from the past.

Who was she kidding? She was in big trouble because the really crazy part was that she couldn't deny that she loved Keaton Cole.

CHAPTER 12

KEATON GLANCED at the screen on the computer as he raced by the living room.

Fucking Fenton had ruined his big moment. For the first time since he'd been twenty-five, he felt love. Honest to goodness love.

It was pure and genuine, making his heart pump blood through his veins like he was a teenage boy all over again. He was pretty sure she felt the same way.

Well, as sure as he could be, considering they were two fractured beings. They were wounded in very different ways, but they shared that bond. Of course, he could have read that situation wrong. He could certainly be coming on too strong.

It had been years since he'd uttered the words, and he certainly didn't take saying them lightly.

Perhaps this was the universe telling him to slow down. He could wait a few days. A couple of weeks...a month. No. He had made that mistake once, and he wouldn't make it again.

He curled his fingers around the doorknob and yanked it open. Jesus, he disliked this man.

"What are you doing here? It's late." Keaton stood in the center of the door and glared, painfully aware he was barefoot, shirtless, and he hadn't bothered to button his jeans. Not that it mattered. This was his home—his domain—and this man had ruined his evening.

"I came to see Trinity." Fenton lifted his chin. The idiot held flowers in one hand. He didn't know Trinity. Not one single bit. Even if he didn't understand why she didn't like flowers, he should have at least been in tune with the concept that she didn't want them, considering they'd dated for a couple of months. But he shouldn't be showing up at his home with a bouquet.

"You've got some nerve to show up here unannounced and uninvited," Keaton said. "She doesn't want to see you." He pointed. "And she sure as hell doesn't want those."

"No offense, but I won't take your word for it."

"You don't have a choice. This is my house, and you're not welcome." He pointed to the man's fancy vehicle. "Now, kindly leave before I make you."

"Not until I speak with Trinity." Fenton widened his stance.

Jesus, this man had a big set of balls.

"Keaton," Trinity's voice rang in his ears.

His heart did a flip in his chest, but he didn't dare glance over his shoulder. He wasn't about to take his eyes off this jerk. He didn't trust Fenton as far as he could spit. "Yes?"

"My dad's on the phone. He's stopping for food on the way home, and he wants to know if we want Chinese or Italian for dinner," she said. "Oh, Fenton. I'm surprised to see you here." Her fingers glided across Keaton's shoulder and curled around his biceps. She leaned into his body.

Keaton glanced down and swallowed. She wore one of his shirts and a pair of his boxers, and she looked so damn sexy in them.

"I've been so worried about you," Fenton said, taking a tiny step forward. "I brought you these. I know how much you love lilies."

Keaton inched closer. No way would he let this man inside his home. Nor would he allow him to speak with Trinity. If that made him a dick, then he'd gladly wear the title.

"Hang on. I need to give my dad an answer." She waved her cell.

"Italian sounds great," Keaton said softly.

"Daddy, why don't you order something from Mario's?" She nodded. "Okay. See you soon. Love you." She pulled the phone from her ear, glanced down, and tapped at her screen as if she didn't have a care in the world.

Keaton furrowed his brow and leaned over her shoulder. She actually had been talking with her dad.

She glanced up. "I'm texting Audra. She wants to know if we want to come to the B&B for breakfast tomorrow. I'm making the executive decision that we'll be there. It'll be fun to hang out with them." She managed the cell quite well with one arm in a sling.

ELLE JAMES & JEN TALTY

"Sounds nice." Keaton nodded, almost forgetting an intruder stood a foot away. He shifted his gaze. "I'm not going to ask you nicely again. Now, leave."

Fenton didn't look at him. He stared at Trinity—really stared at her—and it got on Keaton's nerves.

"Trinity," Fenton said softly. "I need to speak with you, it's important. Can we go for a walk? It won't take long. I promise."

"No," Keaton said. "She's not going anywhere with the likes of you."

"I wasn't speaking to you." Fenton's face hardened. His nostrils flared like a bull. "I'd appreciate it if you'd let Trinity talk for herself."

"We have nothing to say to each other, Fenton." Trinity tucked her good arm through Keaton's and leaned against his shoulder. "And keep the flowers. I don't like lilies. They're your favorite, not mine."

Keaton puffed out his chest. He wasn't normally the kind of man to do that. But damn, he was proud. It was an honor to have her on his arm.

"Please, Trinity. There are things I need to tell you."

"Okay. Speak." She glanced at her cell. "But we've only got a few minutes, so make it fast. Keaton and I need to get ready. We have friends coming over shortly for happy hour."

This was news to Keaton. He figured she was lying, and it scared him how good she was at it.

"Not in front of him." Fenton jerked his head.

"Well, if you can't say it in front of my boyfriend, then I don't want to hear it," Trinity said with a strong, confident voice. "And seriously, don't come to his house again without calling. Actually, don't call me or him ever again. I've put up with this long enough. I broke up with you for a reason."

"You're not safe here," Fenton blurted out. "I've heard things about him, and they aren't rumors. I know people. You need to listen to me."

Keaton wasn't going to stand in his own house and listen to this shit. "Get—"

"I don't need to listen to anything you say." Trinity squeezed Keaton's arm. "You're a liar, a cheater, and the only person you care about is yourself. I don't know what game you're playing now, but I never want to see you again. So, if you don't leave, I will call the police chief." She leaned a little closer. "I've got his personal number on speed dial, and I'm not afraid to use it."

"Remember, I warned you about him." Fenton shifted his gaze, as if to look past both of them and into Keaton's personal sanctuary. Then he turned on his heel and marched off toward his vehicle.

Keaton watched him back out and pull onto the main road. Then he turned, cupped Trinity's face, and kissed her hard. It was wet and sloppy. It wasn't very romantic. He suspected he had bruised her lips as they stumbled backward into the wall. When he broke off the kiss, they were both breathless and gazing into each other's eyes with wonderment.

"You...were...incredible just now. You handled him like a pro," Keaton whispered.

"I'm so tired of him." She pressed her hand on his chest and pushed a little.

He realized he was crushing her arm.

"Shit. I'm sorry. I hurt you."

"That kiss was worth the throb in my shoulder."

He chuckled.

"I don't understand what Fenton's obsession with me is. My dad's not going to fire him. Not unless he screws up, and so far, he's been a model employee. But you should know that I texted Dawson when I heard it was him standing outside."

"That's good. I'm glad you did that. Documenting how much he texts, calls, and shows up will build a potential harassment case."

"Trust me, unfortunately, I know the drill. Only, Fenton hasn't hit that number, and he's never threatened me. He's not like Charlie. Fenton's just a cheater and after my dad's money."

"And therein lies his obsession with you." He arched a brow. "I have to ask. I understand why you think a man bringing you flowers represents him asking for forgiveness for things he's done wrong, but do you have a favorite flower?"

"Definitely not lilies." She smiled and laughed. "When I used to appreciate them, I always enjoyed more of an arrangement of color. But seriously, why does it matter?"

"Because I was raised that flowers at random times are romantic. My dad always brought flowers home to my mom on weird days and for absolutely no reason. When she'd ask why, he'd say it's Flower Friday. Or it's the thirteenth of the month, so you needed thirteen roses."

"That's kind of sweet. However, I need to ask a

dumb question." She cocked her head. "Had they been fighting?"

"No, and I can say that with the utmost certainty because when my folks did argue, they pretty much always did it in front of us kids. My mom has always said the big fights, the ones about how to parent, were done in private, but when they were mad at each other, we all knew. They believed it important to get those feelings off their chests when they happened. Get it over with, forgive, and move on." He shrugged. "It worked for them, but sometimes, I will admit, it made it awkward for us kids."

"My dad tried never to fight in front of me with my mom, but she was a screamer, and she also demanded flowers and gifts after they fought. It was gross."

"I can promise that I will never buy you a gift or flowers to make up for a fight." Keaton kissed her temple, took her hand, and strolled to the kitchen. He needed to express his feelings. He'd given Dawson shit for holding out, and with this case looming over their heads, he refused to make the same mistake twice.

But he didn't want to blurt it out. He did feel the need to make it somewhat special. He wanted both of them to remember the moment.

Unless, of course, he crashed and burned. That was always a possibility.

Keaton pulled down a bottle of wine and poured two glasses. He pushed one of the stools back to the breakfast bar and helped her hop on.

"Can I ask you a question?" She fiddled with her wineglass.

"Of course."

"What do you think Fenton meant by he'd heard things about you?"

Keaton leaned against the sink and sipped his wine. He'd missed this stuff, and enjoying it wasn't strange at all, especially with Trinity. It amazed him how comfortable he'd become having her in his space. He normally didn't like having people in his home—outside of his buddies or his family.

This was his safe place. A space where he could be alone with his thoughts. Alone with his demons—those things he didn't share with anyone. But he'd shared them with her.

"It could have been any number of things," he admitted. "When we first came to town, people gossiped about how we'd all been there when Ken died. There are still a few rumors that float around about that, and Ken is a local hero."

"I've heard all those," she said softly. "But there are things about Ken that have come out that aren't...well... so nice, either."

Keaton had struggled with some of that and knew more was coming down the pipeline—he just didn't know what. He and the guys had all talked about that. Ken was the one man on the team who was different. Far more different than Hayes. More private than any of them.

He'd had a wife and kids, so they'd all chalked it up to that.

But even when Keaton had been with Petra, he hadn't been as close-lipped about his life. There had been times when Ken had spent an entire weekend not hanging out with the team. He'd been with Julie and her family. It wasn't abnormal for a man to do that.

It just wasn't normal—for them.

Keaton grimaced. "Ken made a mistake when he was young. He pivoted. He corrected the course of his life, and we really don't know what he knew about Paul, Benson, and their operation."

"But he knew something," Trinity said. "And I've spoken to Audra about when Ken found her and how he spoke to her that night. It wasn't kind. It wasn't a man begging the woman he loved to come home. I didn't live here for all the crap that Baily went through, but Ken did and said things that make me wonder what he did or didn't know."

Keaton had been wondering those same things. "Part of me wants to believe that Ken wanted Baily out because he knew and didn't want her to get caught in the crossfire, but that makes him guilty of not doing anything. The other part of me—because I knew Ken well—believes he just wanted his sister to get out from under the shit their father left her with."

"But that was Baily's decision, not Ken's." Trinity arched a brow. "And now, we've drifted off topic."

Keaton nodded. "I honestly don't know what Fenton's talking about now. The team and I have gained the town's respect. He's probably just still trying to win you back." He set his glass down, and with his heart in his throat, he closed the gap. "You are an incredible woman. You're sweet. Kind. Intelligent. And I've been an utter moron for the last year. I'm kicking myself because I couldn't see past my own insecurities and fears."

"You really know how to get all mushy." Her smile melted his heart and mended the parts of him that were broken.

"I haven't even warmed up." He kissed her. Slowly. Softly. He pulled away, gazing into her captivating eyes. "And now, I might muck it all up and send you packing, but I won't let another minute tick by without telling you how I feel."

"Oh, sweet Jesus," she said in more of a breath than words. "I'm not sure I'm ready for this—that we're ready for this."

"Is anyone ever really ready to fall head over heels in love?" He traced her lower lip with his thumb. "Because that's what's happening. I'm falling hard for you, Trinity. I can't stop it. And truth be told, it's been happening for a while. It didn't just magically appear overnight. I haven't been able to stop thinking about you—dreaming about you—for months. I've been so afraid of being in love that all I've done is act like a jerk, so your only option was to dislike me."

A tear trickled out of her eye and crash-landed on her cheek. She smiled. "Even when you were being an asshole—which for the record, was almost every day—I always liked you."

And that was it. She liked him—not loved—liked.

Well, everyone had to start somewhere.

He cupped the back of her neck and pressed his lips to her forehead. "Like is good. I can live with that."

She giggled. "I wasn't finished."

"Oh," he said.

"You can be a hard man to get to know, but you're not necessarily complicated once you do. Over the last year, I've seen glimpses of who you really are, which is this sweet, gentle man who cares deeply. I couldn't put my finger on why you were so much harder on me than everyone else. It wasn't the same as with Silas, who I do get cares a great deal about me. But it was different with you. It was like this weird yin and yang. One minute, I thought we were friends, while I secretly wanted more. The next, I figured you hated me."

"I never—"

She pressed her finger over his lips.

"I've been falling for you, too. It wasn't this thing that happened overnight. I didn't wake up one morning and think, God, I love this man. It was gradual. Until it wasn't, and then it hit me like a ton of bricks."

He couldn't help it. He smiled. Wide. And his cheeks hurt.

"But honestly, Keaton. Loving you scares me."

He frowned. "Why?"

She groaned, dropping her head to the center of his chest. "I've never felt real love before. Not anything like this. I've had boyfriends, but they never last. I've been told I'm too much of a princess, or I find out they're only interested in Daddy's money. And Charlie, well, I realized how much I didn't love him when I got pregnant."

He reached down and cupped her chin. "I get how terrifying love can be. I've only felt it twice, and both times, it made me want to jump up and down like a kid waiting to open presents on his birthday while at the same time wanting to run away as fast as I could."

"You feel like that now?"

"A little bit." He chuckled. "I closed myself off to love because of how painful the loss of it can be. At least, that's why I thought I did. But now, I realize it wasn't that at all. I closed up because I was afraid I wasn't worth it."

"I wish I could say that's the most ridiculous thing I've ever heard, but my mother has made me feel as though I'm not worthy of love my entire life. I think I've chosen men who aren't capable of love because of that."

"Well, aren't we a pair?" He kissed her temple. Her cheek. The soft spot under her earlobe. And then her lips. "I do love you, Trinity."

"I love you, too."

He covered her mouth with his in a passionate, meaningful kiss. He nestled between her legs, wrapped his arms around her body, and held her gently. Nothing about this moment would ever be forgotten. Every word would forever be etched into his brain. Every touch. Every kiss. Every swirl of her tongue in his mouth.

He'd never let it go. No matter what happened. He'd die for this woman.

Emotion poured through him, his heart bursting like a dam giving way. It was as if all the pieces of himself that he thought had been lost forever were suddenly found.

The sound of the door lock moving caught his attention.

He jumped, smacking her shoulder.

She groaned.

"Shit. I'm sorry." He reached for his weapon.

But it was only her father.

Monty stepped through the front door carrying bags of food. "Looks like I interrupted...something." He laughed. "Please, don't mind me. Go back to whatever you were doing while I put the food out."

Trinity blushed and buried her face in his bare chest.

His bare freaking chest. Not to mention, he'd never buttoned his pants, and she was wearing his clothes.

They both probably smelled of sex. Thank God Monty had brought garlic bread because now his house smelled like that.

"I should go put a shirt on," he mumbled before kissing her again. It was going to be hard not to put his hands and mouth on her every chance he got now.

"Yeah, it's rude to be at the dinner table like that," Monty teased.

As awkward as he'd felt a few days ago, it had all disappeared. Monty was a ballbuster, and Keaton loved that about the man. He also respected him and enjoyed his company. The two men had gotten to know each other, and Keaton at least believed Monty thought Keaton was a decent choice for his daughter.

With that thought, Keaton strolled to his room feeling more alive than he had in years.

CHAPTER 13

LATER THAT NIGHT, Trinity tucked her hands under her cheek and stared at Keaton. Her life had done a complete one-eighty in less than a week. She'd harbored feelings for Keaton ever since she'd met him, and if she were being totally honest with herself, it was one of the reasons she and Fenton would have never worked out.

His cheating and all his other faults—they had been the push she'd needed to get out of one more lousy relationship. She'd always picked the wrong kind of man. It was as if she were a magnet for them. Or as if she chose that kind of man on purpose, as if to prove to herself it was all she was worth, just like her mother had told her.

But Keaton was different, and she felt that deep in her bones. Keaton was exactly the kind of man her mom told her would never want to marry her, simply because she was too much trouble, too independent, too much like her father.

Keaton lived his life honorably, as shown by his relationships with his Navy buddies and how he treated people. He respected others and lifted them up rather than cutting them down.

Outside of their rocky start, which she understood now, Keaton was the kind of man who didn't give his heart easily, but when he did, he did so freely and without reservation.

Her heart beat rapidly in the center of her chest. Honesty was important to him, and she didn't want to keep secrets. She didn't want to sit on this just because it might not be anything to worry about. Then again, it could be life-changing.

"You're deep in thought." Keaton ran his index finger up and down her arm. "Are you okay?"

"I have to tell you something, and when I do, I need you not to freak out."

He traced her lower lip with his thumb. "I believe we're past all that, considering we jumped from being unable to be in the same room without arguing to barely dating to being in love."

"Yeah, well, I still want the dating part. I want to be taken out to dinner. To go on picnics. To scuba dive together. Everything but the flowers." She patted the center of his chest. After dinner, while sitting on the dock, watching the boaters return, she'd told him she wanted to take things slow. While she loved him and that wouldn't change, she still wanted—needed—the part of a relationship that included long walks and getting to know each other better.

He'd easily agreed. He didn't want to jump into anything other than being in a relationship where they didn't see anyone else but each other, and they'd take everything else one day at a time.

His willingness and desire to take things slow made her love him even more.

"I look forward to it." He kissed her nose. "But now you're avoiding whatever has put that wrinkle on your forehead."

She wanted to resent that he could not only read her emotions but also knew her that well. No man she'd ever had a relationship with had been this in tune with her. It was both refreshing and terrifying.

"I kind of am," she admitted. "It's not an easy topic."

"Perhaps you should treat it like a Band-Aid, then."

"You neglected to bring over my pills," she blurted out.

"What pills?" He raised on his elbow, palming his cheek, and stared at her with an inquisitive gaze. God, he was adorable. When his attention was on her, he didn't waver, and wouldn't, unless a bomb went off.

"A prescription that was in the master bathroom."

"Oh. I'm sorry. I can get them for you tomorrow." He smiled. "Just tell me where they are and what they look like."

"Thanks, but you should know they're important, and I shouldn't miss a dose."

"What does that mean? What happens when you do? Is something wrong?" He sat up taller. His face paled. God, this man was so sweet.

"No, it's nothing like that."

"What is it like? Because now I am freaking out."

"They're my birth control pills, and I haven't taken

any since the morning I got lost at sea." She sucked her lower lip into her mouth and chewed on it.

He blinked. Once. Twice. Three times. Then his eyes went wide. His lips parted, but he didn't gasp. He didn't groan. He didn't even make a hefty sigh. Raising his hand, he began to touch each finger with his thumb.

"What are you doing?" she whispered.

"Counting how many days…" He dropped his hand to the mattress. "I have no idea. It's not like I completely understand these things. But I'm not an idiot, and I do get that we essentially had unprotected sex."

"To be completely transparent, too many days were missed, and we might want to consider a Plan B solution, and that window is pretty short."

He narrowed his stare and flopped back on the bed, fingering his tattoo. She wondered if he even knew he did that. Not that she minded, because she didn't. However, considering the situation, she found it… interesting.

And a little scary. She knew him…but there were so many things she was completely clueless about. This was one of those things.

"I can pick that up, too," he said so softly she barely heard the words. He turned, catching her gaze. "Can I ask you a crazy question, but one that most couples eventually discuss?"

"Okay."

They were a couple. That wasn't weird or scary. But her pulse raced, and her mind scattered. She held her breath in fear of whatever this might be.

"Do you want children?"

"Someday." This could be the beginning of the end. The thing that turned this beautiful beginning into a storm at sea. "You don't want a family," she whispered.

He inhaled sharply. "It's been so long since I've thought about it. After Petra died, all the dreams of having kids went with her, so I never even considered it." He ran his thumb across her lower lip. "I love you. I don't want to be with anyone else. I can't even imagine that. All of that is easy for me to say. To feel."

"But the family part? That's hard?" She swallowed her breath. While that hurt, she couldn't blame him. That death had shaped so much of his life, and she'd be a bitch if she tried to take that away and change his reality and how it had affected who he'd become as a man.

"It's not exactly like that. It's just that I didn't consider it. The idea never even entered my brain, partly because I can't say I've ever been in a real relationship since Petra. While I never dated more than one person at a time, there still wasn't any level of commitment, only an understanding that I was dedicated to being a SEAL, and that's where my heart belonged." He leaned in and kissed her softly. "But understand it's something that's now sitting in the front of my mind."

"But only because I forgot my pills, and I didn't do this on purpose. You've got to believe me. This isn't something I want to deal with right now in my life. But I couldn't not tell you. That would be wrong," she said, practically begging him to hear her words. To not hold what happened against her and hopefully forgive her forgetfulness.

"You've been under a lot of stress." He brushed his mouth over hers in a long, decadent kiss. "We've both been firing on half a tank." He tucked her hair behind her ears. "I don't honestly know where I stand on having a family in the future because I haven't thought about it. We jumped into the deep end, and we need some time to tread water. But what I find fascinating about myself now is that I don't seem to oppose the idea in the future."

Her heart did a backflip in her chest. She had to be dreaming. "I don't want you to change your mind because I was…reckless."

"Babe, I don't see it that way."

She groaned. She wanted to believe him, but she'd been the one who'd forgotten—not him.

He cupped her chin. "And I'm not changing my mind about anything. I'm having a discussion with my girlfriend—whom I love—about something important. I don't know if now would be the right time. We've barely even begun. All I'm saying is that I'm not freaking out."

He had to be too good to be true. He would show his true colors and leave her, or he'd see how unworthy she was. That's what her mother had always beaten into her brain.

"Maybe you're not, but I am." She'd always struggled to fit in—to believe she belonged—anywhere. Returning to Calusa Cove had been one of the hardest things she'd ever done. She'd always loved the sleepy little town. It felt like home, and she wanted the people to accept her as she accepted them.

She'd seen the ugly underbelly of Keaton Cole. She knew some of his darkest secrets. And what she didn't know, she could see etched in the scars on his body.

Keaton was the kind of man that what you saw was what you got. He spoke his mind freely, and perhaps that was one of the things she'd been drawn to—as strange as that sounded. He'd been hard on her for a long time.

But he'd also been right. What was she trying to prove? And to whom?

The people who mattered in her life—her father, Audra, Baily, Keaton, and his friends—gave her the respect she craved. She might not have a long history with them, the tight bond and inside jokes. But she had something special with each and every one of them.

For the first time in her life, she felt like she fit in, that she belonged, that she had found *her* people.

"We're in this together." He pulled her close to his side, tucking her head onto his shoulder. "I look forward to the day this business with jewels is over so we can settle into whatever brand of normal we can find."

"That is if the jewels haven't curs—"

"Don't even say it. I researched that, and while I don't believe anything I have read, there's no point in putting it out in the universe." He kissed her temple. "Now, get some sleep. It's late, and we promised Dawson and Audra we'd be there by seven."

Trinity snuggled in, her arm and leg draped over Keaton's body as if that was exactly where they had always belonged. As if she'd found home. It both electrified and terrified her. She'd been searching for this feeling her entire life. She'd always had a safe place with her father. That was a given.

But what human—what woman—didn't want more? She'd craved a life partner. Someone to share her dreams, hopes, and fears with. Someone she could be herself with. Someone who would accept her for who she was, faults and all.

A tiny voice in the back of her head worried that when all this business with the jewels was handled, Keaton would walk out of her life, that it was the danger that had brought them together and drove him to step in because he couldn't let a bad thing happen to someone he called a friend.

She closed her eyes, holding on to the three lovely words he'd uttered more than once. They had flowed from his lips to her ears and hit her heart like a cannon-ball hurling through the air, smacking their target with precision. There was no reason not to believe he meant them—in the moment.

But moments tended to fade into the background.

Moments didn't always last.

She let sleep overtake her body, doing her best to ignore that little voice because each moment in life built on another. And then another.

And hopefully, this was just the beginning.

* * *

KEATON JERKED AWAKE. An alarm blared in his ears. One constant, loud siren. Only, it wasn't the sound attached to waking him up. That noise seldom went off. He always woke before that happened. He had an internal clock that naturally made his body and mind come alive somewhere between four thirty and five. It had been ingrained in his psyche since the military and hadn't disappeared in civilian life.

He rubbed his eyes and sprang to his feet. Leaning over the bed, he reached for Trinity's good arm. "Wake up." He shook her a little too harshly. "Come on, babe, we've got to get out of the house, now." He turned and pulled back the curtains. Fire surrounded the back of the house. The flames stretched high. They were wild and danced toward the sky. They smacked against the glass like fists punching a wall. It wouldn't be long before it went inside by shattering the pane into pieces.

"Huh. What?" She wiped the hair from her face. "What the hell is that sound?"

"The fire alarm," Keaton said as calmly as he could. His sense of smell registered the smoke. It filled his lungs, constricting his breath.

So did the scent of gas. It was intense and could only mean one thing.

This was no accident.

He snagged his jeans, hiked them over his hips, grabbed his weapon, and snatched up his cell. "Put some clothes on and let's go." His voice was stern—commanding—and he didn't like speaking to her in that tone. But now, his skin felt the heat. He didn't know where the fire had started, except he suspected someone had doused his home with gas and lit a match.

He needed to get to Monty, and they all needed to get out.

Trinity didn't need to be told twice. She did exactly what he asked her to do without question. "My dad," she whispered.

Keaton raced to the bedroom door. Before opening it, he placed his hand on the wood panel. It wasn't too hot. He put his ear to it. He couldn't hear the roar of the flames. Nor did he see smoke coming from under the door. Carefully, he tugged on the knob.

He swallowed, staring at the yellow and orange that glowed on the walls. The fire appeared to be mainly on the outside frame of the home, but it had broken through the barrier and crawled up the walls of his foyer. The curtains were all but gone. He glanced to his right.

The couch had sparks as a few flames grew. More flames danced outside the glass sliders.

"Monty," he yelled as he tapped on his cell, texting the SOS to his buddies. Hayes was working tonight, so he could act immediately, and Keaton wouldn't have to call the fire department, killing two birds with one text.

That worked because Hayes immediately texted with an ETA for his home.

"Monty, can you hear me? We need to get out of the house." He took Trinity by the hand. "Stay close," he said as he inched through the house. Both exits were covered in flames, cutting them off from being able to use them as escape routes.

"Daddy!" Trinity's voice screeched, and she tugged hard at his hand, trying to get to her dad.

"What the hell is going on?" Monty appeared on the other side of the kitchen. "There's a fire outside."

"I know." Keaton nodded. "Can we get out of your window?" he asked.

Monty shook his head. "The fire made its way inside my room." He covered his mouth and coughed. "I tried opening the window, and it won't budge. It's as if it's locked."

"That's impossible," Keaton said. "Stay right here in the middle of the room." He huddled his two house-guests in the safest spot and went to the sliders, jumping over a few flames. That was the safest exit right now. He unlocked the door and yanked.

Nothing. Someone had barricaded it from the outside.

How had he not known? They should have tripped his motion detectors. His alarm should have gone off long before the fire alarms had. "I'm going to have to break the glass," he said. "Go to my bedroom and get some sheets. Douse them in water and wrap yourselves in them."

"Okay," Monty agreed as he grabbed his daughter.

"But Daddy, we can't leave him out here to—"

"You can and you will." Keaton glanced over his shoulder. "I'll be fine." He took the blanket from the sofa and wrapped it around his hand and arm. "Trust me. Hayes and the fire department are on the way." He pleaded with her with his eyes. Begging her to do as she was told.

"Okay." She took off with her dad, thank God.

He stared at his hand. That was dumb. He took his

weapon, gripped it, and rewrapped the blanket to protect his arm. He smacked the glass once. It barely cracked. He did it again. Not much more. A third time provided spider cracks, but it didn't break.

He hit it four... five... six times... and finally, on the seventh hit, the damn thing broke. Glass went flying everywhere.

"Goddammit." He groaned as a piece landed right in his thigh. A big piece, too. Big enough he could pull it out, but also big enough he probably shouldn't.

Blood oozed out around the sides, soaking his jeans. He did what he always did and pushed the pain that tried to register in his brain to a dark corner of his mind. He'd deal with it later.

"Come on, we've got to go. The flames are just getting worse." The smell of gas was worse than the smoke. It was as if whoever had done this took an airplane full and dumped it on top of his house.

"Here." Monty handed him a wet blanket.

"Run toward the center of the lawn. I'll be right behind you," Keaton said.

Bang!

Monty clutched his shoulder. His body jerked backward.

Bang!

"Daddy!" Trinity screamed as her father dropped to his knees. This time, the bullet tore through his chest.

Monty's eyes went wide. He opened his mouth, but all that came out was a gasp and a gurgle.

Keaton shoved Trinity to the ground, covering both

her and her dad with his body, and glanced over his shoulder.

Bang. Bang. Bang.

"Stay down," he said as calmly as he could as the bullets flew over his head.

"Find the jewels and get the girl," a male voice echoed.

"Over my dead body." Keaton lifted his head. A sharp pain vibrated against his temple. It rattled his teeth. His vision blurred.

And then the world went dark.

CHAPTER 14

TRINITY KICKED and screamed but it didn't do anything but piss off her captors. They tied her hands and ankles. They put something over her head, and then they tossed her in a boat like she was a sack of potatoes.

"Did you find the jewels?" one of them asked.

"No," the other man said. "You're a goddamn idiot. That fire is out of control. No way can I search that place in those conditions, and I can hear the fire trucks coming down the street. We've got to get out of here, now."

She focused on the voices—focused on the tone and timbre—but she didn't recognize either one.

"You should have gone in as soon as the alarm was disabled. The fire was overkill."

"We needed to flush them out. We needed to separate him from her so we could snag her and the jewels."

"Well, that didn't pan out, now did it?"

Trinity lay perfectly still. The hum of the engine—an outboard, because she knew boats—filled the night air.

The water was calm, and as they continued to move in whatever direction they were headed, it stayed calm. It stayed that way for a little bit before the boat began to rock.

That could only mean they weren't headed into the Everglades but out into the bay. Perhaps out into the ocean.

Not that either direction was good for her.

Her father had been shot—possibly dead—and Keaton had been left for dead in a burning building. For what? Stolen jewels? Which weren't even in the house but locked up tight in Dawson's safe at the police station. But the bigger question was how the hell was she going to get out of this, because this was not how she was going to die.

The boat picked up speed. They had cleared the channel and were moving north toward Marco Island. She continued to focus on the movements of the vessel. She knew these waters better than most. No matter where she ended up, she'd have a decent idea of where that was if she paid attention. Or at least she hoped she would.

"What good is she without the jewels?" one of the men said.

"We can use her as leverage, and that's what the boss wants."

"Not if her father and boyfriend are dead. Who else in this town would give the boss the jewels to save her?" the man said. "Our boss is going to be pissed, and I refuse to take the blame for your mistakes."

"Relax. All I did was clock the boyfriend on the head.

He's fine. The fire trucks weren't far away. They'll save him. Not sure about the dad, though, and I'm not the one who shot him. You did, and you'll have to take the blame for that."

A guttural sob filled Trinity's throat. She swallowed it down. She would not show these men such raw emotion, not betray the horrible fear they induced. She wouldn't give them the satisfaction. She needed to be strong—stronger than she'd ever needed to be before. She would survive this. She had to.

Another thing she was good at was assessing time. That came from scuba diving and understanding how much time she had been under, how much time she had left in her tank, and how much time it would take to surface safely.

The boat didn't go too fast. Not as fast as her cruiser could have gone. She wasn't exactly sure how fast, but based on what she believed, it was about a twenty-two-foot vessel that cut through the bay at about sixteen knots.

The men no longer spoke to one another, making it easier for her to gauge the time. She was used to silence when she was underwater. She was used to using her breath, her pulse, and her body to calculate time. It wasn't easy, but she'd spent a lifetime learning to do it. By the time the boat slowed and pulled up to…something, she figured they had been driving for about an hour.

If her calculations were correct, they would be somewhere in Gullivan Bay. That could mean any number of small towns, marinas, or even a boat anchored. But it was a place—a location—something to work with.

The engine cut out, and utter silence filled the air until it didn't.

"Did you get the jewels?" an all-too-familiar female voice smacked her ears. It snaked down her spine and made her shudder. Her entire world crumbled in a second.

"Mallary," she whispered.

KEATON SAT on the edge of the hospital bed while a nurse took a pair of scissors to his favorite pair of jeans. He held the ice pack to the back of his head. All he wanted to do was race out of the room and chase after whoever had taken Trinity and shot and nearly killed her father.

He had promised Monty that he'd protect them both. That they would be safe in his home.

He'd failed.

Tears burned his eyes.

Fletcher leaned against the far wall, covered in soot. He wiped his brow.

Doctor Emily Sprouse pulled back the curtain and strolled into the examination room.

"Aren't you supposed to be in the operating room with Monty?" Keaton dropped his hand to his side. He grimaced as the nurse poured some antiseptic on his thigh. The large piece of glass was still stuck in his muscle. The paramedics hadn't wanted to yank it out, and they—along with Hayes—had forced him to take a ride in a damn ambulance instead going with Dawson.

Not that Dawson had too many leads.

Keaton didn't even know if his attackers had come by water or land.

"Monty's stable." Emily leaned over, slapped on a glove, and pressed her finger against his leg. "I'm not the right doctor for the surgery. The bullet is too close to his heart, and he needs a specialist for that," she said softly. "I'll be heading back in to observe. I've known Monty a long time." She glanced up, catching Keaton's gaze. "I was in elementary school when he was the star quarterback in this town. Every girl, including me, had a crush on that man." She smiled. "I made sure he had the best of the best. He's in good hands."

"Thank you for that," Keaton said. "Now, how about making this process go faster so I get out of here? Trinity is—"

"I'm well aware of the situation, Mr. Cole."

"It's Keaton."

The doctor nodded. "We need to get that glass out, flush the wound, make sure no glass is stuck in there, and stitch you up. Then you can go." She held up her index finger. "But I'm more worried about the fact you were knocked unconscious. I'm told you could've been out for well over ten minutes, and it took smelling salts to wake you."

"It's not my first concussion. I'm fine," he mumbled.

"The fact that you can say that with a straight face is worrisome." She arched a brow.

"He's not going to sit idle." Fletcher pushed from the wall. "I'll keep a close eye on him, promise."

She folded her arms. "I know from past experience there's no arguing with you guys, but since it's going to be at least an hour before you can walk out of this joint, you're going to humor me by letting me do a final check on your head. Just a few questions to make sure you're still ornery and coherent. I want to flash my light in your eyes and annoy you."

"Sounds like a reasonable request to me." Fletcher placed his hand on Keaton's shoulder and squeezed. "But after that, he and I are gone, and he's not doing it in a wheelchair. We're not waiting for massive amounts of paperwork. He knows what 'against medical advice' means, and he's been through worse in the Navy."

"I can tell by his scars." Emily nodded, snapping on another glove. "Do you want to feel the needle as I stitch you up, or are you going to let me numb your leg?"

Keaton chuckled. "You can numb it as long as it's just a local. My days of being tortured are over, but I don't want painkillers. I don't need to be a walking zombie."

"God forbid." She went to the tray, snagged a large syringe, and jabbed him with it.

He flinched.

"All right. Let's get this glass out." She glanced at the nurse. "Be ready with the flush. I want to clean out the wound right away. Hopefully, we won't see too much blood when I take this out. If we do, it changes everything."

Keaton held his breath. He'd been through much worse, but he wasn't a fool. He knew veins and arteries ran up and down his leg, and if the wrong one had been nicked, well, that would suck.

Fletcher left his hand on Keaton's shoulder, and he certainly appreciated the support. It wasn't because he was squeamish. It was more because, if he didn't squirt a crap ton of blood, Fletcher knew he might jump off the hospital bed and race out of the room.

His heart pounded in his chest.

The fire. The flames. The smoke. The gas. The gunshots. Trinity's scream. It all played over and over in his brain.

But what really killed him? What devoured him in the quiet hours? It was that he'd failed the two people he'd been charged to protect. The people he'd come to love. One was God only knew where, fighting for her freedom. For her life. The other one was under the knife, also fighting for his life.

And it was all Keaton's fault.

He stared at his leg while Emily slowly lifted the glass. It burned his thigh. Blood oozed from the open wound, but nothing spewed like a volcano, and the glass wasn't as big as he'd thought, the cut not as deep.

The nurse doused the opening with a solution. It was cold. But other than that, he didn't feel much. At least not physically. Emotionally? He was dying inside.

"Looks better than I expected. You need maybe fifteen stitches." Emily took the needle the nurse held out and went to work.

Keaton felt a little pinch and some pressure. But nothing else. He rolled his neck, glancing up at Fletcher.

"Check your cell. I want to know if we've heard anything from Dawson or Hayes."

Fletcher dug into his pocket. "I got a text from Hayes. The fire marshal, the inspector, and the department's fire investigator just arrived. The fire is out, but now comes the hard part. Hayes said his crew is about to leave, and he got someone to cover the rest of his shift, so he's headed this way."

"And what about Dawson? Where's he at?"

"I don't know." Fletcher tapped his fingers on his phone. "I'm texting him now, but when he left the scene at your house, he mentioned going to have a little chat with Fenton."

"He showed up earlier to talk with Trinity." Keaton focused on what the doctor was doing, almost wishing he'd never asked for his leg to be slightly numb. He needed to be reminded of the mistakes he'd made. "I can't stand that man. He lied to and cheated on Trinity. He's an arrogant asshole. But does Dawson have any real reason to believe he'd have anything to do with this? He's not that bright."

"Maybe not," Fletcher said. "But he learned two things in the last few hours."

"What's that?"

"The first one was that Anna overheard him telling some pretty radical lies about you to some people in Massey's Pub the other day."

"What kind of lies?"

"He was telling anyone who would listen that he'd heard you didn't have a stellar reputation in the Navy. That you were actually released from your contract."

Keaton chuckled. "No one is released from the Navy. You're either discharged or you're court-martialed. It's pretty cut and dry."

"I know. That's what piqued her curiosity. So, she brought her drink closer to the table and listened more intently," Fletcher said. "Fenton went on to say we were all discharged because of how Ken died. He then said how he'd learned you had a temper—with women. That one even had to file a restraining order against you, and now she's dead."

Keaton clutched the side of his bed. "I'm going to strangle that asshole with my bare hands."

"That's not what got Dawson's hackles up, because it's all lies."

"Based in truth," Keaton mumbled. "Petra filed a restraining order against a stalker that I did punch, and Petra is dead."

"Do you want me to continue, or do you want to focus on the twisted lies?"

"Please, go ahead." Keaton waved his hand.

"Mallary's stepmother owns a floral shop." Fletcher arched a brow. "The same one that Fenton bought the flowers from, which he brought to the hospital and gave to Trinity."

"How do you know that?"

"Because I fished them out of the garbage," Emily said. "They were so pretty. I didn't want to see them go to waste. I put them on the desk, and Dawson asked me where they came from. I fished out the card and told him."

"Mallary lives on Marco Island. So does Fenton. Not sure why this is relevant," Keaton said, frowning.

"It wasn't—until Dawson went to the floral shop to buy Audra flowers, which was an excuse for him to speak to the family. A picture of Mallary was displayed on the counter. He spoke to her stepmother for an hour yesterday."

"Trinity said Mallary and her stepmom didn't have a very good relationship," Keaton added.

"According to Dawson, her stepmother was heartbroken, both due to the death of her son and now Mallary's disappearance. She blamed herself. Cried up a storm, and you know how Dawson does with crying women." Fletcher sighed. "Anyway, the stepmom then commented about the earrings in the picture. How they were hers, and she'd let Mallary borrow them. But one went missing, and Mallary was always losing things like that. How now she felt bad about being so hard on Mallary for such trivial things."

"While this is all riveting," Keaton said with an exasperated sigh. "Can you please get to the point?"

"Dawson mentioned this to Audra last night before bed. She told him how Trinity found an earring." Fletcher held up one finger. "Just one earring in Fenton's car when they were dating. It was one of many things that made her believe he was cheating on her."

"So, Dawson now believes Fenton was cheating on Trinity with Mallary?" Keaton asked. "That's a stretch. Women lose earrings all the time. Petra was notorious for doing that, which was why she never bought expensive ones."

"I'd normally agree with you." Fletcher nodded. "But Audra went on and on about how Mallary constantly told Trinity she should give Fenton a second chance. That she misunderstood all the text messages that were obviously sexting, and that he explained the earring."

"It makes no sense that the other woman would want the guy she's screwing to get back with the girl-friend." Keaton pinched the bridge of his nose.

"I agree. But we don't know if Fenton is telling the truth and what he might have been telling Mallary."

Keaton sucked in a deep breath and let it out slowly. "If that man touched a hair on her head, I swear, I can't be held responsible for what I'll do to him."

"Do I need to restrain him?" The doctor stood, took off her gloves, and tossed them in the trash.

"Dawson will make sure he follows the law," Fletcher said. "Or he'll personally restrain him."

"Good to know." Emily nodded. "I don't mean to put myself where I don't belong, but it was impossible not to overhear that conversation." She took what looked like a pen out of her pocket and flashed it in Keaton's eyes.

He did his best not to react too harshly to its bright-ness. The last thing he needed was to be told they wanted to hold him for observation.

"Are you talking about the girl who went missing when you brought Trinity in?" Emily asked.

"We are," Fletcher said. "Do you know her?"

"No, but her picture has been all over the news, and I remember seeing her about a year ago when I went to Marco Island with my ex for a romantic getaway. We were at this cute little out-of-the-way upscale, posh resort. It's small—only a few bungalows and right on the beach. She was with this guy. They were all cozy and romantic. I didn't think anything of it, but I vaguely remember the guy. I think it's that man Fenton."

"I hate him even more," Keaton said. "But what does those two having an affair have to do with why someone went after both Mallary and Trinity on *Princess Afloat*? Or why they tried to kill Trinity and now have kidnapped her? That doesn't make sense."

The sound of boots marching in perfect rhythm echoed in Keaton's ears.

That had to either be Dawson or Hayes.

Knock. Knock.

Dawson pulled back the curtain and stepped inside. "Hey, Doc." He looped his fingers in his belt. "Are we about done in here? Can my boy have his walking papers?"

Emily sighed. "I'll go get them, but remember—"

"Against medical advice," all three men said in unison.

The nurse laughed and followed the doctor out of the room.

"What did Fenton have to say?" Keaton stretched out his leg. The stitches already itched.

"That's an interesting story all by itself." Dawson rolled the stool the doctor had been using and planted his butt on it. "At first, Fenton denied having anything to do with Mallary. But once he learned Trinity was missing, he owned up to having a little side action with one of her best friends. But he said it didn't last long."

"What a slime," Fletcher said.

"Does he have an alibi for the last few hours?" Keaton asked. "Did you search his house? Did you—"

"He has an alibi that checks out, and I had no reason to search anything," Dawson interrupted Keaton. "Fenton doesn't deny that he's been in an on-and-off-again relationship with Mallary. He admitted that, for a time, he probably cared about Mallary."

"I really don't want to listen to this," Keaton mumbled.

"It's important." Dawson raked his fingers through his hair. "According to Fenton, Mallary had been chasing him for months, and he ignored her advances. But after a fight with Trinity, he ended up in her arms. He said it only happened a couple of times while he was seeing Trinity, and he constantly told Mallary he didn't want to be with her, but she was relentless and didn't mind being the other woman." Dawson ran a hand over his mouth. "Fenton caved a few times and admitted to spending time with Mallary after he and Trinity broke up."

"I'd have those handcuffs close by next time I'm near that jerk." Keaton hated men like Fenton, and he'd have no problem punching him in the nose, unprovoked.

"A few things don't add up to what Fenton told me." Dawson raised his hand. "I asked the same questions more than once, only I reworded them, and his story changed. He mixed up the timeline regarding his relationship with Mallary. I think he has seen her more than he's willing to admit." Dawson glanced at the watch on his wrist. "I also find it quite strange that he wasn't actually at his home on Marco Island, which I'm shocked that you two didn't think that it would have been impossible for me to make it back and forth in such a short period of time."

"Where was he?" Keaton asked.

"A small sleezy hotel about twenty minutes from here," Dawson said. "He told me it was late last night, and he didn't want to drive all the way home. Bradley, who's off today, volunteered to follow him. As of ten minutes ago, he was headed north, toward Marco Island."

"What is it that you and that cop brain of yours is thinking?" Keaton asked.

Dawson rubbed the back of his neck. "On my way from speaking with Fenton and coming here, I called Ralph's parents."

"Why?" Fletcher asked.

"Keaton mentioned that right before he got clocked, Trinity's kidnappers said, 'Get the jewels and get the girl.' We've always known they were after the jewels, and I get why they'd take Trinity if they didn't have the jewels. But I don't get why they'd want to take both. They don't need Trinity if they have the jewels."

Keaton shifted restlessly. Sometimes, when Dawson got in cop mode, he rambled. "But they don't have them, so Trinity becomes leverage. They can use her to force Monty to pay a ransom," Keaton said, frustrated.

"You're missing my point." Dawson raised his finger. "It's the words they used. Get both. And not to beat a dead horse, but they don't need both."

"Unless they're getting greedy." Fletcher arched a brow.

"It's possible, but my mind has been traveling down this dark, dangerous path for the last twenty minutes. It tells me that Trinity has been a pawn in a deadly game for a while now, and Ralph's parents might have clinched it for me."

"What do you mean?"

"None of us knew Mallary very well. She didn't hang out with us, even when Trinity invited her, so whatever information we got was spoon-fed to us via Trinity." Dawson held up his hand. "Mallary told Trinity that Ralph was a bad influence on her brother and that Ralph and his friends picked on Jared for years. She said she didn't understand why Jared was hanging out with Ralph. She also told Trinity all about the marina babe, Valerie. When all this went down last year, I spoke with Ralph's parents, and they were angry. They didn't like what people were saying, and they were defensive. They've softened a bit, but they are adamant that Jared stole those jewels. That he'd been asking Ralph all sorts of questions about them, like where his parents kept them, and he even asked Ralph to show them to him."

"Wait. That's new information," Fletcher said.

Dawson nodded. "And Valerie—well, it turns out, according to Ralph's parents—that Mallary paid her to be nice to Jared."

"You've got to be kidding me." Keaton shook his head.

"I've yet to verify that, but I can think of only two reasons Mallary would do that. The first one is being a nice older sister who wants her little brother to have friends, but is totally misguided in judgment. The second one is that she was trying to set up a narrative."

"You're giving me a headache." Keaton rubbed his temples. "What kind of narrative are we talking about because all she did was make her brother look guilty."

"Let's look at that night logically," Dawson said. "Whoever else was out there never expected Trinity to be a witness to Jared's boat sinking. They might not have even known it was Trinity until the next day."

"That makes sense, especially if Mallary had something to do with it," Keaton said. "But that means you believe Mallary isn't missing and that she had something to do with what happened the night Trinity got shot."

"It's a working theory." Dawson rubbed the back of his neck. "A weak one at best. But something stinks when it comes to her and Fenton. I'm not exactly sure what it is. I don't have all the puzzle pieces, and the ones I do have don't line up. I called Chloe. She's about a half hour away."

"Well, I can't sit on my ass and do nothing while someone has Trinity doing God only knows what to her." Keaton shivered.

"And I don't expect you to." Dawson stood. "Chloe is off the books for this one. I have to be all official-like, so I'll be with Remy. You, Hayes, Fletcher, and Chloe can all work together." He crooked his finger. "But do not shoot or kill anyone. I don't need the hassle or the paperwork."

"Understood." Keaton nodded. "But I can't make any promises."

CHAPTER 15

TRINITY SAT on the floor in the cuddy of a larger fishing vessel, her hands and feet bound. The air reeked of five-day-old fish. She coughed and gagged as she stared into the eyes of someone she'd once called a friend while she waved a gun in her face. "This was you all along?" She swallowed the bile that bubbled from her stomach to her throat. "Why? Why would you do this?" She blinked, shifting her gaze, not wanting to look her in the eye. She stared over Mallary's shoulder. Something shiny glimmered on the small table.

A knife?

God, she hoped it was a knife.

"You can never just walk away from anything, can you?" Mallary lowered herself, grabbing Trinity's face and forcing her to look into her terrifying eyes. "You had to call the Coast Guard that night. You had to see what was happening at sea in the middle of a storm instead of doing what a normal person would do and turning around to go home."

"Are you kidding me? Normal people don't let boats sink." Trinity squared her shoulders. "Did you kill your brother?" she asked softly. Visions of that night flashed in her brain. The storm. The massive waves. The lightning. The rain. The small vessel bobbing up and down.

Mallary narrowed her stare. "Of course not. I loved Jared. He wasn't supposed to die. He was supposed to be on that boat with Ralph and a few other boys. It was supposed to look like pirates got them. But when my friends got to my brother's boat, they were shocked to find Jared alone." Mallary shrugged. "They had to make the tough call. Someone had to go down with the boat." She waved her gun. "But then you showed up, causing a ruckus, making it impossible for them to snag the jewels. They had to sink the ship and haul ass. But I guess I need to be grateful it was you." She smiled wickedly. "My dear, sweet friend who would do anything for me, including spending a year looking for sunken treasure."

"You used me," Trinity whispered.

"As if you haven't been using me our entire friendship." Mallary rocked back on her heels before sitting on her ass and crisscrossing her legs. "You only became friends with me because I made you 'regular.' If it weren't for me, you'd just be the rich bitch on the block that everyone hated. Because of me, you became relevant. You had friends."

"That's not true."

"Oh, please." Mallary rolled her eyes. "You rolled up to the dorms in your expensive SUV like you were Elle in *Legally Blonde*. You were such an elitist. During our freshman year, everyone talked about you behind your back, and it wasn't to call you sweet names like a princess. Sadly, I wanted to be you. I wanted money. I was so tired of being the girl who smelled like rotting bait. Do you have any idea what it's like to grow up with a dad who runs a fishing charter business? I thought when he married the witch and she owned a floral shop, I'd get to work there, but no, I had to work for Daddy. What a joke."

This was not the Mallary that Trinity had been friends with on and off for years. This was a bitter, angry woman, and Trinity wanted nothing to do with this version of Mallary.

"You tried to kill me." Trinity sucked in a deep breath. Her own rage bubbled to the surface. "Three times."

"Not me personally." Mallary laughed. "And they weren't supposed to kill you. Not without finding the jewels first. I need them. They're the key to my happiness." She leaned closer. "Something you took from me."

"Excuse me? How did I do that?"

"Fenton." Mallary raised her hand—the one with the gun in it—and smacked it across Trinity's face.

The taste of metal filled her mouth. Her eyes watered. Her cheek felt as though a bomb had gone off inside the bone. She groaned. "Fenton?" she managed. "But you always wanted me to get back with him."

"You're such a dumb bitch for someone who thinks she's so damn smart."

"Why don't you explain it to me because I don't understand?" Trinity's cheek throbbed. Her eyes watered. Her insides trembled. But as she sat there and stared at someone she'd once thought was her friend, she honestly wanted to know why Mallary had decided kidnapping and killing her was the answer to whatever problem she had.

Even if she was going to die after finding out the truth.

Mallary leaned closer. Her lip twitched. "Fenton, like most men, believes you walk on water. I can't understand why he loves you, but he does."

Trinity gritted her teeth. "He only wants my father's money, and he's a cheater." She gasped. "He was sleeping with you, wasn't he?"

"Technically, that only happened twice while you and he were together." Mallary sneered. "When you found those texts and my earring, I thought maybe he'd realize I was the better choice. But he didn't. He decided he'd made a mistake and lost the best thing that had ever happened to him."

"But if you wanted him, why encourage me to take him back?"

Mallary laughed. "At first, all I wanted was to crush you and destroy your confidence in him. I would text Fenton when I knew he was with you, hoping you would see the sexy talk. I left my earring in his car on purpose. But after Jared died—after you and Fenton broke up—he still didn't want me. He wanted *you*. Loved *you*. He's been determined to win you back. To prove to you that while working for your dad has been a dream come true, it's not the only reason he wants to be with you, which is a crock. That man cares more about money and prestige, about his place in the world, and these jewels are my way of giving him that."

"Are you kidding me?" Trinity swallowed, choking on some blood. "You think that money will make him love you?"

"It will help him forget about you," Mallary said.

"Hey, boss," a male voice yelled. "Fenton just pulled into the marina. What do you want us to do?"

"Don't let him on this boat, that's for damn sure, but maybe he made good on his word." Mallary jumped to her feet. She leaned over. "Don't go anywhere. I'll be back."

Trinity spat the blood that had pooled in her mouth at Mallary.

She just laughed as she wiped her face and walked away.

Trinity dropped her head back and tried to keep the tears at bay. How had she not seen it? How could she have been so blind and stupid? She sucked in a deep breath and pushed it out through her nose. She blinked, glancing around the small cabin. She needed to find a way out.

The knife! Thank God Mallary hadn't seen it.

She shimmied her way up the wall and hopped across the small cabin. She fumbled with her fingers until she clutched the knife. She managed to hobble back to her spot and began cutting through the restraints. That was priority number one.

She'd figured out the rest once she managed that.

One thing at a time.

* * *

KEATON TOOK the binoculars that Chloe handed him and peered through the lenses. They had perched themselves across the street and up on a hill, overlooking a marina on Gullivan Bay.

"That's the boat my buddies at the Coast Guard saw a few mornings ago. It crossed into the Bahamas later that day, but there was no word on it returning to US Waters," Chloe said. "It's registered to Riggs Oppenheimer. He's been a fishing charter captain out of Marco Island for twenty years, and my contacts just informed me he has a connection to Fenton."

"Obviously, since Fenton is parked down the road," Keaton said with a little too much sarcasm. "We need to have Bradley stop him if he enters the marina."

"I agree," Chloe said. "Eight years ago, Fenton hired Riggs. Since then, he's hired Riggs exclusively for fishing charters. But Riggs also knows Mallary and her family. Riggs got his start working with her dad."

"Wonderful," Keaton mumbled.

"Also aboard that vessel that morning was Eddy Ives," Chloe continued.

"I take it he has a connection to Fenton as well," Fletcher said.

"Just Mallary and her dad. He worked as a mechanic at their shop until about five years ago. Now he owns his own engine repair shop," Chloe said. "Wille Avery, now he's the man we need to be worried about."

"Why?" Hayes asked.

"Ex-Army," Chloe said. "My contacts tell me he was

given an other-than-honorable discharge. I pulled in a few favors to find out more, and he was sent packing for breaches of military orders."

Hayes snorted. "We all sat in front of a review board for that—twice—but it wasn't because we didn't want to follow orders. It was because if we did, civilians would've died."

Keaton set the binoculars aside. Whatever was going on down there, he couldn't see it. "Do you know more?"

"Yeah." Chloe nodded. "This asshole got lucky he didn't get court-martialed. He broke the chain of command more than once. He put his men in danger. He put civilians in danger, and according to one of the team leaders I spoke with personally, he's reckless and a menace."

"This just keeps getting better," Keaton muttered, glancing at his watch. "How far out is Dawson?"

"Ten minutes," Fletcher said. "He had to ditch the uniform and fly under the radar of the locals. This isn't his jurisdiction, and he's putting his job on the line."

"He doesn't have to participate." Keaton rolled his neck. "We're not even a hundred percent sure Trinity is on that boat."

Hayes slapped him on the back. "Maybe not, but that looks an awful lot like Mallary, and she's holding a weapon. It doesn't appear she's being held under duress."

Anger boiled over. He snagged the binoculars and slammed them against his face. "I'm going to—"

"Don't finish that statement," Chloe said. "I might be off duty, but I'm still an FBI agent." She crooked her finger. "But now that we have a visual on something, I get to put my official hat back on and make some calls on your behalf."

"I'm not waiting for your friends to show up. That could be too late," Keaton said.

"I'm not asking you to." Chloe arched a brow. "But since we just happened to be in the area and saw a girl we thought was dead, I can call a few people I trust for backup. That way, whatever does go down will be official, and no one will get away with anything today." She smiled.

"I think I'm 'hearting' on your girlfriend." Keaton chuckled.

"How many times do I have to... Never mind. Sorry for my friend, Chloe," Hayes said.

"He's cute, so he's forgiven." Chloe pulled her weapon from an ankle holster and checked the chamber. "Since none of them would know me, I'll go meander down by the docks. You boys take cover behind that building over there." She pointed. "Have Dawson meet you there. We'll text in five to ten with a plan."

"How about I just go walking up to the boat?" Keaton said. "That's a plan."

"Might be what we go with, but for now, let's keep watching." Chloe jumped to her feet. She held Hayes's gaze for a moment.

That moment wasn't lost on Keaton or Fletcher.

"Be safe." She squeezed Hayes's biceps.

"You, too." He nodded, raising his hand, but before it landed on anything, he dropped it to the side.

"Looks like Fenton is on the move. Let's roll." Keaton wasn't sure he could wait ten minutes. They didn't know if Trinity was on that boat, but Mallary was, and that was a start.

* * *

KEATON PACED BEHIND one of the storage buildings in the marina with Hayes, Dawson, and Fletcher. His heart pounded in his ears. "What the hell is taking so long?"

"Chloe didn't want to risk anyone on that boat having a visual of her and Fenton together." Dawson stuffed his hands in his pockets. "She made contact and said he should be driving by in less than a minute. The plan is for him to make the turn around this building and park over there, which is out of sight from the docks."

"Unless he keeps going because he's guilty as sin," Keaton mumbled.

Dawson shook his head. "Chloe says he wants to talk. She texted and said he looked scared shitless."

Fenton's car took the corner. He pulled into a parking spot, bolted from the driver's seat, and raced toward them, panting.

Keaton took two steps, but Fletcher grabbed him by the forearm, yanking him back. "Let Dawson handle this."

"Would you be standing down if it were Baily who was missing?" Keaton turned and glared.

"You're running way too hot, and the last thing we need is for you to sucker punch him." Hayes placed a gentle hand on Keaton's shoulder. "We need you to be calm."

Keaton took in a long, slow breath and nodded.

"Care to explain why you're here?" Dawson asked as Fenton approached. "Is there something you didn't tell me this morning when I questioned you?"

"Yes and no." Fenton wiped his brow. His face dripped with perspiration, and it wasn't even that hot out. "I suspected a couple of things but wasn't completely sure. Now I am."

"That's called obstruction of justice, and it's an arrestable offense," Dawson said.

"Then arrest me, but you'll be wasting valuable time." Fenton raised his hand and pointed toward the docks with a shaky finger. "Mallary is alive, and she needs help."

Keaton stole a glance toward Dawson, who shook his head. "How long have you known she wasn't missing or dead?" Keaton asked.

"She texted me a couple of days after she went missing," Fenton admitted. "I was gobsmacked. She's being held captive for ransom, but Trinity wouldn't give up the jewels."

"No one ever contacted Trinity, or the police for that matter," Dawson said, planting his hands on his hips. "Why didn't you come to me when she reached out?"

"She told me her life was in danger, and then the next day, I got an alarming message from some man who said they were going to kill Mallary if I didn't do what they asked."

"And what was that?" Dawson asked calmly.

"Find out where Trinity was and who was staying with her. I gave them that information." Fenton wiped his hand over his mouth. "I'm sorry. I had no idea they would set Keaton's home on fire and kidnap Trinity, but Mallary's life is also in danger, and you have to help her."

"Is Trinity on that boat?" Keaton clenched his fists at his sides.

"I don't know. I saw a man standing guard with a gun, and then that FBI agent sidetracked me." Fenton blew out a puff of air. "I'm glad you're here. You have to help Mallary."

"How did you know to come here and that Mallary was on that boat?"

"The phone number," Fenton said softly. "After I learned about the fire, I found the message from the man who called me, and I searched the number. I couldn't believe it, but it was from someone I knew. Someone I had taken my boat to for service a few years ago. It got me thinking about Mallary and her past. How the guy I always used for fishing charters—Riggs—was connected to Eddy, the service guy, and he was always a bit shady. It's why her dad fired him. He thought he was using his charter boats for his own side gigs—like pirating."

"Still doesn't tell us how you knew she'd be here," Keaton said.

"Because Mallary told me to come here. She said she could see out the window, and she knew the marina," Fenton shouted. "They have Mallary. Maybe they have

Trinity, too. You have to do something. We can't stand back here and do nothing."

"We need more," Dawson said. "This isn't adding up."

"After you visited me this morning, I called the number that Mallary first reached out on. She answered. She was so scared. I told her I wanted to help, and she said the only way I could help was if I had the jewels. She asked me if I knew where they were. I told her I suspected Keaton had them and that I would get them. I would do anything to make sure she was safe. I might not love the woman, but I don't want anything bad to happen to her."

"So, you thought you'd come here, alone, and save her?" Dawson asked.

"Okay, so not my brightest move, but I didn't exactly expect a tattooed man with a machine gun." Fenton slumped his shoulders. "What would you have done in my shoes?"

"Called for backup, for starters," Keaton mumbled. "And I'm still struggling with your story."

"It's not a story, man. I'm telling you the truth. Mallary—"

"Is not who she seems." Chloe came around the corner. "Earlier, we saw Mallary with a weapon."

"What? You didn't tell me that. You're lying." Fenton stared at Chloe. "That can't be. She's being held against her will. They kidnapped her for the jewels from the *Flying Victoria*. They tried to kill Trinity..." Fenton let his words trail off. His eyes grew wide. His face turned bright red. "No. No. That can't be right. Are you suggesting that Mallary has been behind all of this? Why?"

"You're going to stand there and pretend you weren't in on it with her?" Keaton took a step closer.

"Me? Why the hell would I blow up my life over jewels from a stupid sunken ship? Why on earth would I go along with kidnapping? That's crazy." Fenton stared at Keaton.

"Oh, I don't know," Keaton said. "Maybe because Trinity rejected you, and you wanted revenge?"

"That makes no sense." Fenton shook his head. "I love Trinity. I was doing whatever I could to win her back." He held up a shaky hand. "That certainly doesn't include hurting her friend or stealing jewels. How would that help me get her back or extract this so-called revenge? If I wanted that, I would've done something to you, and no, I didn't set fire to your home because she was in... Oh my God," Fenton said softly. "I can't believe I didn't see it before." He covered his eyes with his hands.

"See what?" Dawson asked calmly.

"Mallary and her games. I'm so stupid." He shook his head and dropped his hands to his sides. "She was always playing stupid games, like agreeing to be the other woman when I was dating Trinity. Or how she'd tell me that she understood how important money was to me, and that's why Trinity was more important when that wasn't the truth at all."

"But you did say you wanted Trinity for her father's money," Keaton said.

"That was taken out of context." Fenton glared. "I

will not apologize for my success in the business or wanting to go as high as possible. But that's not why I was with Trinity, and I have always regretted saying those words and being with Mallary while I was with Trinity. Two things I can't apologize enough for." He shifted his gaze toward the water. "If Mallary is behind all this, and she does have Trinity, then she's a woman who no longer has anything to lose."

"Why do you say that?" Dawson asked.

"Because Mallary has always wanted what Trinity has, and that's money and the respect of her family. If it's the jewels she's after for money, she won't have that. And her father hasn't appreciated the way Mallary has lived her life. My God, I've been such a fool." Fenton stuck his hands in his pockets. "I know saying sorry isn't enough, but I truly am. What can I do to help?"

"Stay out of our way," Dawson said. "And I'll need a full statement when this is over."

"I'll do anything." Fenton nodded, staring at Keaton. "I hope you'll be able to forgive me."

All the air in Keaton's lungs flew out like a flock of birds taking flight. He hated this man. Despised him. But if everything he said was true, the only thing this dude was guilty of was being an asshole—and stupid—and every man was guilty of that at least once in his life.

But forgiveness, in this case, wouldn't come easily to Keaton. "If anything bad happens to Trinity, I will personally hold you responsible."

"I suppose I'd feel the same way if I were you," Fenton mumbled, nodding like a freaking bobblehead.

"I hate to break up this party," Chloe said. "But we

need a plan, and we need to act." She glanced at her watch. "The Coast Guard is in place, and honestly, there are way too many civilians in this marina to do this here."

"Bradley has secured two speedboats." Dawson jerked his thumb over his shoulder. "Me, Keaton, and Fletcher on one. Chloe, Bradley, and Hayes on the other." He pointed his finger at Fenton. "You are to stay right here. Do not move. If you signal them or do anything to make me regret not slapping handcuffs on you, so help me God, you will regret ever meeting me."

Fenton held up his hands. "I won't. I promise."

"You better not." Keaton inched forward. "Because if you do, it's not Dawson you need to worry about." With that, he turned on his heel but paused without taking a step and glanced back. "Hang on."

"What?" Chloe asked.

"We're forgetting one thing," Keaton said. "We don't know if Trinity is actually on that boat, but I think we can use Fenton to find out."

"I'll do whatever you want," Fenton said.

"What are you thinking?" Chloe asked.

"She wants the jewels, and Fenton here led her to believe he could get them. She likely saw him pull in." Keaton rubbed his jaw. "Let's have him call and tell her that he got them. During the rush at my house, while they were taking Monty and me to the hospital, he was able to get in and get them. But when he got here, he saw Bradley and got scared, so he rented a boat, and he'll meet her out at sea, but..." Keaton raised his finger.

"I want him to ask about Trinity, whether the kidnappers have her, too."

"Let's do it," Chloe said.

Fenton pulled out his phone.

"Put it on speaker." Keaton waved his hand.

It rang twice. "Hello? Fenton? Is that you?"

"Mallary? Are you okay?" Fenton asked in what could only be described as incredible acting. As if he cared. Maybe he did because one didn't turn off feelings that quickly.

"Barely," she whispered. "I'm so lucky they haven't found this phone."

"I have good news," he said. "I've got the jewels."

"You do? How did you manage that?"

"Trinity's dad was hurt really bad. Last I checked, he was still in surgery. And Keaton, they had to take him to the hospital, too. While all that was going down, I poked around and found them. But when I got to the marina, a cop was hanging around, so I got scared. I didn't want to do anything that would upset those who kidnapped you. I will call them now and tell them I rented a boat and to meet me out in open water. I think that's safer."

"You're probably right," she whispered.

"Did you know that Trinity is missing now, too?"

"She's here," Mallary said. "You can save us both."

"Okay. Hang tight. I'm on my way." Fenton ended the call. "That bitch. She plans on killing me, too."

Keaton coughed, pounding his chest. "What makes you believe that?"

"And you don't?" Dawson glared.

"Just asking the question as to what brought him to that conclusion so fast." Keaton raised his hands.

"What else is she going to do with me after I bring her the jewels I obviously don't have," Fenton mumbled. "Don't you think I should call the other number now to make it all legit? Otherwise, they might think something is up."

"Good idea." Keaton nodded, rolling his neck. He still didn't like the guy, but he hated him a little less.

That call lasted only four seconds. The man grunted a few coordinates at Fenton and then hung up.

Chloe stuck her head out around the side of the building. "They're firing up the engines. They took the bait. Let's roll."

That's all Keaton needed. Trinity was on that boat, and he wouldn't wait another second to get to the woman he knew he didn't want to live without.

CHAPTER 16

TRINITY TWISTED and turned the knife. It dug into her skin, making her wince every time it drew blood, but with the last flick of her wrist, her hands broke free from the restraints. Her shoulder throbbed, and her arm felt like a dead weight against her body without the sling.

The engines roared to life.

Oh no! Her chance at freedom was being snatched from her grasp before she even had the opportunity to try to escape.

The boat rocked as it pulled away from the slip.

She stared out the porthole. She knew exactly where she was—a popular marina lined a channel leading into Gullivan Bay.

Where was Mallary taking her and why? What was the plan? Had Fenton boarded the boat? What did he have to do with all of this?

So many questions, and she didn't have any answers.

The only thing she knew for sure was that she was going to die if she didn't do something. But what?

Don't be reckless. Don't act impulsively.

What would Keaton do? Well, he'd be prepared with a weapon and a plan. She had neither. But she did have a window. And there were other boaters. She hobbled around the cuddy in search of a pen and paper. She opened every drawer...every cabinet...and found nothing.

She had to find a way to signal a vessel as she passed them. Pressing her nose against the porthole, she watched as the boat accelerated into the open waters.

The door rattled.

She spun, losing her footing, and fell on her ass. She groaned when she used both hands to cushion the blow, causing her bad shoulder to explode.

"Well, lookie who found a way to escape her restraints." Mallary waved her gun around and laughed.

"You won't get away with this." Trinity lunged forward.

"I wouldn't do that if I were you." Mallary pointed her gun right at Trinity's chest. "You are literally of no use to me now."

"Why not?"

"Fenton has the jewels. He's meeting us out at sea. Once I get them..." She shrugged. "You're shark bait."

"Just like that. You're a stone-cold killer."

Mallary inched closer, pressing the gun into Trinity's gut. "This isn't my first rodeo." She smiled. "Mommy didn't swallow a bottle of pills and kill herself."

Trinity covered her mouth and gasped.

"That's right." Mallary smiled a wicked, deadly grin. "Sure, I painted this picture of how close we were, but the truth was, I hated my mother. She was selfish and not much better than wife number two. Can you believe she thought that me working on my dad's slimy boats was a good idea? My mother thought I should be groomed to take over the family business. Like I want to smell like fish guts all day." Mallary scrunched up her nose.

"And Amber? Did you kill Amber, too?" Flashes of that college party from so many years ago bombarded Trinity's brain like a cattle prod.

"Damn, what a leap, but yeah." Mallary shrugged. "She was sleeping with Tim, and he should've been mine. Not to mention, you and she were becoming a little too buddy-buddy after all the hard work I had put into you. Talk about not showing respect." Mallary shook her head. "You know, I thought about putting an end to you when you chose to move back to Calusa Cove instead of coming to Marco Island when that dipshit Charlie did a number on you. I couldn't believe you slapped me in the face like that."

Trinity lifted her shaky hand. If she was going to overtake Mallary, it was now or never. The boat rolled up and down with the ocean waves. It moved at a good clip, heading out to sea. Thus far, she'd only seen two other men onboard. Big men. With big guns. But one would have to be behind the helm, driving. One thing at a time. Just breathe.

She sucked in some oxygen as her fingertips brushed

against the cold metal. Her heart landed in her throat like a cement brick. She couldn't swallow if she tried, so she didn't bother.

"You're a fucking bitch," Trinity said, curling her fingers around the grip of the gun. She shoved Mallary hard.

"What the hell?" Mallary's eyes went wide with shock as she slammed against the table.

The boat hit a wave, and she rolled to the side.

It was all Trinity could do to balance herself with her legs while holding the weapon in her good hand. Her father had given her a million lessons on how to shoot, but she'd been better with a rifle.

However, when it came to a handgun, she wasn't the worst shot. She just didn't like guns, which is why she didn't own one. After this, she might change her mind. It was Florida, and almost everyone she knew had one, Baily included.

Mallary twisted and turned her body, pushing away from the table, and stepped closer.

"I won't hesitate to shoot you," Trinity said.

"Then do it." Mallary sneered before lunging at her.

Trinity jerked to the side. Mallary missed her completely and smacked into the wall.

"You bitch." Mallary wiped the blood from her cut lip. "You're going to pay for that." The cold, dark stare that danced from her eyes made Trinity's heart drop to her knees. Mallary inched closer.

Trinity held the weapon as best she could with both hands. Her shoulder was useless, but she needed to steady her aim. She needed to be willing to pull the trigger because she knew, without a shadow of a doubt, she was staring back at death.

"Fisherman's Run, this is the Coast Guard. We are investigating a possible violation of boating laws. Please stop your vessel immediately and have your registration ready. We will board your vessel for inspection," a man's voice crackled over the radio.

That was music to Trinity's ears.

The boat slowed.

"Jesus," Mallary muttered. "You better let me go topside." She cocked her head. "My partners are going to need me to smooth this one over."

"You're not going anywhere," Trinity said. "Not until the Coast Guard opens that door and I can tell them what's really happening here."

"Who are they going to believe? The woman holding the gun? Or the woman saying, 'Oh my God, she's going to kill me. Please help me.'" Mallary waved her hand in front of her face for dramatic effect. "Now give me the gun." Without a care in the world, Mallary closed the gap with her arm stretched out.

With her heart in her throat, Trinity shifted her aim and squeezed the trigger.

Bang!

Mallary jerked backward into the wall, grabbing her shoulder. She glanced down at her hand, and blood trickled through her fingers. "You fucking shot me?"

"And I'll do it—"

Bang! Bang! Bang! Bang!

Rapid fire sounded—machine gun fire.

The boat picked up speed.

Men shouted.

Trinity fell to the ground as the boat lurched. She slid toward the back of the cabin, rolling like a sack of potatoes.

Bang! Bang! Bang! Bang!

More yelling, but she couldn't make out the voices. Or the words. The boat pitched to the starboard. Then to port.

Trinity gripped the weapon with all her might as she and Mallary tumbled about inside the cabin, lunging at each other. Mallary grabbed her hair and pulled. She punched her in the shoulder and then kicked her side.

Trinity gave as good as she got, but her one arm was freaking useless.

Mallary knocked the gun from Trinity's hand as the boat pitched again.

More gunfire. More shouting. Cussing. It was utter chaos.

And then, as if it were magic, the boat slowed. It was as if someone had yanked the throttles to neutral. It rocked in the swell of the ocean waves.

"Where the fuck is she?" Keaton's voice echoed in Trinity's ears. It was loud, sweet, and sent one big warm shiver up and down her spine.

"I'm down here." She jumped to her feet, but Mallary grabbed her ankle, and she face-planted to the fiberglass floor with a thud. "Ugh." She groaned. Her eyes watered. Her nose felt as though it flattened right into her brain.

The door flung open.

She lifted her head. Her vision blurred, but she knew

Keaton's frame when she saw it, as he stood in all of his glory, pointing a weapon at...

"Drop it," Keaton said.

"You shoot me, I'll shoot either you or her, it doesn't matter." Mallary laughed.

Bang!

"No," Trinity whispered.

Keaton's body flung backward.

Bang!

Dawson appeared at the door. "Mallary's down. I need help with Trinity, and will someone please help Keaton? I don't need to hear his moaning."

"He's been shot." Trinity tried to scramble to her feet, but everything spun around her like she was on that stupid ride at the amusement park that made her vomit every single time. "He's not moaning. He's dying."

"No, I'm not," Keaton said with more of a breathless groan than anything else. He crawled to the opening. "I need help getting this damn thing off. I can't freaking breathe."

"Is he always this big of a baby?" Chloe came up behind Keaton while Dawson knelt beside Trinity.

"Take it easy." Dawson forced her to sit back at the table. He flashed a light in her eyes. "You definitely have a concussion, and that nose is broken. You popped a few stitches, and it looks like she got you with a knife in the thigh."

Suddenly, her leg burned.

She glanced down, and her entire body screamed at her as if she'd walked into a minefield. But she honestly didn't care. "Keaton!" She grabbed Dawson by the shirt. "Why isn't anyone—"

"Babe, I'm fine." Keaton tore some big vest thing off his chest. He tapped on it. "Chloe and her friends made us all wear these things. I just got the wind knocked out of me, that's all. Not even a scratch." He took her by the chin, tilting her head, and grimaced. "You, on the other hand…well, you might need a plastic surgeon."

"Lucky for me, my daddy's rich." She stared into his sweet eyes. "Don't you ever scare me like that again. I thought you were dead."

"I'll try not to." Gently, he kissed her forehead.

She glanced over her shoulder. Dawson was now kneeling over Mallary. "Is she…"

Dawson nodded. "It couldn't be helped."

"You should know she confessed to two other murders." Trinity leaned into Keaton's strong body as he lifted her off the bench.

"You've got to be kidding me." Dawson sighed. "You can tell me all about it after a doctor has seen you and you've had a chance to visit with your dad."

"My father? He's okay?" she asked.

"We just got word he's in recovery, and he's going to be just fine." Keaton carried her up the small set of stairs and out into the warm Florida air. The two men who had been on the boat with Mallary were lying in pools of blood.

A bunch of official-looking people were huddled in the corner of the vessel, chatting with Chloe and Hayes. She had no idea who they were, but she'd be forever grateful to them.

"I don't think I'll ever ask for anything exciting to happen in my life again," she whispered. "And I could use a vacation."

"How does Oregon sound?"

"Boring," she said. "Let's go."

"My cousin Foster will love that." Keaton handed her to a burly Coast Guard man before hopping onto their vessel. They laid her down on a stretcher, and another man began poking and prodding at her, checking her vitals and all that stuff.

She took Keaton's hand. "And Fenton? How does he fit into all of this?"

"One of her pawns, and while I still don't like the guy, he's not responsible for this."

She palmed his cheek. "How bad do I look?"

"You're beautiful." He smiled.

"No, seriously, because I feel like I have snot for brains."

He chuckled. "You look like you need a new nose." He brushed her hair from the side of her face. "But that doesn't change how much I love you."

"You can bring me flowers in the hospital this time."

"Is that all I'm gonna get?"

"I love you, too, Keaton Cole."

"Wow. My whole, entire name."

"Because I love you with my whole heart." She closed her eyes and wished for this ride to be over and to be at the hospital. As much as she enjoyed all of this with him, her body hurt. And it hurt a lot.

* * *

THE FOLLOWING MORNING, Trinity stared into the mirror. She looked like a horror show. If she wanted one, it would be six months or so before she could get a nose job. That all depended on how crooked this thing ended up. Right now, it was the swelling and bruising that made it look so damn ugly. But it could have been worse.

She could have been dead.

Or Keaton.

Watching his body fly backward after Mallary pulled the trigger had been one of the most horrifying experiences, only second to when her father had been shot.

Knock. Knock.

"Come in." Trinity stepped from the hospital bathroom and padded back to the hospital bed. She'd forced Keaton to go with his friends down to the cafeteria and eat some real food with the understanding he'd bring her back a milkshake.

There was something to those milkshakes that Hayes was constantly slurping on.

"Good afternoon, Trinity," Emily said with a sheepish grin.

Trinity had always thought one of the reasons she'd gotten such good care the last time she'd stayed in this place had been because her dad had money, not because he had a freaking girlfriend.

As in Doctor Emily Sprouse, of all people.

She couldn't believe her old man had kept that juicy piece of news from her, but she supposed he did so because Trinity could be a pain in the butt.

And Emily was younger. But she was so sweet and kind, and Trinity was thrilled for her dad.

"Are we here on official doctor duty or as my dad's girlfriend?" Trinity winked, and the effort hurt, but it was worth it to see Emily blush.

"I'm so sorry we kept our relationship from you." Emily sat on the edge of the bed. "He wanted to tell you, but I was worried. He kept telling me that you'd accept me and that our age difference, which is barely ten years, wouldn't bother you, but it being so new, I wanted to—"

"Emily, it's fine. I get it. I do. You're a private person, and I respect that. I do accept you. I think you're good for my dad. He adores you, and it's obvious you care about him."

Emily smiled and nodded. "I do. I never thought I could feel this deeply about anyone. But he's so special." She cleared her throat. "However, I'm here right now as your doctor, and I have a bit of a touchy, personal matter to discuss with you."

Trinity stiffened. "I don't like the sound of that."

"It's not bad. It's just that I wouldn't want to discuss this in front of anyone but the patient, and Keaton wouldn't leave your side—all night."

"Now, you're really scaring me." She touched the side of her cheek. Sometimes, when she talked, her face hurt.

"Like with every patient, we run a standard blood test, and your hCG levels came back elevated. I had the lab techs run them again and also run a pregnancy test to confirm—"

"Pregnant?" She grabbed Emily's arm. "I'm pregnant?" Trinity had forgotten all about the missed pills and unprotected sex. The plan to pick up a different option had all flown out the window when she'd been kidnapped. "How is that possible?"

"Seriously?"

"No." Trinity shook her head, which was a mistake because it just made it seem like a rocket blew up in her head. "It's just that it's only been like ten days since all this crazy stuff went down, and I couldn't take my pills because... Well, that doesn't matter. And we only had unprotected sex like once, though I'm not the greatest at taking my pills daily or at the same time every day when I'm not in a relationship, and I've only been in an official relationship with Keaton for like two weeks." She paused her rambling. "Are you sure?"

"I'm sure your pregnancy levels are elevated. When are you supposed to get your period?"

"Yesterday," Trinity said softly.

"We can confirm with an ultrasound, but based on our findings and everything you've provided, I'd guess you're barely four weeks. We'll need to do some testing with OB/GYN to confirm that date." Emily rested her hand on Trinity's thigh. "That is, if you want to continue with the pregnancy. There is no judgment here. I'm certainly not going to say anything. This is one hundred percent your decision. Right now, you have options, but understand that in this state, we only have a couple more weeks before the decision is taken out of our hands and there are some hoops we'd have to jump through."

Trinity sucked in a deep breath and let it out slowly. "I wouldn't make that decision without Keaton."

Emily jerked her head back. "I mean no disrespect to your boyfriend. He's a fine man, but this is your body."

Trinity placed her hand protectively over her stomach. "I have no idea how he'll react to this news, and I'm still in shock, but is it weird that I'm already attached to the idea of it?"

"No, not at all." Emily smiled. "I want you to know that no matter what happens between me and your dad, you will always have a friend in me and if you need to talk, all you have to do is call."

"Thanks. I appreciate it."

"I need to see some other patients." Emily stood. "You know how to reach me."

Trinity ran her hand across her taut mid-section.

A baby.

No, she couldn't think of it that way. Not yet. Too many things could go wrong with the pregnancy. Or Keaton might not want it—something she had to allow herself to consider—even if she knew without any doubt, she wanted it.

So much for having calm in her life.

CHAPTER 17

A WEEK LATER...

KEATON ROLLED his truck into Trinity's driveway, rubbing his chest. He had no idea what she would think of what he'd done to his tattoo. It didn't change his past. He hadn't gotten rid of Petra's name. But he'd felt the need to add Trinity, so he had.

Hopefully, she'd appreciate it.

Part of him hated that he'd moved into one of the free cabins at Dawson's place. But he couldn't live at his house anymore. That place needed to be bulldozed and rebuilt.

However, he'd half-expected Trinity to invite him to stay with her, and when that invitation hadn't come, it had crushed his heart a little. It shouldn't. They had promised each other to take things slow, date, and do all the everyday things couples do when they first get to know one another. Just because they loved each other didn't mean they needed to work at warp speed.

But the heart wanted what the heart wanted.

Trinity waved from the front porch. The swelling on her face had gone down. Her nose wasn't bent quite as badly as he'd expected. The bruising had disappeared. Her shoulder was healing.

Her father was now home, and he was the lucky dog. Emily had moved in with him. Keaton wasn't jealous. Not one bit. Okay, he was over the moon jealous.

But he didn't let it show because Monty and Emily were good people and deserved a little slice of heaven.

Keaton had no doubt that he and Trinity would get there. They loved each other. They had a good relationship. They would be going to Oregon together in a couple of days to visit Foster. Life was good.

He slipped from the driver's seat and jogged up the steps. "Hey, babe."

"Hey, yourself." She set her book aside. "How was work?"

"Pretty boring, which is exactly how I like it these days." He leaned over, giving her a damn good kiss. It was hard, romantic, wet, and sloppy. It was every emotion he could muster into a kiss on the front porch where all her neighbors could see. "What did you do today?"

"Don't get mad, but I spoke with Fenton." She crinkled her forehead.

"Not mad." He eased onto the plush sofa. "What did he have to say?"

"He officially resigned from my father's dealership,

though my dad said he'd give him a good recommendation."

"That's nice of him."

"Even though I think Fenton is a jerk, it's the right thing to do." She patted Keaton's leg. "And Fenton apologized for like the millionth time."

"You're a very kind and forgiving woman. I wouldn't speak to the man."

"Yet I know you have." She lowered her chin. "And don't deny it."

He raised his hands. "I won't. But if he told you that we spoke, he should've also told you that I told him to stop calling you and telling you that he loves you. That does piss me off."

"No, he didn't mention that, but he didn't tell me he loved me either, so there's progress."

"Progress would be for him to go away. If Dawson could've found something plausible to arrest him with that would have stuck, he—"

"Don't go raising your blood pressure." Trinity laughed but lowered her gaze, and her cheeks turned red. "At least not right this second because I might be doing that in a minute."

Keaton arched a brow. "What exactly does that mean?"

"I have been searching for a way to tell you this for a few days."

"Blood pressure going up." He jerked his thumb toward the sky but laughed. These days, it took a lot for this woman to make him mad. She could fluster him.

She could make his blood run hot, but angry? No, that would take a flat-out lie.

"Remember when I had to go stay at your place, and you forgot to bring over my pills?"

He nodded, crinkling his nose.

"And you were going to get them and pick up a Plan B option, but then I got kidnapped. You remember all that, right?"

"I do, but why are you bringing it up?" He jerked his thumb over his shoulder. "You're at home. Pills are up in the bathro—" He tapped his chest, which squeezed and tightened. He struggled to suck in oxygen. "We never got the Plan... What are you saying?"

"I'm pregnant," she whispered.

He opened his mouth, but no words tumbled out. He slammed it shut, cleared his throat, and tried again, but got the same result. He blinked and inhaled sharply. A vision of her with a swelled belly filled his brain, and his heart immediately swelled. He swallowed.

"Don't freak out." She inched closer. "Breathe, Keaton. Come on, don't panic on me now. We have options if you don't want this—"

"Don't want it?" He glared. "Of course I want it. I love you. What on earth ever gave you the impression I wouldn't want a baby with you?"

"Oh, um, I don't know. The fact you might have mentioned you weren't sure about having kids. Your past life. My life. The fact that we've barely begun dating..." She stared at him with a questioning gaze. "Wait. What? You want us to have this baby together?"

"That's what normal couples do." He cupped her

chin and leaned closer. "You do love me, right? Or am I missing something here?"

"I love you. This is just a lot coming really fast, like warp speed."

"I've never been able to live like a turtle, so it works for me."

She chuckled, burying her face into his neck. "This is crazy."

"Maybe, but now we have some really tough decisions."

"Like what?" She glanced up.

"For starters, am I going to rebuild my house for us to live there? Or do you want to live here?" He pressed his finger over her lips. "It doesn't have to be decided today. But one thing we do need to figure out is the wedding, because do we really want to let Audra and Dawson get the jump on us?"

She jerked her head back. "Why, Keaton Cole, that isn't even a proposal. Maybe I don't like flowers, but I like jewelry. Not to mention, I've always wanted the white dress and stuff, and what's with this idea that you just think because I'm pregnant, I'm expected to marry you? Do I need to start with the name-calling?"

His smile quickly turned into a full-on laugh.

"Do not make fun of a woman with raging hormones." She poked him in the chest.

"Ouch, that hurt." He rubbed the tender skin. "And not just because of those daggers you call nails." He lifted his shirt. "I promise you, I will go buy you a ring and get all mushy, but I think this says it best."

She lowered her gaze and reached out to touch the

addition to his tattoo. A second infinity sign with her name, looped in with the first and around both of them was a heart, locking them together.

"Do you like it?" he asked.

"I don't know what to say," she whispered. "It's… beautiful." She kissed him softly. "I suppose I can forgo the proposal after that, but I want a ring. However, I'd prefer to pick it out. No offense."

He raised his hand. "None taken."

"And, unlike Audra, I want the dress. A big, fancy, white… Oh crap."

"What?" He palmed her cheek. She was so flipping adorable when she got like this, and he would forever be grateful that he was the lucky bastard who got to love her for the rest of his life.

"I don't want to waddle down the aisle like a beached whale."

"That's not possible."

"Looks like you get your quickie wedding." She jumped to her feet, yanking him by the biceps.

"Where are we going?"

"We have to start planning. I mean, it won't be but a few months before I start showing, and that means we've got only a few weeks to lock down a venue, deal with caterers, and—"

"How about we elope?"

"Have you met me?" Trinity planted her hands on her hips. "Besides, I've always dreamed about my daddy walking me down the aisle." She patted his chest. "Look, pal. You tattooed my name on your chest. You knew what you were getting into when you got involved with me. Now let's get to it."

"Yes, ma'am." Keaton followed her into the house with the biggest grin. He wasn't sure if he'd ever smiled like that before. If she wanted to get married on the moon, he'd find a way to give it to her. All that mattered was that they were together.

She paused at the front door and turned. "You're really okay with all this?"

He nodded. "I love you. I wouldn't have it any other way."

A tear cascaded down her cheek.

"Aw, don't do that. I hate it when you cry."

"I know, but they're happy tears, and I had this thought because I'm going overboard and being a princess." She rested her good hands on his shoulder. "We could get married at my dad's house. We could see if Audra and Dawson wanted to make it a double wedding. She can wear whatever she wants, and I can still have my white dress and be on my dad's arm. We can toss that together pretty quickly."

"Sounds like a plan." He brushed his lips across her mouth in a hot, tender kiss. She'd made his life whole again. She made him want to be a better man. Without her, he'd been walking around with one foot in the past.

Calusa Cove—and Trinity—had become home.

MURDER IN CALUSA COVE

EVERGLADES OVERWATCH BOOK #3

New York Times & USA Today
Bestselling Author

ELLE JAMES

USA Today
Bestselling Author

JEN TALTY

EVERGLADES ⚓ OVERWATCH

MURDER
in
CALUSA COVE

USA Today & NY Times best selling author
ELLE JAMES
USA Today best selling author
JEN TALTY

CHAPTER 1

HAYES BENNETT LAY in his bunk at the fire station and stared at his cell. He didn't know what was worse—the fact that she'd called things off in a message or that it bothered him so much.

He had no problem admitting he cared. He cared about every single woman he'd dated. Of course, he did, or why bother taking them out in the first place?

But he didn't care...enough.

He wasn't the kind of man to have long-term commitments—except for his career and brothers-in-arms. Those were the only two things that mattered more to him than his own beating heart. Some might consider that sad, especially since Hayes had a massive family. He was one of twelve—well, eleven now—and that thought brought him back to the confusion that spread through his veins like the fires he was called to fight.

No woman since he'd been a young man had ever gotten under his skin like Chloe had, not even Betsy. If he had ever honestly really cared about any girl, it had been her. Okay, it had been her kid, Fedora. He smiled, remembering how adorable that teenager had been, and he missed her a lot.

When he'd ended the relationship with Betsy, Fedora had hated him—despised him, actually. It wasn't until he'd left the military that he'd received a heartfelt letter from Fedora. She was in college, had a boyfriend, and plans...big plans.

Hayes was glad for that and grateful she'd been able to forgive him for walking away from her mother.

While the relationship had been mostly good, Hayes had only been twenty-eight. Betsy had been thirty-eight and had a fifteen-year-old kid.

Hayes didn't do children, no matter the age, and he hadn't loved Betsy.

That was the cold, hard truth.

Love.

It was the one thing the world believed Hayes avoided. Except the world was wrong. It wasn't that he tried to skirt it. Or sidestep it somehow. It was that the kind of love Hayes had experienced as a child had come with conditions and manipulations. His parents and the community he'd grown up in didn't know or understand what real love was all about, because if they did, they wouldn't tie it to hell and damnation.

Not that Hayes had any idea about love—though he could see it with Dawson and Audra, and now Keaton and Trinity. They all had a love so pure it was like a flipping fairytale.

But it didn't make Hayes want to believe in love. He didn't trust it.

So, why was his chest sore over the fact that a woman—Chloe Frasier, a reserved FBI agent who held her emotions closer to the chest than he did—had rejected him. Why did it bother him so much?

The siren blared.

His colleagues jumped from their bunks, landing on the floor with thuds.

Well, that was a question he'd have to ponder another time. He hiked up his pants and raced into the locker room, collecting his gear and emptying all external thoughts from his brain. When duty called, Hayes knew how to compartmentalize better than most.

"Let's roll," Bear, his captain, said.

Hayes climbed into the passenger seat of the engine truck and glanced at his buddy, Carter. "Where are we headed?"

"Purdy Street. The old Crab Shack's on fire." Carter shook his head as he reached for the ignition. "The town wanted to bulldoze the place and maybe build a small park or something, but Dewey's been throwing a fit about that. He believes the Crab Shack is some kind of historical monument. Damn restaurant shut down six months ago, but for years it wasn't doing well and about the only person who ever ate there was Dewey."

"Why didn't Dewey buy it?" Hayes buckled himself and chuckled. Dewey Hale was an interesting character, as were most of the folks born and raised in the small town of Calusa Cove. Dewey loved the area, and it showed in the way he told all the old tall tales about pirates and ghosts hidden way up in the Everglades. Or in how he volunteered during hurricanes and storms. He seemed to be always looking out for his neighbor... and making sure people didn't dare touch the mangrove. He got ornery when anyone did that.

Of course, the mangrove was protected, and no one but a qualified trimmer could go near it, and in these parts, that person was Dewey Hale.

But the man was strange. He lived alone and always had, according to everyone. He kept to himself mostly, and unless you got him in the evening down at the Pub or just hanging by the marina, he was just the mangrove trimmer that appeared in weird places when you least expected it.

Carter chuckled. "While we all think Dewey is secretly rich, considering he has freaking Grady White fishing boat, of all things, I doubt he has the funds. He comes from a humble background, and for as long as my family has known Dewey, which has been my entire life, he's grumbled about every little thing that changes this town right down to painting new yellow lines in the street." Carter honked the horn as he eased out of the station house. "My dad told me that Dewey's first job when he was ten years old was shucking crabs for old man Tomey, and he doesn't want to see the place get torn down." Carter palmed the wheel and gave the big engine some gas.

"Change is bound to happen, even in this town."

"Yeah, but Dewey lives in the dark ages. He's still complaining that a woman runs Mitchell's."

"That's sexist." But not surprising. Hayes had seen that first-hand a few times when he'd been in the marina and Dewey had needed something. It was as if he refused to deal with Baily, only wanting a man to help him, scoffing when she was the only one around, and mumbling how her dad would be disappointed. He'd even gone as far as to tell Fletcher to get off his ass and either marry her, or knock her up, which was beyond rude."

"That's Dewey, but he's not a bad guy, just backward." Carter flicked on the lights. "Probably why he's been single his entire life. I can't remember ever seeing him with a woman except this nice lady who used to play the organ at the local church. That didn't last long because she moved, and Dewey didn't seem heartbroken over it anyway."

"He doesn't date at all?" Hayes asked.

"I don't know. Maybe. I mean, I don't pay attention. Dewey keeps to himself except for occasionally hanging out with Silas." Carter shifted his gaze. "My old man told me once that Dewey had a girl back in the day and that she broke his heart, but that was when he was like twenty."

Hayes knew all about how one woman could change a man's view on love.

The rest of the eight-minute drive to Purdy Street was done in silence. It was a single station alarm, and there were no expected casualties. That was always a plus.

But it didn't make fighting the fire any less dangerous. Any number of things could go wrong.

As soon as Carter rolled to a stop, Hayes leapt from the vehicle, pulled his jacket over his shoulders, thrust his arms inside, and plopped his hard hat on his head. His heart danced in his chest. The blood in his veins raced through his body. It was chaos, but his mind was clear.

"Working fire," his captain called. To most, that seemed like an obvious statement, but all it meant was that firefighting operations had commenced. "Fire attack," Bear shouted, waving his arms.

Hayes snagged the hose, hooked it to the truck, and twisted the knob. He looped the hose over his shoulder and jogged toward the fire. He was used to running toward danger from his military days. He scanned the area, first assessing the wind and then the size and scope of the flames.

"Over here." Jenson waved. "Water on the fire." Another command that had seemed odd at first, but essentially it meant Jenson believed he'd found the main source.

Hayes rounded the corner and stared at the back kitchen door, which had been knocked down, or blown off, or had simply fallen off. He couldn't be sure, but flames spewed out like hungry fingers in search of more food, and to a fire, that meant anything that could burn. He adjusted the hose, turned the knob at the end, and braced as water coursed through it, smacking against the flames and pushing them back.

Other firefighters attacked the fire from different angles. They shouted commands and projected their progress as the fire slowly dissipated into smoke and ash. Hayes and Jenson inched closer into the kitchen, dousing the flames as dark smoke billowed into the air, circling toward the sky like a signal to the world that soon every flame would be nothing but a hot ember.

It took forty minutes to put the fire out, which had mostly been contained to the kitchen and half of the old dining area. Hayes let out a long breath as he turned, sucking in a deeper one. He always felt as though he'd smoked a dozen cigars after fighting a fire. He knew he smelled like ash. It probably clung to him for days.

He coughed, set his helmet on the side of the engine truck, and took the water his captain offered, chugging vigorously, as if he'd been depleted of every ounce of hydration.

"Do you mind doing the primary and secondary search?" Bear arched a brow. "We have to go through the motions."

"I don't mind." Hayes nodded. "Can I have Carter at my six?"

Bear shook his head. "He's still going through investigator school. He needs the experience with Jenson, and we still need to figure out what caused this fire." Bear pointed his finger. "Your buddy, the Chief of Police, is here. I don't have a problem if you take him with you." He shrugged. "He's a cop. He won't do anything stupid."

Hayes laughed. "You don't know him like I do."

"Maybe not, but he's marrying Audra McCain." Bear smiled, letting out a big laugh. "I had the biggest crush on that fiery redhead in high school, but she was dating Ken, and they both scared the crap out of me."

"I've been meaning to ask you something, and since I've got to wait for it to cool down in there, mind if I ask it now?" Between what had happened with Audra about six months ago, and then Trinity just a month ago, strange revelations about his old pal Ken had come up—things that Hayes and the guys didn't like.

Things that made Baily uncomfortable—and angry—making it more tense between her and Fletcher.

"Shoot." Bear leaned against the engine truck and wiped his brow.

"How well did you know Ken?"

Bear lowered his gaze. "That's a weird question coming from you. Wasn't he one of your best friends? Aren't you tight with his sister?"

"All true." Hayes nodded. "But there are some things that have come up that have been … concerning."

"I thought Ken's involvement with Benson and the drug running was all sorted out."

"For the most part, but as you can imagine, that was shocking to all of us." Hayes needed to be careful how he worded this, not just because he didn't want to say things that would upset anyone or stir up trouble, but he was about to accuse his friend—a dead man—of being a secret keeper.

That's exactly what Hayes had been doing for years when it came to his twin and his love life. It had taken him years to explain to his buddies why he didn't do relationships or children, and it wasn't just his religious upbringing or his twin dying right next to him.

All it had taken was one teenage girl to betray him, a

twenty-two-year-old girl to lie to him, and he was done with romantic love for good.

"Small towns like this one will do crazy things to even a good man." Bear arched a brow. "Most kids spend their youth dreaming about the day they'll leave this place for some big city with a nightlife and something more to do than a makeshift movie night at the docks. Those who never leave, either do so because it's all they know, or…" he tapped his chest. "Because it's in their blood. It's who they are. If they leave and come back, well, they found out what's out there isn't necessarily better."

"Where do you put Ken in that speech?"

"Somewhere in the middle." Bear ran a hand down his dirty face. "He wanted out, no doubt about that. He talked about it all the time, and he thought at first it would be through college." Bear sighed. "I had no idea Benson and his old man were running drugs. Everyone in this town still feels like a fool."

"They ran a tight shop and used a chain that had been in place for decades, which was built on blind loyalty to the cartel. Unfortunately, small towns like this are ripe for shit like that, and I wanted to know if you thought Ken could've been involved in something else that we don't know about."

"Ken got in trouble just like the rest of us. He wasn't some goody-two-shoes, that's for sure. But he walked away from Paul and Benson and followed Fletcher— that's something." Bear scratched the side of his face. "What makes you believe Ken could've been doing something else, and why does it matter?"

Hayes didn't like discussing Baily's business behind her back, and he wasn't even sure he understood the dynamic between her and her brother. "I'm just trying to wrap my head around some things."

Bear glanced over his shoulder as a Range Rover drove past. "Jesus," he muttered. "My first thought when I heard this place was on fire was that some kids were smoking weed in the building, but knowing that guy is still hanging around town, it makes me wonder if it wasn't set on purpose—by him."

Hayes squinted. "Are you talking about Decker Brown?" He didn't care for the man either, but he also didn't know him all that well. He'd seen him around town, hanging around the marina and Baily, but it wasn't like he'd gotten to know anything about Decker on a personal level. The only thing he knew about Decker was that he was a rich land developer working on a big project on Marco Island. Plus, he had a thing for Baily, which was what had Fletcher on edge.

"You know him?" Bear asked.

"Not really, but what about him has your hackles up?"

"He showed up at the town hall meeting the other day, and one of the items on the docket was what to do with this place." Bear waved his hand toward the rubble of what was left of the Crab Shack. "Old man Tomey had no family, and in his will, he left it to the town. I don't begin to understand the legalities of that or even the possibility of the land going up for auction, but when a land developer sits in a town meeting when something like that is being discussed, I get nervous.

The last thing Calusa Cove needs is a man like that building something that brings in too many outsiders and in a permanent way. I get we're a poor town with little to offer in the way of tourism, but we don't need someone like him."

Hayes didn't necessarily disagree. However, the town was hanging on by a thread, and his airboat business would benefit from the town having a bit of a facelift. Dawson had done a bang-up job with renovating Harvey's Cabins, and now that the bed and breakfast was fully operational, it did bring more people to town, staying more than a night—but then they packed up and moved on to their final destination —wherever that might be because there was nothing to do in Calusa Cove.

Having another restaurant, a park, or any other reason to entice visitors couldn't be seen as a bad thing. That said, Hayes understood the town's trepidation. They didn't want to become a highly populated area. They didn't want condos, and they especially wanted to avoid the dreaded snowbirds. Their way of life wasn't for the faint of heart. Their town survived on grit and hard work. Their citizens were humble, proud, and enjoyed their peaceful lives.

"Dawson didn't mention anything about Decker being at that meeting." Hayes polished off his water. "Decker's told Baily he likes staying here because it's far enough away from his job site that he can clear his head, but close enough that it's not a bad commute." He rolled his shoulders.

"Maybe so, but I don't like land developers of any

kind." Bear let out a long sigh. "We had one come through a few years ago. Ask Baily about it. They wanted to buy the marina from her and all the businesses up and down that stretch of land. God only knows what they wanted to build. They put a fair amount of pressure on that girl, and I know her brother wanted her to sell, but she held her ground, something I, for one, am grateful for. I just wish it wasn't so hard for her. Ever since that big marina down the way opened up, her business has taken a big hit."

Hayes didn't need to be reminded of that. It affected him and Everglades Overwatch because that marina also had an airboat tour company they now had to compete with. It was frustrating as hell. They had come to Calusa Cove to honor their fallen brother and to help his sister rebuild the family business. While they had done that, the new marina put a big damper on things.

"Baily told us about that." Hayes nodded. "I'm still shocked at how much pressure Ken put on her. We had no idea."

"Ken never wanted to be part of that marina," Bear said. "He didn't want it to be his legacy, and he didn't want that for his sister. He always wanted her out of this town. Well, at least the Ken I knew did. But I lost touch with him, as everyone did, when he left for the Navy."

"But you kept in touch with Fletcher."

Bear raked a hand over the top of his soot-filled hair and cocked a brow. "It's not like you didn't know that since I first met you, something like ten years ago. But it always struck me as odd that when Ken came home, he acted like he was better than this place—him and that fancy wife of his."

Hayes pulled up a few memories of the times the team had come to Calusa Cove. Ken hadn't been filled with the same kind of fondness for the town that Fletcher had been. Where Fletcher had enjoyed taking the guys on tours and showing them his old stomping grounds, Ken could barely wait to leave.

"You didn't like Julie?"

"I only met her a couple of times, but let's just say she looked down on me and my town." Bear jerked his thumb over his shoulder. "We can talk more about this over a beer when our shift is done. Right now, I need you to do a preliminary search so we can start the fire investigation."

"I'm on it." Hayes collected his gear, snagged an extra hard hat and jacket for Dawson, and made his way toward his buddy. "Hey, man." He shoved the hat at Dawson.

"What's this for?" Dawson took it in his fingers and glared at Hayes.

"Preliminary search." Hayes shrugged. "Come on."

"Audra is going to feed me to the gators if I come home smelling like a campfire this close to the wedding." Dawson chuckled. "She and Trinity are already worried that you're going to reek of it and Keaton's going to smell like fish guts."

"Isn't that what cologne is for?"

"Right, because we've all used that before."

Hayes entered the Crab Shack first, checking for hot spots and not finding any, thankfully. He glanced toward the ceiling—what was left of it. The fire had mostly been contained to the kitchen, but there was some damage to the main eating area, and part of the roof had caved in—but that was more from years of neglect than anything else. There was an old door in the far-right corner. It was opened about two inches. Hayes stepped over a few singed two-by-fours. He tested the handle before pulling it open.

He gasped, jumping backward, stumbling over the rubble. His heart hammered in his chest. He swallowed. He'd seen dead bodies before. He'd stepped over them on the battlefield. He'd pulled one or two from a burning building or an overturned vehicle on the side of a road. He'd killed men while in the military. He'd seen his fair share of carnage, death, and destruction.

But nothing could have prepared him for a body hanging in a closet as if it were a coat.

"What the heck?" Dawson caught him before fell on his ass. "Jesus," he mumbled. "You okay?"

"I am, but she is definitely not." Hayes wiped the sweat from his brow as he lifted his radio and pressed the button. "Bear, we've got a mayday." He let out a long breath, staring at the young woman being held up by a hanger and a rope. She had shoulder-length brown hair. Her face looked bruised and swollen. Her clothes were torn. Dried blood clung to her body like dried paint.

And she was missing her ring finger.

"You've got to be kidding me," Bear's voice boomed over the radio. "Good thing I sent Dawson in there with you."

"I need to declare this a crime scene and call State."

Dawson pulled out his cell. "We need to rope off the area, and I can't have anyone else but your investigators inside this building."

"Yeah, I know the drill," Hayes said.

"You should call Chloe." Dawson pointed to the dead girl's hand. "This is the work of her killer, but I can't make that leap right off the bat based only on a missing finger because she barely got her bosses to declare the few cases she has over decades a serial killer, and this scene doesn't quite fit, but I don't give a shit if you call her and muddy my waters. I doubt Lester with State will either."

Hayes had spent a few nights—and mornings— talking about the Ringfinger killer with Chloe. To say she was obsessed would be putting it mildly. It consumed her every waking thought and probably her dreams as well. It was the case that she couldn't crack. The one that haunted her and made her feel like a failure as an agent.

He understood. He and the rest of the team had held themselves responsible for missions that had gone sideways, for lives lost.

For Ken.

He tore his gaze from the dead girl. "My phone is in the engine truck."

"Remy's outside. I'm sure he and Bear have connected and are barking out orders. I'll stay here and keep this contained until State and Remy can get inside. Let me know when Chloe and her team will get here." Dawson rubbed the back of his neck. "And here I thought being a cop in a small town meant I wouldn't have to work much."

"You do know that this case will be taken right out of your hands."

Dawson let out a dry chuckle. "Right, because I'm going to wash my hands of it. You know me better than that."

Hayes rested his hand on his longtime friend's shoulder. "Let Chloe handle it. Enjoy your wedding and honeymoon." He turned and made his way out of the Crab Shack, knowing damn well that Dawson wouldn't be able to enjoy much of anything.

This murder, no matter whose jurisdiction it fell under, had happened on his watch, and Dawson would take that personally.

Once back at the engine truck, Hayes found his cell and pulled up Chloe's contact information. He tapped the screen a little too harshly. He worried Chloe might not take his call. She'd been adamant their *fling* was over. As much as he didn't want that to be the case, he had no choice but to accept her decision.

But this had nothing to do with his feelings.

"Hayes?" she answered on the first ring. "Are you okay? Is everything okay?"

He blinked. That wasn't the greeting he'd expected. "Yeah, I'm fine."

"You sound tired. What's wrong?"

"I was called to a fire tonight, and we found a body," he blurted out.

"That sucks."

"The victim is missing their ring finger. Dawson

called State because he doesn't have the resources to deal with the crime scene, and while we know you've been working on a serial killer case, it's not something that's been publicized, so it wasn't something he could just leap to. However, it could take a day or two before it lands on your desk, so we thought we would skirt the system and give you a call."

"That's a convoluted way of getting yourself into trouble," Chloe mumbled. "But thanks, I appreciate it. We can be there in a couple of hours, or less."

"We?"

"Um, yeah. Just like State, we have a team that'll work the crime scene, deal with witnesses—"

"Okay, that was a dumb thing for me to say." He leaned against the hood of the engine truck as the local news crew pulled up. "Crap. You might want to hurry. Our resident busy body is here, and if she gets wind of the magnitude of this story, she'll pull out all the stops."

"Are you talking about Stacey Mohawk?"

"That's the one, and last I heard, she's got stars in her eyes—as in, she wants to be picked up by national programs. She's twisted a few stories, trying to make a name for herself."

"She did right by Trinity."

"That's because the story was over by the time she reported on it. There was nothing for her to screw up or taint. But she's still driving Dawson nuts with the fallout from the Massey case and the bullshit around Mo and Anna. It's as if Stacey's trying to find ways to make their lives miserable. Mo is paying his debt to society, and Anna didn't do anything wrong."

"You're barking up the wrong tree, Hayes. Now let me go so I can gather the team and get there."

"Okay. See you soon…and Chloe?"

"Yeah?"

"I know you said we're done, and I respect that, but you don't have to stay at Harvey's Cabins or a hotel. I have a guest room; you're welcome to stay with me."

"I'll take that under advisement." The line went dead.

Hayes lifted his gaze to the night sky and let out a sigh. It was going to be a long night.

Thank you for reading Pirates of Calusa Cove by Elle James and Jen Talty. Please click here to read more of Murder in Calusa Cove

ABOUT JEN TALTY

Jen Talty is the *USA Today* Bestselling Author of Contemporary Romance, Romantic Suspense, and Paranormal Romance. In the fall of 2020, her short story was selected and featured in a 1001 Dark Nights Anthology.

Regardless of the genre, her goal is to take you on a ride that will leave you floating under the sun with warmth in your heart. She writes stories about broken heroes and heroines who aren't necessarily looking for romance, but in the end, they find the kind of love books are written about :).

She first started writing while carting her kids to one hockey rink after the other, averaging 170 games per year between 3 kids in 2 countries and 5 states. Her first book, IN TWO WEEKS was originally published in 2007. In 2010 she helped form a publishing company (Cool Gus Publishing) with *NY Times* Bestselling Author Bob Mayer where she ran the technical side of the business through 2016.

Jen is currently enjoying the next phase of her life...the

empty nester! She and her husband reside in Jupiter, Florida.

Grab a glass of vino, kick back, relax, and let the romance roll in…

Sign up for my Newsletter (https://dl.bookfunnel.com/82gm8b9k4y) where I often give away free books before publication.

Join my private Facebook group (https://www.facebook.com/groups/191706547909047/) where I post exclusive excerpts and discuss all things murder and love!

Never miss a new release. Follow me on Amazon:amazon.com/author/jentalty

And on Bookbub: bookbub.com/authors/jen-talty

ALSO BY JEN TALTY

ABOUT ELLE JAMES

ELLE JAMES also writing as MYLA JACKSON is a *New York Times* and *USA Today* Bestselling author of books including cowboys, intrigues and paranormal adventures that keep her readers on the edges of their seats. When she's not at her computer, she's traveling, snow skiing, boating, or riding her ATV, dreaming up new stories. Learn more about Elle James at www.elle-james.com

Website | Facebook | Twitter | GoodReads | Newsletter | BookBub | Amazon

Or visit her alter ego Myla Jackson at mylajackson.com
Website | Facebook | Twitter | Newsletter

Follow Me!
www.ellejames.com
ellejamesauthor@gmail.com

ALSO BY ELLE JAMES

Nala's Hero (#10)

Mika's Hero (#11)

Bayou Brotherhood Protectors

Remy (#1)

Gerard (#2)

Lucas (#3)

Beau (#4)

Rafael (#5)

Valentin (#6)

Landry (#7)

Simon (#8)

Maurice (#9)

Jacques (#10)

Everglades Overwatch Series
coauthored with Jen Talty

Secrets in Calusa Cove

Pirates in Calusa Cove

Murder in Calusa Cove

Betrayal in Calusa Cove

Raven's Cliff Series
with Kris Norris

Raven's Watch (#1)

Raven's Claw (#2)

Raven's Nest (#3)

Raven's Curse (#4)

Brotherhood Protectors Yellowstone

Saving Kyla (#1)

Saving Chelsea (#2)

Saving Amanda (#3)

Saving Liliana (#4)

Saving Breely (#5)

Saving Savvie (#6)

Saving Jenna (#7)

Saving Peyton (#8)

Saving Londyn (#9)

Brotherhood Protectors Colorado

SEAL Salvation (#1)

Rocky Mountain Rescue (#2)

Ranger Redemption (#3)

Tactical Takeover (#4)

Colorado Conspiracy (#5)

Rocky Mountain Madness (#6)

Free Fall (#7)

Colorado Cold Case (#8)

Fool's Folly (#9)

Colorado Free Rein (#10)

Rocky Mountain Venom (#11)

High Country Hero (#12)

Brotherhood Protectors

Montana SEAL (#1)

Bride Protector SEAL (#2)

SEAL's Vow (#4)

Warrior's Resolve (#5)

Drake (#6)

Grimm (#7)

Murdock (#8)

Utah (#9)

Judge (#10)

Delta Force Strong

Ivy's Delta (Delta Force 3 Crossover)

Breaking Silence (#1)

Breaking Rules (#2)

Breaking Away (#3)

Breaking Free (#4)

Breaking Hearts (#5)

Breaking Ties (#6)

Breaking Point (#7)

Breaking Dawn (#8)

Breaking Promises (#9)

Hearts & Heroes Series

Wyatt's War (#1)

Mack's Witness (#2)

Ronin's Return (#3)

Sam's Surrender (#4)

Hellfire Series

Hellfire, Texas (#1)

Justice Burning (#2)

Smoldering Desire (#3)

Hellfire in High Heels (#4)

Playing With Fire (#5)

Up in Flames (#6)

Total Meltdown (#7)

Take No Prisoners Series

SEAL's Honor (#1)

SEAL'S Desire (#2)

SEAL's Embrace (#3)

SEAL's Obsession (#4)

SEAL's Proposal (#5)

SEAL's Seduction (#6)

SEAL'S Defiance (#7)

SEAL's Deception (#8)

SEAL's Deliverance (#9)

SEAL's Ultimate Challenge (#10)

Cajun Magic Mystery Series

Voodoo on the Bayou (#1)

Voodoo for Two (#2)

Deja Voodoo (#3)

Texas Billionaire Club

Tarzan & Janine (#1)

Something To Talk About (#2)

Who's Your Daddy (#3)

Love & War (#4)